CW00496478

THE
LEIGHTON
MEADOW
KILLINGS

A gripping murder mystery

GAYNOR TORRANCE

Jemima Huxley Crime Thrillers Book 4

Joffe Books, London
www.joffebooks.com

First published in Great Britain in 2022

This paperback edition was first published
in Great Britain in 2022

Cover art by Nebojša Zorić

ISBN: 978-1-80405-303-4

PROLOGUE

The compartment had been partitioned off from the rest of the trailer, hidden from view behind piles of cellophane-wrapped boxes, stacked on pallets and loaded neatly in rows. Every one of these contained legitimate goods complying with current regulations and accounted for with the necessary paperwork. The owner of the stock would have been horrified if she had had any inkling of the other cargo that was making the journey alongside her goods.

The driver had taken great care to conceal the internal modifications. It was a risky business and essential to ensure it appeared that nothing was amiss. The secret compartment contained an area smaller than a prison cell designed to house a single person. The people responsible were determined to utilize the minimum amount of space, so as not to arouse the suspicion of a zealous customs officer, should something go wrong at the British port and the guy paid handsomely to look the other way was not on shift.

Five young women had been bundled into the back of the truck on a side street just off Wenceslas Square. They were not paying for passage but would command a premium price from a certain client.

There was no CCTV in the area, and they had not put up a fight, as a cocktail of drugs had ensured their compliance. They were sophomore students at Charles University in Prague, emboldened by having negotiated their first year away from home without encountering any problems. Their misplaced confidence had cost them dearly.

Each came from a good family and up to that point had led a charmed life. Their downfall was that despite their intelligence, none of them was streetwise. Convinced they had one another's backs, they had partied recklessly, each relying on the others. So, when two British men approached them in a nightclub, the students had failed to spot the danger. The men were well behaved and sober, seeming to pose no threat. When they'd offered to buy a round of drinks, no strings attached, the women had happily accepted.

The two groups had socialized for a while, and the five friends left the club ahead of the men. As they headed towards the student accommodation, staggering and giggling, the men caught up with them. From the moment they had entered that side street, their fate was sealed. The drugs kicked in. Unable to resist, they were steered towards a waiting truck and bundled inside. They were already unconscious as one of the men screwed a false panel into place. A few hours later, legitimate cargo was stacked in front of it.

Throughout the journey, the hidden compartment had soured with the smell of human excrement, sweat and decay. When the modifications had been carried out, no thought had been given to the need to expel carbon dioxide and replenish oxygen levels. It was a death trap for the only asthmatic among them.

Many hours later, Dominika's eyes fluttered open. She gasped, dragging foul air deep into her lungs. Moments earlier, she'd felt as though she was drowning. Now she realized that there was no water — only stench and darkness. She sensed that the end could be near, and although she didn't believe in God, she prayed for help. Her lips barely moved as she muttered a string of words, but a panicked voice inside her head drowned out the sound of her speech. Its message was clear. It would soon be over. There would be no bright future ahead of her. Or even an unremarkable one. There was no hope.

Despite the debilitating brain fog caused by the ever-increasing toxicity levels, Dominika was determined not to give up without a fight. Her eyes strained as she attempted to make sense of her surroundings, an impossible task, as everywhere was pitch black. There wasn't a sliver of light in any direction to provide context to her surroundings.

It didn't help that her thoughts were muddled and fuzzy. She prided herself on having a sharp intellect and the capacity for lateral thinking. The combination usually enabled her to get quickly to the nub of any problem. She had never felt as helpless as she did at this moment. She had no memory of recent events. Her mind was blank. Anything could have happened to her. The not knowing was terrifying.

A wave of fear rose from the pit of her stomach, and Dominika fought the urge to scream. It suddenly didn't seem wise to attract attention when she didn't know where she was or who was nearby. Someone could be watching, revelling in her fear, and she wasn't about to gratify the sick individual responsible. She swallowed hard and pressed her hands over her chapped lips to prevent any sound from leaving her mouth.

As Dominika's breathing slowed, she regained a sufficient level of composure to lower her hands. It occurred to her that she could use other senses to explore her immediate environment. She touched her body and realized that she was still clothed. She ran her hands over the garments. They felt familiar, and she began to recall that these were the clothes she had worn when she had gone out on the town with her friends. There was a possibility that she still had her mobile phone.

She frantically searched, but she failed to find the device. Her heart sank. There was no chance of alerting an outsider.

Wiggling her digits and carefully moving her limbs, Dominika established that she appeared to be uninjured. She was lying down and, as she sat up, her hands touched the smoothness of the surface beneath her, while directly behind her was another solid surface.

Huddled in the darkness, she could make out the distant hum of an engine and feel a rocking motion. It suggested she was in a vehicle, though, whether on the road, rail, sea, or in the air, she had no idea. As she pondered, she became aware of the occasional stifled whimper of another being. She wasn't alone.

As she weighed up the risk of announcing her presence to whoever was nearby, the other person dared to speak, and Dominika realized that it was her friend Agata. Just as she was about to say something, the engine cut out, and a door slammed. There was the sound of muffled voices. She could not hear what they were saying, but it sounded like a conversation between at least two, if not more, men.

'Agata, if they open the doors, we've got to run for it,' whispered Dominika. She was unsure whether she'd actually spoken the words out loud or just thought them. She forced herself on to her feet in preparation for whatever she was about to face. Psyching herself up to bite, gouge, kick and scream. She was determined to do what it took to have a chance of escape. Having invested so heavily in working towards her life's goals, she wasn't about to sit back and allow someone to steal her future from her.

At the sound of more doors opening, she was surprised to find that there was still no light. The vehicle rocked slightly. There was the hum of machinery and the sound of another vehicle. The noise was distinctive and vaguely familiar. She desperately tried to recall where she had heard it before.

She eventually realized that it was at her uncle's warehouse. It was the sound of a forklift truck, suggesting that someone was moving something. With no clear idea how long she had been standing there, Dominika heard the machine back away. Immediately she could feel at least two people step inside the trailer. Footsteps approached, and there was the sound of a screwdriver. Within seconds, thin strips of light appeared up ahead. The voices were close, and they were speaking English.

Dominika shifted her weight from foot to foot in readiness to make a move. The fuzziness in her head was clearing rapidly as cortisol and adrenaline flooded her body. She visualized what she had to do. She kept her head down so as not to be dazzled by any brightness when the door finally opened. If the men's voices were anything to go by, she was probably thousands of miles from home. In a foreign country, where she knew no one and where there was little chance of rescue. But for now, none of that mattered. She needed to block out her fear and focus on just one thing. Her sole priority was to escape. To put as much distance between herself and these men as possible. If she could do that and find a safe place to hide, she might stand a chance.

As they removed the metal panel, Dominika realized that the light she had seen came from torches, as apart from those shafts of brightness, it appeared to be dark.

'Grab 'old of this and help me shift it. It's too 'eavy for me to do it by meself,' said a gruff male voice.

The fingers from two sets of hands were visible, wrapped around the edge of the metal plate as they manoeuvred it through ninety degrees to allow access to the hidden recess.

It was now or never. Dominika launched herself forward, forcing her shoulder into the sheet of metal. The men toppled backwards. As she jumped out of the vehicle, she was thankful that she had chosen to wear decorative training shoes instead of the more obvious strappy heels for a night out on the town.

'Eh, what's going on?' shouted a man standing somewhere in the shadows up ahead. From the tiny speck of light, it was clear that he had been looking at something on his mobile phone.

'Stop her! She's getting away!' The warning came from someone else.

Dominika had to make a snap decision, though she had no idea where she was, or in which direction she should head.

The only thing she knew for sure was that she needed to put as much distance as possible between herself and these men. A small cloud of dust rose into the night air as she skidded to a halt and turned sharply, changing the direction she was taking. With no socks to grip the inside of her training shoes, her feet slid uncomfortably. She wished she'd had the fore-sight to check the laces and tie them more securely.

With her vision impaired by the darkness, Dominika had no idea whether the route she had chosen was her best chance of escape. But there was no time to reflect on the choice she had made. As soon as she set off, she was commit-ted to following that course.

'She's getting away!'

'What are you waiting for? Get after her! We'll have our hands full with the others. Stop the bitch before she has a chance to attract anyone's attention. If she's spotted, it'll be over. My old man will kill us if we mess this up. Shift your arse, now!'

As Dominika picked up her pace, she battled to dispel all negative thoughts from her mind. Despite feeling weak, iso-lated, and vulnerable, she knew that she needed to focus and think clearly if she was going to outwit her captors. She had to banish her fears — which was easier said than done. With every stride, her emotions threatened to overwhelm her.

She hated leaving her friends. Wished they'd made a run for it too, as they could have supported each other. But they had made their own choice. Just as she had made hers.

Her father had once told her that at critical moments in life you either fought or took flight. He'd explained it wasn't a conscious choice. Instinct just kicked in. It was most likely the reason she had made a run for it while the others stayed put. At that critical juncture, Dominika wasn't prepared to stand by and meekly allow those vile men to use and abuse her. It was her life. Her choice.

She headed across rough ground, then down a track that took her on to a lane where the surface was smoother. It gave her the confidence to increase her stride. Since she was eight years old, she had been a member of a running club and had competed in numerous races over the years. Barring injury, she did not doubt that she could outpace her abductors if they pursued her on foot. Though if they followed her in a vehicle, she knew that she had no chance.

The key was to banish negative thoughts, which was easier said than done when your life depended on it. Just as in competitive races, Dominika cleared her mind and focused on her strides. She could feel her shoes getting looser but she had no time to stop and tighten the laces. She kept running without looking back, doing her best to concentrate on her action and regulate her breathing.

The darkness of the night sky and the lack of street lights hampered her ability to see the ground. She was trusting her footing to luck, which gave out on her as her left shoe landed on the edge of a pothole. It threw her off balance and she stumbled.

Somehow she managed to correct her centre of gravity and stop herself falling, but lurched precariously, and as she raised her leg for the next stride, her trainer flew off into the hedgerow. In other circumstances, she would have stopped to retrieve it. But in the darkness, it would have taken too long, and time was not on her side. Her foot was sore and hurt more each time it landed on the asphalt. She winced with every step and tried to rise above the pain as she kept on running.

Spotting a house ahead, there was a moment of indecision as she thought of hammering on the door. She desperately needed help, and there was a possibility that the occupant might come to her rescue. But then it occurred to her that the building was in darkness, and there may very well be no one inside. It was also a considerable risk to take. The house was reasonably close to where the truck had stopped. So, whoever lived in the property could be linked to her abduction. Such a possibility made up her mind. It was too dangerous, and if she didn't keep moving, she would allow her abductors to catch up with her. And if that were to happen, her fate would be sealed, as they were unlikely to make the mistake of leaving her unguarded ever again.

At the sound of an approaching vehicle, her heart almost stopped. It was somewhere behind her, and from the engine noise, she realized it was a motorcycle. She didn't stand a chance of outrunning it. She needed to get off the road.

The engine revved up a gear, rapidly closing the distance between them. It was impossible to blot out thoughts of the inevitability of being captured. Dominika wished she had taken her chances at the property she had just passed, but it was too late now. The motorcycle was gaining ground, and she wouldn't have enough time to double back.

She cursed her stupidity. If she was going to find a way out of this mess, she would have to trust someone. Despite what had happened to her, she believed that most people were honest and decent. So, the odds were in her favour. If a stranger witnessed her obvious distress, they would be inclined to help her out.

Her body was starting to feel the strain as lactic acid built up. She longed to stop and double over to relieve the pain. In normal circumstances, Dominika would have had no problem running for a prolonged period, and at a far faster pace than she was currently able to achieve. But she was light-headed and weak from hunger. Her legs were heavy and not as cooperative as she needed them to be. What had started as a sprint had slowed to a jog. With each additional step, it became increasingly difficult for her to raise her legs sufficiently to make much progress. Each restricted movement increased the chances of stumbling as her feet barely cleared the ground.

Struggling on, she spotted a large structure set back from the lane. In a few steps, she drew level with a lychgate and realized that the building was a church. Despite her secular lifestyle, the sight of a place of worship filled her with hope. God was looking out for her. If the church was open, she could seek sanctuary inside. Dominika was sure that a priest wouldn't turn her away, and even if the building was locked, the churchyard would provide plenty of hiding places. She could move stealthily among the gravestones as the darkness would help to shield her.

The most direct route to the church would be to take the path where she stood. But that route would undoubtedly leave her more exposed, and Dominika knew that she had very little time until the motorcyclist drew level with the lychgate. The risk was too significant, and she instinctively veered diagonally, weaving her way through the gravestones, keeping low to avoid detection. The motorcycle engine slowed, and she crouched behind a monument, hardly daring to breathe. Primed for a confrontation she had little hope of winning, Dominika all but gave up hope.

After lingering for a while, the engine revved louder, and the motorcycle continued along its original path. It was a lucky break, and moments later she reached the wall of the church. The sound of the engine had faded into the distance. Twenty or so steps would take her to the door of the church, where she would hopefully be able to slip inside without attracting any unwanted attention.

Her hand clamped around the handle, the metal rough against her skin. She held her breath as she pressed downwards and gently pushed. Relief flooded through her as the door yielded. Though, still afraid of attracting attention, Dominika only opened it sufficiently to allow her to squeeze through the gap. Anything more seemed rash.

She carefully shut the door behind her, wincing at the sound of the latch engaging. In reality it wasn't loud, but in the circumstances, making any sound seemed reckless. The air inside the vestibule was noticeably cooler than the temperature outside. It made her shiver. As she opened the inner door and stepped into the church itself, she became aware of the overpowering smell of incense and her nose wrinkled.

The area was almost dark, with just a few candles lit by those who had called earlier to remember a loved one, burning low but not yet extinguished. Their flames would be long gone by the time the sun rose to welcome the new day. She stood still and listened hard, but apart from the sound of her breath, it appeared that she was alone inside the church. She had no idea whether churches in this country were routinely left unlocked overnight. Somehow, she thought not, and it occurred to her that the door might have been an oversight. She had nothing to base this assumption on but wanted it to be true. If that were the case, it should be safe for her to remain inside and wait for daylight, as the priest and possibly members of the congregation would start to arrive. There would be safety in numbers as they could surely not all be in on the abduction.

Dominika selected a pew about halfway down the aisle. It was in shadow, where the light of the few remaining candles did not reach. She sat down and slid along the seat, picking up a kneeling pad to use as a cushion on which she could rest her head. She was suddenly nauseous. Terrified. Exhausted. This hard wooden bench seemed like the best location to wait out the remainder of the night, safe from prying eyes. It would give her time to formulate a plan about what to do next.

She wondered how her friends were doing. Hoped they were safe and wouldn't be punished because she had dared to run away. When morning came and people arrived, she'd tell them what had happened and ask to be taken to a police station. Everything would be all right. The others would be set free and they would all return home.

The residual effects of the drug and the stress of her recent escape soon took their toll. Dominika's eyes felt heavy, and she struggled to stay awake. It was a battle she could not win, and in no time at all, she was asleep.

During a dream of happier times, Dominika heard a noise that startled her. Groggy and disorientated, her eyes snapped open and the events of the night before flooded back. Her eyes were bleary, and she hastily rubbed them. The first thing she noticed was that the sun had risen, and although its rays were weak, it allowed her to make sense of her immediate surroundings. Though, without raising herself up, which would undoubtedly alert anyone to her presence, she had a somewhat limited view.

Hearing approaching footsteps, Dominika's heart rate increased. The urge to move coursed through her. Every fibre of her being screamed at her to make a run for it, but as her eyes darted about, desperately searching for an escape route, she realized there was nowhere to go. The end of the pew was flush against the wall. Without clambering over the seat, the only way out was towards the aisle, but the stranger was already closing the distance between them. Her only hope was to hide beneath the wooden bench, or even the one in front of that. She felt blindly with her hand for a gap she could squeeze into between the wood and the floor. There was none. There was nowhere to go. She was trapped.

She felt as though her heart was about to burst through her chest. There was a buzzing in her ears as fear gave way to full-blown panic. As much as she wanted to escape, Dominika knew that it was far too risky. She'd let her guard down by falling asleep. It was a mistake she shouldn't have allowed to happen.

She had no idea if there was only one other person in the building or a group of them. Whoever was there could be willing to help her. Alternatively, they could be searching for her to take her back to the others.

Dominika lay on her back, barely daring to breathe as she pressed her body on to the smooth wooden pew. She willed the laws of physics to change and allow her to pass through the solid wooden surface. The footsteps slowed, though they did not stop completely. Whoever else had entered the church was either hesitating or looking around carefully as they progressed down the aisle. Each step brought them closer.

A shadow fell across her and Dominika stared up helplessly, her eyes wide. A scream died in her throat as a bolt fired from a crossbow pierced her heart.

Her killer smiled in satisfaction. He stepped forward to soak one of his hands in her blood, then smeared it across his forehead and cheeks.

CHAPTER 1

Almost eight months earlier

With hindsight, each officer on Detective Chief Inspector Kennedy's squad would reflect on this particular evening with varying degrees of regret. And each would blame themselves for not having done things differently.

If only they'd gone to another restaurant . . .

If it had been any other night . . .

If one of them had accompanied her . . .

But regrets were pointless, as they didn't change a thing. And at the time, no one appreciated that the clock was counting down to a chance encounter that was about to change Detective Inspector Jemima Huxley's life for ever.

That evening started well. Each member of the Cardiff Major Incident Team was having an enjoyable time. They'd closed a big case, which had taken weeks of effort and determination, and a vicious criminal network was no longer operating on the city streets. Unusually, there was nothing in the pipeline requiring their immediate attention. Instead of going home to their respective families, they grasped the opportunity to kick back and spend a few hours enjoying one another's company.

The conversation and laughter died down as DCI Kennedy tapped his knife on the side of his glass to quieten the others. 'I'd like to toast the best bunch of people I know. Each of you is exceptional in your own way, and I'm proud to head up such a team of exemplary officers and fine human beings.' As he uttered the words, his eyes burned with pride. He could have easily been mistaken for a father praising his offspring.

The team raised their glasses, each readily echoing Kennedy's sentiments. Detective Sergeant Dan Broadbent was the longest-serving member. Jemima had been the next to join the team. Broadbent had initially resented her and gave her a hard time, but he was forced to change his opinion when she saved his life, selflessly putting herself in harm's way to protect him. It won his respect and his loyalty, both of which he didn't offer up freely.

It was much later when Detective Constables Finlay Ashton and Gareth Peters had been drafted in, along with two other officers, to help solve a particularly harrowing and perplexing case of multiple murders at the local manor house Llys Faen Hall. Following a shake-up in the force, Finlay and Gareth joined the squad on a permanent basis, with Finlay subsequently going on to pass his sergeant's exam and become a detective sergeant alongside Dan.

Over the years, these five police officers had forged a relationship closer than many families. It was based on mutual respect, an absence of egos and a genuine sense of friendship. Though they observed it in their day-to-day oper-ations, the chain of command had not prevented them from treating one another as equals. Their many successes had resulted from acknowledging that each individual brought with them different strengths and weaknesses. Each of them was prepared to speak their mind without fear of retribution from someone higher up the ranks. It was a case in point that the whole was greater than the sum of the parts.

As they waited for the food to arrive, they chatted inces-santly. It was as though they had not seen one another for a lengthy period and had much to catch up on. After the waiters brought their chosen dishes, the noise died down until the only audible sounds from the table were occasional mutterings of satisfaction. As usual, the food was delicious. At the end of the meal, everyone was uncomfortably full, having eaten far too much, spurred on by the intoxicating cocktail of aromas and the dishes' tempting presentation. It was a perfect antidote to the stress of their working life. Good food, great company and a succession of tall tales and terrible jokes were precisely what each of them needed.

Glancing at the oversized clock above the kitchen entrance, Jemima reluctantly decided to call it a night. She needed to get home as her father was looking after James, her adoptive son, and she'd promised to return no later than nine o'clock. Lately, she'd started to feel like Cinderella, weighed down with responsibility wherever she went. Life had been emotionally and financially challenging since her husband Nick's unforeseen meltdown and sudden departure. It had rocked her world. Yet there was no way she would ever consider letting him back into her life again. Even if Nick crawled over broken glass and swore that he was a changed man. Not after the way he'd let James down when the boy had needed him most.

James was fortunate to have Jemima in his life, and she felt the same way about the child. Against all odds, they'd bonded the moment they'd first met, and over the years, those feelings had only intensified. She loved the boy fiercely, as though he had been born to her. Though, given the pressures of her job, there were inevitable occasions when she wished for a little more freedom. Even a rare few hours of socializing with her colleagues required a great deal of organization on the home front. Spontaneity had become a thing of the past. Any break in routine required prior notice, imposing on either her father's or her sister's goodwill.

Jemima pushed her chair back and reached for her jacket. Darkness was fast approaching. A gentle breeze whipped up as she said her goodbyes, closed the restaurant door and stepped out on to the grimy pavement on the city side street. It was time to return to real-life domestic responsibilities. Being either a single parent or a police officer was a challenging prospect. Combining the two was sheer madness. Life was a constant juggling act.

The others were planning on making a night of it. Dan Broadbent had a pass from his wife and was determined to make the most of his few hours of freedom. Kennedy's partner, Sally Trent, was there. Although she wasn't officially part of the squad, she had worked with them on the Llys Faen Hall case. As Jemima walked past the window, Gareth Peters gave her a cursory wave. Finlay Ashton was on top form, quite animated as he told another joke. Jemima had always admired his sense of humour, as he had a way of delivering punchlines with panache and perfect timing. Broadbent's raucous laughter could be heard, even out on the street. He'd had a bit too much to drink, which always made him loud. It made Jemima smile. They'd had a table next to the window, and she looked back to see him wiping his eyes with the back of his hands as he rocked precariously on his chair.

Jemima knew she was lucky to work with such a great bunch of people. Each of them had a good work ethic and a keen moral code. It wasn't unusual for petty grievances or resentments to fester in any squad. But after her initial run-in with Broadbent all those years ago, there had never been any further issues. They had gelled like a family, and there was no doubt in her mind that they had each other's back.

The smile faded on Jemima's lips as she turned away. With a quick check of her watch, she realized that she needed to hurry. The car park would shut soon. If she didn't get there in time, the barrier would be locked and she'd be stuck. If that were to happen, she'd be forced to wait god knows how long for a bus or take a taxi. Not to mention whatever premium the car park would undoubtedly charge for an overnight stay. With only her wage to rely on, she had to be sensible. Money was tight. James was a growing lad, and every penny counted.

The street was quiet, even for this time of the evening. Jemima took out her headphones, selected some music and set off at a reasonable pace, bunching her hands into loose fists to shove them into her jacket pockets.

As she approached a junction, a jogger passed her at a steady pace. It suddenly occurred to Jemima that she could significantly reduce the amount of time it would take to reach the car by taking a shortcut down a few alleyways. The area wasn't a known trouble spot, so it wasn't much of a risk, especially if she walked faster. She was confident that it should only take ten minutes at most to reach the car park. Whereas if she stuck to the main streets, it would be at least double that. And it wasn't as if she couldn't handle herself if someone tried to mug her.

Without hesitation, Jemima set off along the alley. If she'd had more time, it wouldn't have been her route of choice. But familiarity with the area bolstered her confidence. She soon regretted her choice of shoes, though. Kitten heels made walking briskly more problematic.

She felt happy and relaxed as music blared through the headphones and blocked out all extraneous sounds. Jemima hadn't thought to glance over her shoulder, so there was no way she could have known that someone was behind her. She was so focused on reaching the car park that she was clueless about the imminent danger, her feet pounding the pavement to the beat of the song.

Without warning, someone charged into her, slamming her head into a brick wall. The impact knocked her out.

As she regained consciousness, Jemima started to moan. She sensed, rather than knew for sure, that something was wrong.

Her assailant's slender fingers gripped a handful of her hair as he hauled her upright and pushed her forward, pressing the weight of his body against hers. He pulled up her dress and ripped her panties. His merciless thrusting sped up, forcing her forehead across the brickwork like cheese across a grater, the blood running from her raw skin.

She groaned, and he echoed the sound she made. His delight soon turned to disappointment at how quickly the sexual act was over. After he withdrew, he couldn't help but run a fingertip down the inside of Jemima's forearm, stopping as he reached her wrist.

Jemima trembled, terrified about what this man would do next. She hadn't seen his face and had no idea who he was. Yet she knew she was no match for him. When it mattered most, her years of one-on-one combat training had turned out to be worthless. She hadn't been able to struggle, cry out, or fight back. This man could kill her right now, and there was nothing she could do about it.

Without warning, he yanked her head back and thrashed her face into the wall.

All thought disappeared.

CHAPTER 2

Jemima gradually became aware of sounds. At first, they were merely a jumble of unidentifiable noise. Eventually, they separated into an assortment of cadences, and she recognized that these were actual voices. 'Wh-what's 'appenin'?' she muttered.

It felt as though weights were pressing on her eyelids, making it impossible to open her eyes. As the fog slowly dissipated, her thoughts became more cogent, and she realized that she wasn't dreaming. It panicked her. She summoned up the effort to will her eyes to open.

Her eyelids remained leaden and uncooperative. It was a monumental battle, but one she was determined to win.

At last they opened, and a sickening pulse of pain exploded inside her skull. It was like looking at the sun. The light was dazzling, and her head hurt like hell.

'She's back with us!'

The voice was close, shrill and unrecognizable. It made no sense to Jemima. She was sure that she had been with Broadbent and the rest of the squad. But there was no time for her to dwell on that particular thought. She was about to vomit. And as she struggled to sit up, she turned her head and felt the contents of her stomach rise.

'Don't worry, let it all out,' said the stranger, with a more soothing tone this time.

As Jemima blinked away the fogginess and her surroundings came into focus, she saw Broadbent standing next to someone in a white coat.

'You're in a hospital. You've sustained a head injury.' It was the reassuring voice she'd heard moments earlier.

'Dan?'

'Don't worry, you're safe now,' he said.

Emotion was evident in the timbre of his voice. To Jemima, even in her current state of confusion, Broadbent was clearly upset. His voice was noticeably higher than usual, and the way he'd said '*now*' caused her to panic. Years of being a police officer had taught her to pick up on subtle nuances in speech. Slight inflections in tone or the odd word here or there might pass many listeners by, but the trained ear would expose a whole new meaning to what was being said.

'What happened? How did I end up here?' A growing sense of dread settled then metastasized in the pit of her stomach.

'There's no easy way to say this. You were attacked,' said Broadbent.

'You were found in an alleyway,' interjected Kennedy.

Jemima's mind whirled. Even without knowing the facts, she appreciated that whatever had happened to her had to be serious.

'You've had a nasty blow to the head. So, it's best if you rest,' said the doctor. She spoke softly and smiled sympathetically. She turned her attention to Broadbent and Kennedy. 'Now, I think you should both step outside for a while,' she instructed.

The insistence implicit in the woman's tone gave Jemima even more cause for concern. The reason she was in the hospital had to be something more than just a blow to the head. And then the awful truth dawned on her. She'd been raped.

Kennedy and Broadbent were reluctant to move away from Jemima's bed, as they were keen to speak to her at the earliest opportunity. Accepting that the doctor wasn't about to back down, they stood directly outside the door to Jemima's room.

'Shout when you're ready to kick things off. We'll be just outside,' said Kennedy. He regretted the turn of phrase as soon as he said it. It sounded as if he was eager to get a team meeting underway instead of interviewing the victim of a serious crime.

As Jemima's vision cleared, she could see the two men through a gap in the curtains that had been haphazardly drawn around the bed. And as the medication kicked in, her headache subsided, enabling her to hear every word they said.

Broadbent made a phone call, and Jemima soon realized that he was speaking to her sister, Lucy. She was apparently not taking the news well, as Broadbent told her to calm down and focus. Jemima could imagine Lucy's reaction. Her sister would fall apart. She somehow managed to live a charmed existence where nothing bad ever seemed to happen. News of Jemima's attack would force her to confront a reality any normal person would not wish to encounter.

Jemima drifted off for a while and woke when she heard a female voice. When she opened her eyes, she saw that Sally Trent had joined Kennedy and Broadbent. It was unsurprising, as, given her role, Sally would need to interview Jemima soon.

Moments later, Dan raised his hand to acknowledge the arrival of Jemima's sister. 'This is Chief Inspector Ray Kennedy and Sergeant Sally Trent. We were together at the restaurant this evening,' said Broadbent by way of an explanation.

Lucy ignored social pleasantries. 'Where's Jem? Why aren't you with her?' Her voice was flat, and her brow furrowed with the strain of the situation. It aged her considerably. She was unaccustomed to dealing with the fallout of violent situations and appeared shell-shocked and out of her depth. All that mattered to her now was that she got to see her sister.

'She's just there.' Broadbent nodded towards the bed just inside the nearest doorway. 'Keep your voice down. You don't want to alarm her, and she's able to hear you. The doctor's seeing to her now. She told us to wait out here.'

'Jem shouldn't be left on her own. She's going to need someone to support her, and that's where I come in,' said Lucy. 'So why are you lot still here? You should be out there trying to find the scum that attacked her.'

'It's not that simple,' said Kennedy. His eyes didn't waver from Lucy's face as he spoke in a low and controlled voice. He was more than used to dealing with agitated relatives who were happy to accuse the police of not doing enough to find the perpetrators of a crime. 'Jemima's one of our own. She's like family to us. There's no question that we're pulling out all the stops, but there are procedures that need to be followed, and we're not about to cut corners on this. Until we've spoken with Jemima and established what happened to her, I'm afraid that everything else is just conjecture. At the moment, all we know for sure is that she was attacked, and she's sustained physical injuries consistent with that fact. Though from what we've ascertained by speaking with the person who found her, it's possible she was raped.'

Lucy gasped in horror. Her hands flew to her mouth to stifle a shriek. She lurched towards the nearest wall and leaned against it, as though she didn't trust herself to be able to remain upright without some additional support.

'I appreciate that it might look as though we're standing around here wasting our time, but we're not. We've already got people out examining the scene. They'll gather together any physical evidence they can find. And as soon as we're able to talk to Jemima, we'll find out exactly what happened and hopefully get a description of her assailant.'

'With all due respect, even I know that your team doesn't specialize in this sort of thing. And look at it from Jem's point of view, she might feel awkward speaking about the attack.' It was a statement, not an accusation.

'That's where I come in,' said Sally. 'I've known Jemima for a while. We've worked together before, but I'm not part of this team. I'm based in the sexual crimes unit. I'll be the

21

one taking her statement and supporting her through the process of collecting trace evidence from her body. She'll know the score, and with a bit of luck, we might get some of the attacker's DNA.'

'She'll need my support. Will I be allowed to sit with her while this happens?' asked Lucy.

'Sure, as long as Jemima gives her consent. But the decision has to be hers. If she declines, please accept her decision without argument. After what she's been through, she'll be fragile. It's important that she feels she's in control of things.

'If she agrees to you sitting in, I would ask that you remain silent throughout the entire process. It's important Jemima relays everything in her own words. You need to appreciate that everyone reacts differently. Sometimes a victim wants a close friend or relative with them when they give their statement. But there are occasions when the presence of a loved one is an inhibiting factor. I think you'll agree that the last thing any of us wants at the moment is for Jemima to feel pressurized or uncomfortable?'

'That goes without saying. She's my sister, and I just want to support her.'

'Glad we're on the same page. I'll speak to Jemima alone. Talk her through the procedure, and ask if she's content for you to sit with her while she gives her witness statement,' said Sally.

'That's fine, but I need to see her first. I've let her down in the past, but not this time.'

They all sensed there would be no arguing with her and appreciated it was the right thing to do. After all, each of them had Jemima's best interests at heart. They all knew her well enough to know that she wouldn't thank any of them for telling Lucy that she needed to join the back of the queue.

CHAPTER 3

As her colleagues waited for news on Jemima, Lucy's arrival changed the dynamic of the group. With a civilian present, it was no longer possible to discuss operational matters. Once the scarce facts had been imparted to Lucy, the four of them stood in awkward silence. Everyone was eager to do something yet forced to endure this unwelcome hiatus as they waited to be given the green light to be able to speak to Jemima.

They each had different ways of dealing with their worry and frustration. Broadbent resorted to biting his nails. It was something he'd done as a child, and although he'd broken the habit, he reverted to it at times of extreme stress.

Kennedy paced back and forth like a caged beast, clenching his fists and scowling at the thought of what he'd like to do if he ever caught up with the man who had done this. Of course, he knew deep down that it would never happen, as he could lose his pension if he ever acted out this particular fantasy. Still, it helped.

Trent was the most composed. Her connection with Jemima wasn't as close as Kennedy's or Broadbent's. Her days were spent dealing with the aftermath of sexual assault cases. Every case was harrowing. Victims and their families were devastated by these crimes. And although she empathized with them, Sally had become somewhat inured to the fallout. It was a professional self-preservation stance. She had learned long ago that failure to detach herself from their situations would compromise her effectiveness. It could also have a detrimental effect on her mental health.

Lucy stared helplessly at the gap in the curtains surrounding her sister's bed. She fought a silent battle to control her imagination, which threatened to run riot. If she had been alone in that corridor, she would have fallen apart. But waiting alongside her sister's colleagues, she felt the need to demonstrate some composure. She didn't want them to pity her. This was Jemima's pain, not hers.

They all looked up expectantly when another doctor bustled along the corridor and headed towards Jemima's bed. There was a tense few minutes as they waited for an update. When they were informed that Jemima could have a visitor, everyone stepped forward at the same time. But Lucy was determined to be the first at her bedside.

'You'll have to wait. I'm her sister, and right now, that takes priority over the investigation. If Jemima feels otherwise, I'll let you know.' Her eyes flashed defiantly as she held their collective gaze. Before anyone had the opportunity to object, Lucy strode the few steps from the corridor to her sister's room. In her eagerness to close the distance between them, her heels ricocheted loudly and rapidly like a burst of gunfire from an automatic weapon.

Her legs suddenly began to wobble as she approached her sister's bedside. She took a deep, ragged breath, under no illusion that her distress was inappropriate self-indulgence. Whatever she was feeling needed to be buried then and there. There had been many times when Jemima had come through for her. Now it was Lucy's turn to be the strong one. She had to be there for Jemima. Be her sister's rock and see her through what would undoubtedly be the worst time of her life.

In what took an effort of almost Herculean proportions, Lucy clamped her lips together until they were nothing more than thin, virtually bloodless lines. It looked odd, but it was necessary, as she didn't want to cry. She needed to keep a lid on her emotions and not give in to the sheer panic threatening to rip her heart out as it clawed away deep inside her chest. The moment she set eyes on her sister's injured face, her resolve crumbled.

Over the years, Lucy had marvelled at Jemima's resilience and determination. Her sibling was quite literally a force of nature. In normal circumstances, Jemima was the one that people turned to for help and support. Few were aware of her troubles. They only saw what she wanted them to see. Many of those who thought they knew her recognized her strength of character, resilience and level-headedness. They also admired her capacity to think on her feet. This combination of traits had helped her come up with workable solutions to many problems. It had proved particularly useful over the years when she had found herself pitted against some of the most devious and dangerous people plaguing society. What had started out in the early days of a career in law enforcement as a desperate desire for self-preservation had soon become a way of life. And being someone who cared deeply for others, it wasn't unusual for Jemima to go out on a limb to help those in need.

Throughout her career, Jemima had overcome several physical injuries sustained in the line of duty. But those injuries were nothing compared to this latest attack. There had been many occasions when she'd faced adversity. Some problems had proved hard to overcome. Yet this seemed insurmountable, and Jemima wondered if she would ever be able to come to terms with it. She'd gone from being reasonably contented to what was undoubtedly the lowest point of her life.

Despite the analgesic having a positive effect, Jemima's headache remained. The viciousness of the attack was there for all to see. Her face was raw, bloodied and swollen. And since regaining consciousness, Jemima had quickly realized that even the slightest movement caused a significant amount of pain. If that wasn't bad enough, her insides also felt as though they had taken a battering.

The physical injuries were more than enough for anyone to contend with. Still, they paled into insignificance with what was going on inside Jemima's head. Even during the best of times, she sometimes struggled to keep it together, and when that happened, her mood turned dark, and she resorted to cutting herself in an attempt to regain some sort of control over her life. Jemima was convinced that throughout the coming weeks and months, that would only get worse.

The overwhelming majority of people were unaware that at times of extreme stress, Jemima resorted to self-harming. It was a trait she was ashamed of. Yet it was one she clung to as it grounded her when she felt at her most vulnerable. For many years, she had somehow managed to keep this self-destructive ritual hidden from everyone, including her estranged husband, Nick. The secret had finally come out when he discovered her unconscious on the bathroom floor. She had taken things too far, with the self-inflicted wounds visible and a bloodied razor blade held loosely between a limp finger and thumb.

Once Nick overcame his initial shock, he had wasted no time in calling the doctor. Jemima was distraught that her secret was out, though she understood why Nick had sought medical help. But the following day he went a step too far, betraying her by telling her superior officer, Ray Kennedy, what she had done. There had been no need for him to do this. If she had been the one to discover Nick in such a compromising situation, she would not have considered jeopardizing his career in such a manner. It caused a rift that could not be mended. Her husband should have had her back. He should have lived up to their marriage vow about supporting each other *'in sickness and in health'*. Instead, he'd chosen to stab her in the back. It was a wound that went far deeper than the cuts she had inflicted on herself. It was nothing short of betrayal and had been the beginning of the end of their relationship.

Forced to confront the enormity of everything that had just happened, Lucy's distress was something Jemima could do without. She was grateful that her sister had come to support her, but knowing their personalities, Jemima would ultimately end up trying to make Lucy feel better. And given what Jemima had just been through, she didn't have the energy or the inclination to consider anyone else's feelings.

Throughout their lives, Lucy had let Jemima down on more occasions than she cared to remember. Yet Jemima's loyalty had remained unwavering. Jemima was brave. She fought other people's battles and cleared up their messes along the way. Whereas Lucy skilfully sidestepped trouble as she travelled along the sunny side of the street.

There had been only one occasion when Lucy had been unable to shy away from something as awful as this. It was when her friend Violet had been targeted by a stalker. And even then, Lucy had remained on the periphery of things, scared to death that she would be dragged into events that could cause her harm. She had given Jemima a hard time, accusing her of not doing enough to resolve the situation. But Jemima had put her life on the line to see that the man responsible could no longer target women.

One of Lucy's greatest fears was being raped. When it happened to a close friend of hers, Lucy had seen the devastation it caused. Because of that, she took her personal safety seriously, carrying an attack alarm wherever she went. It was a sensible precaution, even though she had so far managed to avoid putting herself in any real danger.

Seeing how broken and battered Jemima looked in the immediate aftermath of the attack, her fear intensified. It broke Lucy's heart to see her sister this way, but she had to deal with it. She couldn't look away. She would have to take care of Jemima.

In those first few moments, Lucy remained sufficiently self-composed to purposely remain outside Jemima's field of vision. She wanted her sister to know that she was there but didn't want her to see the tears streaming down her cheeks.

Though, masking the distress in her voice was proving far harder than she had anticipated.

'Oh, Jem.' It was all she could trust herself to say, but the words caught in her throat, and she began to sob uncontrollably.

Despite her injuries and her current state of mind, Jemima recognized that it was a big deal for Lucy to come to the hospital. Her sibling was squeamish. The sisterly show of support meant everything. As Lucy's fingers touched Jemima's hand, Jemima grabbed them and squeezed as though her life depended on it.

'Don't cry, Luce. You must stay strong for me. I can't do this by myself. It's a lot to ask, but I need you. James doesn't know it yet, but he'll need you too. He can't see me like this. We have to protect him,' whispered Jemima.

Jemima's heartfelt plea caused Lucy to stop crying. Even now, having just been attacked in such a brutal way, Jemima's primary concern was for James.

'You can move in with us. Ellis is hardly ever there.' Lucy was referring to her husband, Ellis Fisher. As a cameraman with a film production company, his job often required him to be away from home for months at a time. It was a lifestyle that would put a strain on many a marriage, but the arrangement suited them both. 'There's plenty of room, and I can keep an eye on both of you. I'm not taking no for an answer. You've always said you love Leighton Meadow. You'll get the peace and quiet you need to get yourself back on track,' said Lucy. There was no hesitation in her voice. The offer was a practical solution and something that she could easily do.

'Thank you. Take James back to yours, but don't let on that anything's up. When they discharge me, I intend on going back to mine.'

'No, Jem, it's—'

'It's my call, Luce. I need some space. It'll be in everyone's best interests for me to be on my own for a while. What if I start cutting myself again? I don't want James to see me like that. He'd be terrified. No child should have to face something like that.'

'But you can't deal with this alone.'

'I have to. There's no other way. Tell Dad what's happened. He'll check in on me.'

'Mum will too.'

'No. I don't want her to know.'

'This isn't the time to hold a grudge.'

'I said no! Promise me you'll say nothing to her.'

'Fine, I promise.' Though Lucy had no intention of doing what she said. As far as she was concerned, it was only right that their mother should know. She knew that her mother and sister had always had a fractious relationship. But she also believed that a family pulled together in times of crisis. And there could be no greater crisis in their family than this attack on Jemima.

'Are my squad still here?' pressed Jemima.

'They're outside waiting to see you. Sally Trent's with them.'

'That's good. Now you need to go home, Luce. Ask them to come in.'

'But—'

'But nothing. There are things they need to be getting on with. I want this bastard caught before he attacks someone else.'

'You need to rest,' countered Lucy. It was all very well for Jemima to consider what was best for any ensuing investigation. Still, it didn't mean that it was in Jemima's best interests at the moment.

'Tell them to come in, and then go and speak to Dad. I'll need you to have your best game face on tomorrow when James moves into yours. I'm relying on you, Luce. Please don't let me down.'

CHAPTER 4

Jemima swallowed hard as a ragged breath caught in her throat. The happiness, laughter and camaraderie at the restaurant seemed like a lifetime ago. The way she felt now, it was impossible to imagine finding anything to smile about ever again. All because she had let her guard down and had believed she was more than capable of taking care of herself. It was a stupid mistake that she would regret for the rest of her life. There was no one else to blame. She had allowed this to happen.

She had been hurt many times in the past. But overcoming injuries sustained in the line of duty was different. They were the result of confrontations Jemima had knowingly entered into. This attack was dehumanizing. She had been targeted. Whether an opportunistic assault or not, she had been unable to defend herself and the rapist had quickly rendered her helpless. This faceless man had treated Jemima like a piece of meat and had left her for dead in the alleyway.

The abuse was callous, and the attack savage. Yet Jemima's humiliation was far from over. She was a proud woman who cared deeply about what others thought of her. But being a victim as well as a police officer meant that she had no anonymity. There were few secrets at the station.

Officers were notorious gossips. Everyone she worked with would soon know what had happened to her. There would be no escaping their pitying looks. No being normal ever again. She would be the rape victim they would never forget about.

Jemima was thankful that she had no memory of the attack. Though she knew that the gap in her consciousness would fuel her imagination and haunt both her waking moments and her dreams. It was a terrifying thought that she was unaware of such crucial moments of her life. Anything could have happened during that time. He could have filmed the attack and put it up on the internet for all to see. If it were uploaded, she didn't know how she could ever face anyone again.

All Jemima wanted to do was curl up into a ball and let the world fade away. This man had treated her as a disposable commodity, there to meet his own needs. He'd thought of her as nothing more than worthless. He wouldn't care that by violating her, he had stripped her of her independence and self-confidence.

As these thoughts swirled around inside Jemima's head, she was consumed by self-loathing. Over the years, her mother had frequently told her that bad things happened to bad people, and that's why Jemima's life was the way it was. She'd brushed it off as just the usual bile her mother took pleasure in spouting at her, but perhaps the woman had been right all along.

Jemima suddenly wanted to be rid of her skin. Every inch of her felt vile, dirty and contaminated. She wanted to scrub her entire body, to rid herself of any trace of the beast who had done this to her. She had an overwhelming desire to claw at her skin but knew she had to put that thought out of her head. She had to endure his presence a while longer if they were to stand any chance of getting his DNA. But Jemima's thoughts turned to the razor blade, craving its cut. The desire was always present, lurking in the depths, ready to surface at moments of extreme vulnerability. And right now, it promised to bring some relief and give her a level of control.

Even in this disturbed state, Jemima knew she could not allow herself to travel that particular path again. She had James to consider, and the boy had already been exposed to an excessive amount of trauma in his young life, what with his birth mother dying unexpectedly and the man he had always thought of as his father abandoning him. For many years now, Jemima had been his one constant. And no matter how low she felt, he was unquestionably her top priority.

The battlefield of scars littering her body had faded as the cuts healed. These pale lines of thickened skin were an enduring reminder of her inner turmoil. When Nick had outed her darkest secret, Jemima had been forced to face up to her demons and attend counselling sessions. She had initially been reluctant, resentful and sceptical. But Ray Kennedy had insisted that participation in these sessions was the only way she would be allowed to return to work. She had eventually come to acknowledge that the wounds to her psyche were far more profound than those of the epidermis. The former required constant tending and would hurt until the day she died. She had made so much progress that she no longer attended regularly. Instead, she booked ad-hoc sessions as and when she felt she needed them.

Jemima lay in the hospital bed, willing herself not to cry. The last thing she wanted was for anyone to see her like this, especially her friends and colleagues. As a police officer, Jemima was aware of the procedures that had to be followed. But as a victim, she wanted nothing to do with this. It was a mind-blowing conflict of professional ideology and personal interest. One she was currently too fragile to deal with. Should she stand by her beliefs? Or should she look after her own self-interest?

'How're you doing, kiddo?' Kennedy's voice was unusually soft and trembled with emotion. It was not the way he would have addressed any other victim.

'Oh, you know . . .' she replied. In all the years Jemima had served under him, Ray Kennedy had never once called her 'kiddo'. He was a man who was always at pains to act professionally. It meant that at that moment, he didn't see her as a police officer. He was treating her as a family member. When the realization hit home, something shifted inside her. The others were the police officers. She was the victim. If she was to get justice, it would be down to their efforts. Not hers. For the second time that evening, she had no control over what would happen. It was like being cast adrift in a stormy sea, buffeted by gigantic waves as she struggled to keep her head above water.

'Did you see your attacker?' asked Kennedy. Having asked her how she was feeling, he didn't want to embarrass either of them any further. He wasn't good at the softly-softly touchy-feely stuff. That was Sally's role.

'No. He came up behind me. Until he r— until he attacked me, I didn't even know he was there. I had my stupid headphones on.'

'You must have had some sense of what he was—' pressed Kennedy.

'Enough now, Ray,' interjected Sally. Her voice was low but firm. This was an order, not a request. She was the only person who could get away with cutting him off like that. Despite being two ranks his junior, she was the person who shared his bed. They had known each other professionally for many years, though, on a personal level, more recently. But Kennedy adored and respected Sally and accepted her judgement that he had overstepped the mark.

For many years, Sally Trent had been part of the sexual crimes unit. She was so determined to make a difference to victims of these crimes that she had turned down the chance of career progression. Had she been career-minded, it would have undoubtedly resulted in her having to leave the unit.

As a serving officer, Jemima knew the score. Her colleagues were aware of what had happened to her. Her chance of privacy had been snatched away the moment they had been alerted to her fate. There would be no hiding. Within the next few hours, she would have to speak to one of the police officers who routinely interviewed rape victims. It would be emotionally stressful and humiliating, but Jemima was determined that Sally Trent would be the officer she dealt with. Better she spoke to someone she had a personal connection with, and she trusted Sally. As the woman was Ray Kennedy's significant other, there would be a negligible chance that this would become station gossip. That was the only positive thing that Jemima had to hold on to.

'Guess there's not much we can do here at the moment,' said Broadbent. He shifted uncomfortably on the spot, looking anywhere other than directly at Jemima.

'No, I think you and Ray should take yourselves off. Perhaps coordinate things at the scene? I'll stay with Jemima and take things forward at this end.'

The sense of relief was evident on the face of both men. If Jemima could not give them any helpful information, it was a waste of valuable time standing around in a display of moral support. Each of them was confident that Jemima knew the score, and she would want them out there, helping to locate evidence that might lead them to find out who attacked her.

Broadbent and Kennedy muttered their goodbyes, but there was no response from Jemima. Sally focused her attention on her, and began to make preliminary enquiries. 'You know that I'm here in my work capacity. What I need to know is whether or not you're prepared to make a statement?'

'I don't want to, but I don't have a choice,' sobbed Jemima. As the words tumbled out, what little self-composure she'd managed to retain dissolved into tears.

Sally reached out and gently took her hand. When the crying showed no sign of abating, she sat on the edge of the bed and put her arms around Jemima. 'I'm so sorry, Jem. I wish I could make it all go away, but we both know that's impossible. Though, I'd like you to believe me when I say you have a choice. You've just had your world turned upside down. You're the victim of a heinous crime. It's incidental that you just so happen to be a police officer. Don't get the two things confused, Jemima. You have rights, just like any other victim. You don't have to make a statement if you don't want to.'

'I have to, Sally. Not only did that bastard rape me, but he knocked me out. I'm grateful someone found me and called for help. But the moment they did, it set off a chain reaction. Because of who I am, I feel as though I'm being railroaded into an inevitable investigation. If I wasn't a police officer, I'd have a choice over whether or not I wanted things taken forward. As things stand, the guys are already working the scene. I'd lose their respect if I didn't go down the official route.'

'Believe me when I say that there isn't anything you could do that would cause those men to think badly of you. They're there for you because we're family. We have one another's back because it's the way we survive. And as a serving officer, you have that mentality too. It's the unwritten rule. An attack on one of us is an attack on us all.' Sally took Jemima's hand once more.

'Jemima, if you don't wish to take this forward, then that's how it will be. No one's going to pressure you into going down the official route. You know the procedures we have to follow. So you have the advantage of being able to make an informed decision. I promise you that there'll be no comeback on you if you don't want us to pursue this. It's entirely your decision.'

'We both know it's not that straightforward, Sally.' Tears rolled down Jemima's cheeks. Yet she somehow managed to keep her voice under control, as she was determined to have her say. 'By now, everyone at the station will know what's happened to me. As much as I wish I could, I can't just walk away and pretend it never happened. I didn't ask for any of this. OK, I was stupid and let my guard down. But I didn't deserve this. No one does.

'The thing is, we spend our lives persuading others to do the right thing. We convince victims to make a statement and testify in court, so that we can stand a chance of getting the criminals off the street. We airbrush out the fact that there are no guarantees. They are putting their lives on the line so that we can play our hand. If the case doesn't go our way, we tell ourselves that we'll get another shot at them if they commit another crime. But that's it for the victims. They don't get another shot at justice. It's easy to be pragmatic when you look at things through the eyes of a police officer. But I've just started to appreciate that it's a hell of a big deal when you're the victim.'

Jemima took a deep, shuddering breath, then swallowed hard. Her effort to keep her emotions in check was taking a considerable toll. She lay there without speaking for a while, grateful that Sally had no need to fill the silence. On the surface she appeared reasonably calm. In reality, she was silently screaming. Eventually feeling more composed, she continued speaking. 'If I walk away from this without doing everything I can to help you find this bastard, then I'd be a hypocrite, and I don't think I'd be able to do my job again. No, I must see this through. What if somewhere down the line, he attacks someone else? If that happened, I couldn't live with myself knowing that I might have stopped him if only I'd had the courage to do something about it.'

'Are you sure? It's a huge decision. Don't just go with your conscience or any misplaced sense of duty. Think hard before you answer because it won't be an easy path to follow, Jemima. Even if we find the guy and make an arrest, you know what it'll be like to testify in court. His defence team will dig up everything in your past to try to discredit you. Any secrets you have could potentially be out there for the whole world to see. You feel violated now, but you'll have to relive it in front of a packed courtroom with the press present. They'll treat you like fodder. The only crumb of comfort I can offer is that the attention will eventually die down.

'You also need to know that a significant proportion of rape victims say that the process of giving evidence is as brutal as the actual attack.'

'What would you do if you were me?' asked Jemima.

'I'm not going to answer that. We're all different, and the decision has to be yours.'

At that moment, the doctor returned to Jemima's bedside. 'We'd like to keep you in tonight. It's a precaution as you lost consciousness. So far, we've only dealt with your visible external injuries—'

'I was raped,' interjected Jemima.

'It appears so,' said the doctor. 'What I was about to say is that we have a private area where I can examine you. I'd recommend you let me take some samples and run some tests. Unfortunately, there's a risk that your attacker could have passed on a sexually transmitted infection.'

Of all the thoughts swirling about in Jemima's head, the possibility of contracting an STI hadn't been among them. Suddenly struck with terror at the possible implications, she zoned out from what the doctor was saying.

'Jemima? Jemima, are you listening to what I'm saying?' asked the doctor.

The mention of her name focused her attention. 'Yeah,' she muttered, somewhat unconvincingly.

'So, you're happy for DS Trent to photograph your injuries?'

'Y-yeah.' She frowned. Having missed some of what the doctor said, she wasn't inclined to ask her to repeat it.

'I'll make the arrangements.' The doctor walked away.

'Get some rest,' said Sally. 'I've a few calls to make and things to organize. I'll be back as soon as I can.'

Jemima was exhausted. The prospect of sleep seemed impossible. Yet sleep she did. She jerked awake when Sally gently touched her shoulder and called her name. Those first few seconds of consciousness were bewildering and confusing. It didn't help that the skin around her eyes was bruised and swollen and severely restricting her vision. But Sally's voice was familiar and reassuring.

'There's no rush, but Dr Svenson's informed me that everything's set up to get the examination underway. We're ready as soon as you are. I've got a wheelchair, so you won't have to walk to the suite. We'll be taking this forward in a private area, so there's no risk of anyone walking in on us.

'I'm sure you already know that there'll be evidence on your clothes, and we'll need to take them. But your sister somehow had the foresight to bring in a change of clothes, so at least you can still wear your own stuff.'

'Thanks.' Her lips barely moved as she muttered the response.

'You have my word that everything will be done respectfully,' said Sally. 'Dr Svenson will undertake your physical examination, record your injuries and take swabs. I'll sort out the photographic evidence so that we'll have a record for any future prosecution.

'I've too much respect for you to sugar-coat it. You'll find this hard. It's inevitable. But, if it all becomes too much for you, then we can take a break. And don't forget that you can put a halt to it at any time.' The sound of Sally's voice was both soothing and reassuring.

'Let's get on with it. I know the score,' said Jemima. She was about to undergo another violation of her privacy and just wanted this over and done with.

The physical examination lasted well over an hour, as Jemima's injuries were photographed, measured, treated and recorded. The wounds were worse on her face, which appeared to have taken the full force of the impact that had rendered her unconscious. There was significant bruising between her thighs, and semen was found inside her vagina. It had also dried on the skin of her inner thighs.

CHAPTER 5

Present day

It didn't take a detective to figure out that this was one of the good days. They had been hard at it for weeks when they'd finally got a break leading to an arrest in the early hours. It was often that way, the inevitability of having to slog your guts out for weeks on end. Often going round in circles, getting nowhere fast, following up what appear to be viable leads only for them to fizzle out. The worst-case scenario was that they could not identify the culprit, and the case would be added to an ever-increasing pile of unsolved crimes. But in this instance, they had got lucky, and it felt good. Although they were confident that they had the right person, everything rested on the interview, which had ended up being as tense as any cup final.

There was a sense of relief and camaraderie as Kennedy, Ashton and Peters exited the small viewing room. It had been far too hot inside the cramped space, despite the air-conditioning unit pumping out cool air. Each of them could have walked out whenever they chose. But they were so invested in the outcome that they had all been prepared to put up with the discomfort.

There had been a couple of hairy moments at the start of the proceedings. Still, it had soon turned into a master class of how to tie a suspect up in knots once Jemima, ably assisted by Broadbent, had goaded him into talking. There was good reason the solicitor had advised her client to answer every question put to him with those two frustrating words, '*No comment*'. If a suspect needed to lie, then once he had started down that path, it became necessary to embellish the facts and often add further untruths. Opting for that particular course of action required a cool head and an excellent memory to ensure not getting caught out. Not an easy thing to pull off under pressure.

Now the scrawny, overprivileged seventeen-year-old had been charged with the murder of an elderly couple. He was a pupil at a local private school. His parents had stumped up for the very best legal representation, a solicitor named Prudence Dwight. She was short, stocky and fierce as an attack dog. And unfortunately for the police force, she had an exceptionally sharp mind, which had enabled her to triumph in many encounters with less well-prepared officers.

The teenager's arrest was the culmination of weeks of painstaking work. And as events unfolded, it became clear that the lad had killed the couple and stolen the man's military service medals. It was a sickening case. Especially as he showed no remorse for what he had done.

As the three men watched the events unfold, you could have heard a pin drop. When the admission eventually came, Ashton and Peters high-fived each other. Kennedy was also delighted and let out a long sigh of relief. He pushed his chair back, stood up and stretched. 'Right, back to it, you two,' he ordered, before heading back towards his office.

Ashton and Peters were already at their desks when Jemima and Broadbent walked into the room. It was easy to see that Broadbent was pleased with himself. He'd adopted a confident swagger and was grinning from ear to ear. Jemima's walk was more waddle than swagger. Unsurprising given the fact that she was heavily pregnant and looked as though she was smuggling a beach ball under her clothes.

'Couldn't have played it better myself,' said Ashton.

'Yeah, great work, guys,' said Peters. 'I've just made you a cup of ginger tea, guv. Thought you might appreciate it, what with the heartburn.'

'Thanks, Gareth. It's exactly what I need and so thoughtful of you. I don't suppose you'd fancy being my birthing partner when the time comes?' she asked.

'Tea maker, willingly. Occasional babysitter, possibly, but only if there's a packet of Jammie Dodgers on offer. As for a birthing partner, the answer's never. But I know you're only kidding,' he said with a nervous laugh.

Jemima's pregnancy had come as a shock to everyone. Not least to herself. Having spent so many years trying to come to terms with her inability to conceive, she had finally discovered that the fault lay with her husband. And when Nick Huxley found that he had always been infertile, it had sent him over the edge. He'd walked out on Jemima and James — the boy he had always believed to be his biological child. It had been at a time when James had needed Nick more than ever, as his birth mother had recently died in a road traffic collision. Jemima had been the one to pick up the pieces, doing everything she could to help James feel safe and loved as he tried to come to terms with his mother's death and his father's abandonment.

History had shown that nothing in Jemima's life ever ran smoothly. And although her desire to give birth to a child was soon to happen, it had come at a considerable cost. She had no idea who the father was as she had been raped by an unknown, opportunistic assailant. And so the pregnancy, although a blessing, was also a curse.

The attack on Jemima had impacted everyone who knew her. She was the victim, but the event had had a ripple effect that had changed many lives and highlighted strained relationships.

Dan Broadbent had been incandescent with rage. Although she was his boss, he considered Jemima to be family. She was even his son's godmother. It hadn't been so long ago that Jemima had mentioned to him that she thought someone was watching her. She had no proof that that was the case. It was more a feeling, which she explained away as transference of emotion, as they were investigating a stalking case at the time. Broadbent had told her not to dismiss her concerns. He'd advised her to trust her gut, but as the weeks passed and nothing had happened, he'd put it out of his mind.

It sickened him that he'd let her down that evening. Dan had thought of offering to walk with her to collect her car from the car park. But he'd stopped himself from doing so as he knew that Jemima would feel slighted. It wasn't as if he would have offered to accompany any of the men back to their car. And his wife, Caroline, had suggested that he make a night of it. It was a welcome and generous gesture, as she was the one who was always stuck at home with their young son while he went out to work.

The moment Kennedy took the call, they had all realized that something awful had occurred. As he had listened intently, his face had darkened. When he finally spoke, his voice had cracked with emotion. A few seconds passed as they had each tried to get their heads around what had happened. It was as though they were all frozen in time.

Broadbent had been the first to recover. He had thrown money on the table, gathered up his belongings and headed for the door, telling the others that he was going to the hospital. Kennedy had left hot on his heels. He had appreciated that Broadbent was not in a good place and didn't want him to do something he might later regret.

Peters and Ashton had headed to the crime scene. After all, Jemima was one of them, and there was no way they were going to sit back and allow anyone to mess things up. No one attacked one of their own and got away with it. But despite throwing everything at the case and even bringing in Kennedy's significant other, DS Sally Trent, who specialized in sexual assault cases, they had got nowhere.

They'd started out with high hopes, as the rapist hadn't used a condom. But despite having markers to work with, they had failed to find a match on the national database. Jemima had been unable to provide any useful information as she hadn't seen or heard her assailant. It was frustrating and demoralizing. Still, they had kept at it until another case took priority, and they were forced to put the hunt for Jemima's attacker on the back burner. But every officer on the squad had a long memory. Whenever there was a spare moment, they kept returning to it, hoping that they would spot something they had previously overlooked.

When Jemima was discharged from the hospital, she had taken some time off work. Having already agreed that James would stay at Lucy's house, Jemima had returned home alone. In those early days there was no disguising her obvious facial injuries. Yet these cuts and bruises were superficial and quick to heal compared with the damage to her psyche. She needed the headspace to try to process — then come to terms with — what had happened.

The anguish of being alone with her dark thoughts soon proved overwhelming. Shame, anger and grief filled every conscious moment. Having spent less than twenty-four hours at home alone, she acknowledged that Lucy's assessment of what was best for her had been correct. If she was going to find a way back from this without resorting to cutting herself, she needed the support of people who cared about her. And when she turned up on Lucy's doorstep, bags in hand, and witnessed the welcoming smile on her sister's face, she knew that it was the right decision to move in with her sibling. At least for a while.

In recent years, she had fought many personal battles in a bid to turn her life around. Unsurprisingly, the rape was a significant setback. Jemima had suddenly found herself under so much pressure, having to try to put it out of her mind to be there for James. The boy had been through so much with the death of his mother and Nick, whom he still believed was his father, abandoning him. Jemima had been determined not to allow her adopted son to see that anything was up with her. The last thing Jemima wanted was for James to feel insecure. So it was agreed by everyone that James would be told that Jemima had been injured while she was on duty.

Jemima's sister, Lucy, had been exceptionally supportive, as had their father. Whereas their mother, Celia, had been a nightmare. She blamed Jemima for the rape, berating her for disgracing the family. Lucy had been horrified when she had overheard her mother's vicious tirade. Still, Jemima hadn't been surprised, as her mother constantly mistreated her.

Since regularly attending counselling sessions, Jemima had been forced to confront issues that she had long since accepted as the way things were. Her mother had brought her up to believe that she was a constant source of disappointment, a daughter she was invariably ashamed of. One of the surprises about talking about things was the realization that Celia Goodman was a narcissist, and her treatment of Jemima was neither normal nor acceptable. It was the reason that Jemima loathed herself and self-harmed.

Throughout her formative years, her mother had virtually brainwashed Jemima into believing that she was inadequate. *'Bad things happen to bad people'*, was one of Celia Goodman's favourite sayings. It was something she had whispered into her daughter's ear during the few moments she had deigned to spend alone with her following the rape.

Since the attack, there had been many occasions when Jemima had picked up the razor blade. It was always at times when she was alone, occasions when she was plagued with dark thoughts that wouldn't go away, no matter how hard she tried. She wanted to find the inner strength to rise above her immediate problems. Hold it together for James and show him that no matter how far you fell, you could still struggle back from adversity. But wanting and doing were poles apart.

On the occasions when things got too bad for her, Jemima locked herself in the bathroom. She'd sit on the tiled floor as she pressed her back against the door, slowing flipping the blade between her fingers. Over the years, she'd lost count of how many hours she'd spent doing this. Problems that seemed insurmountable faded into the background as she stared transfixed by this tiny implement that held such power over her, yet paradoxically gave her a feeling of control.

In the weeks after the rape, Jemima had been aware that she was spiralling out of control. She needed help, as she wasn't equipped to deal with this on her own. Yet despite her therapist being a great support, it was still a constant battle. There were occasions when she had felt so overwhelmed that she had relented and given in to the compulsion to slice through her skin. She had hated herself for doing it, yet at the same time, it had given her a feeling of relief.

It wasn't just the physical assault that messed with her head. There was the fact that she had become pregnant as a result of the rape. In similar circumstances, it would have been unsurprising for a woman to opt for a termination. But Jemima had spent so many years longing for a baby of her own. Suddenly faced with what might be her only opportunity to have a baby, she had decided to proceed with the pregnancy. It had been far from an easy decision, as she was worried that, given the conception's circumstances, she might not bond with the baby when it was actually born.

As with most things in life, everyone seemed to have an opinion about what she should do, when all Jemima wanted was to be left in peace to decide for herself. The last thing she needed was for people to heap more pressure on her. At first, she hadn't wanted to think about it, but she had known that she needed to make a decision before she arrived at a time when the decision would no longer be hers to make. There had been so much to come to terms with, so much to think about that it was hardly surprising she had kept changing her mind.

In the end, it was the joy on Lucy's face as she interacted with her own children that had finally made up Jemima's mind. Jemima wanted a piece of that, and when she'd explained to James that she was expecting a baby, the young lad had initially asked if she had a new boyfriend. Sensing that the question would inevitably be asked, Jemima had already steeled herself to provide an answer. She was determined not to lie or distress the boy and wanted to keep the explanation surrounding the pregnancy as vague as she possibly could. But the prospect of having a little brother or sister proved so exciting that James raced off to tell his cousins before Jemima had a chance to explain, and he hadn't raised the question again.

The decision had been made.

Jemima was relieved when Lucy had insisted that she and James should continue to live with her after the baby was born. She had a sizeable eight-bedroomed property and a live-in nanny. It would be a perfect solution, as it would enable Jemima to continue with her career even after the baby arrived.

CHAPTER 6

Jemima sat at her desk and sipped the mug of ginger tea Gareth Peters had so thoughtfully made. Her abdomen was so large these days, it made ordinary things such as walking around, getting dressed, or even manoeuvring into an upright position monumental tasks. As the baby changed position, her stomach rippled. It was a strange yet comforting feeling that she had come to love. Jemima smiled and gently ran her hand across her belly.

There weren't many weeks left before she'd be forced to go on maternity leave. She was already taking more of a back seat, as it wasn't as if she could get stuck in the way she used to. It proved difficult enough to raise her legs to walk up the stairs, let alone launch herself at an armed assailant and bring them down with a combination of kick-boxing moves.

DCI Kennedy strode into the room. 'Listen up, people!'

Everyone knew from his sombre tone that he was about to tell them of a new case that had just come to his attention.

'There's been a murder — young woman, by all accounts. Huxley, isn't your sister's house in Leighton Meadow, close to St Agnes's church?'

'Yeah. That's the village, and the church is about a hundred yards away. Why?'

'Well that church is our crime scene,' said Kennedy. 'The four of you should get yourselves over there. I've other things I need to attend to.'

As usual, they took two cars. Broadbent always travelled with Jemima, while Ashton and Peters shared a vehicle. Dan was relieved that in recent months, Jemima had always chosen to sit in the passenger seat. He'd lost count of the times his fingers had almost melded to the seat when he was forced to endure Jemima's penchant for speed. In his opinion, she had a habit of taking unnecessary risks.

In reality, they had only once been involved in a crash when Jemima was at the wheel, and she had not been the one at fault. The collision had occurred as they were taking a suspect to the police station. They had the right of way and were mid-junction when a drugged-up driver ran a red light and went straight into the side of their vehicle. Jemima had lost consciousness, and Broadbent had been trapped. They had both had to be cut out of the vehicle. It had allowed the suspect to flee the scene and murder an elderly woman and rape her granddaughter later in the day. In fact, the effects of that crash had unexpectedly continued to play out years later in a shocking confrontation that had seen Jemima and Broadbent hospitalized for injuries sustained in the line of duty.

Right now, they were heading for the small village of Leighton Meadow in the Vale of Glamorgan. It was located less than ten miles from Cardiff and was where Jemima lived. Not that she could have ever afforded to live there on her wages. Despite earning a decent salary as a police inspector, it was nothing compared to her sister. Lucy had set up a business that was so successful, she had money to burn. In the last few decades, property prices had rocketed in these villages, pricing out most people. On the rare occasion when something went on the market, it was snapped up almost immediately, even those properties that required a significant amount of work.

Traffic eased as they left the city behind. Still, the noise of vehicles was incessant until they were able to turn off the trunk road and continue their journey along a series of country lanes.

In the short time she had lived with her sister, Jemima had discovered that village life was the antithesis of city living. It was far quieter for a start, with more of a community feel. People knew one another and stopped for a chat if they happened to walk by. It was a throwback to what life had been like when people were less self-absorbed and actually had conversations and made real connections. At first, it had seemed alien and often intrusive. But as Jemima had discarded the cloak of city life and adapted to her new circumstances, she had actually discovered that it was a more enjoyable way to live. She and James were becoming part of something, and it was a good feeling.

St Agnes's church was located on the edge of Leighton Meadow. It was a building that Jemima frequently passed, though she had not been inclined to visit. Religious establishments made her feel uneasy. The very idea of surrendering to such an ideology seemed nothing more than mass brainwashing. It defied logic yet appeared to offer comfort and hope to people who desired a sense of belonging. There had been a few occasions in her life when Jemima would have acknowledged that particular appeal. But in those moments, she reminded herself of the evil and corruption that religious institutions were keen to hide.

'Pull up on my sister's driveway. We'll walk from there.' It was the most Jemima had said for the entire journey. Her thoughts had been preoccupied with knowing that she would have to spend time inside the church and most likely have to interact with the vicar. She just hoped that he wouldn't rub her up the wrong way.

'Won't she mind?' asked Broadbent.

'I've already texted to let her know. Anyway, you could fit at least ten cars on that driveway and still have plenty of space for her clients. The church car park's small, and I guarantee the SOCOs won't thank us if we take up space there unnecessarily.'

As they parked up, Ashton and Peters pulled in beside them. In the distance, Lucy looked up and waved. She was sitting at her desk in the impressive log cabin, which served as her home office.

'How's the corporate hamper business doing?' asked Peters.

'Fine, as far as I'm aware. Lucy's always run off her feet and never seems to have a shortage of clients,' said Jemima. Though, as she spoke, she experienced an unexpected pang of guilt. She realized she hadn't once enquired about the business her sister had set up from scratch. It took up so much of her sister's time, as Lucy worked every available hour to make a success of it. Yet despite being under enormous pressure since the rape, Lucy had always been there for Jemima.

She put the inconvenient thought out of her head. 'Come on, it's this way.' There was work to be done. Now was not the time to ponder on things that could be put off until later.

They walked along the lane towards the church to find that a couple of uniformed officers were already in attendance. A patrol car had pulled into the car park and still had its lights flashing. It was a sure way to attract any villagers who happened to not be working that day. Sure enough, Jemima spotted three familiar faces up ahead. As soon as they saw her, they wasted no time heading in her direction.

'You can all head up to the church. I'll follow once I've had a quick word with the neighbourhood watch brigade,' said Jemima. She drew a deep breath and plastered what she hoped looked like a genuine smile on her face. 'Ladies, Mr Mundell.' She nodded hello.

'What's going on, Jemima?' asked Rosie Forbes, the younger of the two women.

'I'm sure you'll appreciate that I'm not at liberty to divulge information about an ongoing investigation. All I can say at the moment is that there's been an incident at the church. Now, if you'll excuse me.' Jemima turned and walked away without saying another word. There was little point in telling them to go home, as this was probably the most

50

exciting thing to have happened in the village for many years. If anything, their numbers would swell as word got around that something awful had happened. Jemima wouldn't have been surprised to return to this spot in a few hours to discover that they'd brought camping chairs and a picnic.

She headed through the lychgate. 'Don't tell them anything, and don't allow them on to the church grounds.'

'Goes without saying, ma'am,' replied the uniformed officer.

The rest of the team hovered outside the main entrance of the church. They knew better than to set foot on a crime scene ahead of Jemima. Whenever possible, she preferred to be the first one over the threshold. Not because she got some sort of power trip out of it, but because she found it helpful to take in every aspect of the murder scene without it being crowded with other people. There was always the chance that someone had disturbed things or even gone as far as touching the body. But the fewer people, the better, as there was less chance that evidence had been compromised. And she found that seeing the scene in its natural state helped her to identify with the killer. It was not something she was particularly fond of, but she often found it a valuable thing to do.

Sensing her approach, Broadbent turned and stepped towards her. As he did so, Jemima spotted someone sitting on a wooden bench inside the vestibule. She heard Ashton say something to the person but was too far away to make out the words.

'This is Father Mason Roy,' said Broadbent. 'He had the unfortunate experience of discovering the body. He's a bit shaken up at the moment.'

Jemima approached the priest. At first, she could only see his full head of hair, as his elbows were on his knees and his head in his hands. When he looked up and their eyes locked, her breath caught in her throat. She was taken aback by how attractive she found the man to be.

Despite being sufficiently self-aware to acknowledge her prejudice against religion, Jemima had gone there expecting to feel disdain, possibly even contempt for the clergyman. Yet this instant spark of attraction was confusing, as she loathed everything his calling stood for. She immediately experienced a pang of guilt and silently chastised herself. The feeling was inappropriate under the circumstances. It seemed doubly wrong given the fact that she was so heavily pregnant. Still, it was proof that despite everything she had endured over the last year or so, she was still capable of feeling attraction towards members of the opposite sex. It was the first time since Nick had walked out on her that she'd felt that way about any man. The unexpectedness and intensity of the feeling shocked her.

She shook it away, needing to focus. 'I'd like you to talk me through what happened this morning, Father Roy.'

'It started out as a typical morning. I came along just before nine o'clock to open up. That's when I discovered that the door was unlocked. My first thought was that someone had broken in during the night. We've been lucky so far, but you hear about it all the time. People thinking there may be money on the premises. Or wanting to steal the chalice and other paraphernalia — it's sad, but there's money in metals. Then there are the ones who are after the communion wine. But I soon realized that it wasn't the case as there was no damage to the door or the frame.'

'So you'd left the church unlocked overnight?' asked Jemima.

'Me? No.' He shook his head emphatically.

'Who did?'

'That'd be Winston Mundell. He's got a key to the church, and he was here yesterday evening, along with a few others, for the weekly bell-ringing practice.'

Jemima had lived at Lucy's for long enough to have heard the weekly efforts of St Agnes's campanologists. There was no doubting the fact that they were an enthusiastic collection of people. But from the sound they produced, it was evident that they needed a lot of practice.

'And is Mr Mundell in the habit of leaving the church unlocked?' asked Jemima.

'That's the kicker. As far as I'm aware, he's not done it before. This is the first time I've arrived in the morning and found the door unlocked.'

'Gareth, go and have a word with Mr Mundell. He's one of the people I stopped to speak with on my way in. Find out what he's got to say for himself,' said Jemima.

As Gareth Peters set off towards the lychgate, Jemima turned her attention back to Father Roy. 'What happened when you went inside the church?'

'The sun was up, so I didn't need to put any lights on. Everything appeared to be the way I left it. There was no suggestion that anything was wrong as there was nothing out of place. The unforgivable thing is that I didn't notice her at first. I was so focused on getting to the vestry, I didn't think of glancing across each of the pews. It's awful to think that she was just lying there, and I walked straight past her. A young woman lost her life in my church, and I didn't know.'

'Surely there's no reason you would have expected to find a body?'

'None at all, but it doesn't stop me from feeling guilty. This building is where we come together to commune with God. It's sacrosanct. You'd think that as a member of the clergy, I'd know if some heinous act had been committed within these walls, but I didn't. I had no idea.'

'Don't beat yourself up about it. You had no reason to think that anything like this had happened. It's not exactly an everyday occurrence.' Jemima witnessed the pain in the man's eyes. She suspected that this had been the only occasion he had encountered a murder scene. Members of the clergy were used to dealing with the aftermath of tragic events. However, their pastoral role meant that they were at least one step removed from the horror and depravity the police and many others had to face.

'Was anyone with you when you went inside?' pressed Jemima.

'No, I was alone.'

'And has anyone else entered the building since you discovered the body?'

'No, I've seen enough television programmes to know that it makes things far more difficult if there's any contamination of the scene.'

'One last thing, did you approach or touch the body?'

'I didn't need to. From my vantage point in the aisle, I could see she was dead.'

Jemima nodded. 'The church and the grounds will be off limits to everyone until we've had a chance to complete our examination of the scene. Sergeant Ashton will accompany you to the vicarage and take a written statement from you. I'd ask you not to discuss this morning's events with anyone, as it may compromise the investigation,' she said.

CHAPTER 7

Jemima took a deep breath to steel herself for what she was about to face. She shivered as she stepped over the threshold into the main body of the church. It was an involuntary reaction to the noticeable change in temperature. As cooler air kissed her skin, goosebumps erupted along her forearms. She distractedly raised her hands to rub them away as she cast a critical eye over the murder scene.

Thoughts of the gorgeous vicar began to fade as she focused on the reason she was there. Being attracted to a member of the opposite sex was an unnecessary and confusing distraction. But as her hormone levels were all over the place, Jemima was more susceptible to mood swings and strong feelings overwhelming her when she least expected it. This instance was especially bewildering as, in her opinion, clergymen were not to be trusted until proven otherwise. And under the circumstances, that particular view seemed apposite. There was no denying that, given Father Roy's responsibility for the building where a murder had recently taken place, he was currently their only suspect.

Still, Jemima knew that she could have lost herself in his eyes . . .

As she resolved to put the enigmatic priest out of her mind, she forced herself to study the church's interior. And as Jemima raised her gaze, she noticed that the sun's rays showed off the beauty of the main stained-glass window. The vibrant colours were a stark contrast to the otherwise sombre interior. They drew the eye away from features that were predominantly hewn from stone and wood. In beams of refracted light filtering through the interior space, millions of dust particles floated in the air.

The atmosphere inside the old building was noticeably stale, and she wrinkled her nose in disgust. There was an overriding smell of incense. But although Jemima found it off-putting, it was preferable to the smell of a corpse. At least the cooler temperature would help slow the level of decay. Throughout the pregnancy, Jemima's sense of smell had heightened, often causing her to feel nauseous. And the last thing she wanted was to display weakness by vomiting at a crime scene.

Despite her unfamiliarity with the inside of a church, Jemima agreed with Father Roy's statement that there was no obvious sign that anything was amiss. Nothing appeared to have been disturbed, and there was no sign of a struggle. It confirmed the plausibility of his assertion that he had walked past the body without noticing it. This was his place of work, so he would be familiar with every inch of the building. No one would make that walk each morning glancing from side to side to see if something was wrong. You'd have to be paranoid to act that way.

Jemima breathed shallowly as she walked slowly down the aisle, wincing at the volley of ricochets the heels of her shoes repeatedly struck on the stone floor. It seemed inappropriately loud and disrespectful in the context that she was heading out to acquaint herself with the recently deceased.

A few steps more and she spotted the corpse — a svelte figure, more girl than woman. She lay on the far end of a pew, no doubt a deliberate attempt to hide in the shadows. A bare arm dangled towards the floor. With the index finger extended, it appeared as though she was pointing at the blood that had flowed from the fatal wound. From the expression

56

on her face, it was easy to see that she had been afraid. Her eyes were wide and her mouth open. In the end, her chosen hiding place had been her downfall. The safety of knowing that no one could creep up on her had also allowed no means of escape without revealing her whereabouts. She'd found herself trapped, and there was nothing she could have done about it.

A metal bolt, which Jemima suspected had been fired from a crossbow, protruded from the corpse's chest. The choice of weapon was problematic. There was no requirement to have a licence or even register the fact that you owned such a weapon in the UK. It was crazy, as anyone could get their hands on such a lethal weapon with virtually no controls in place to prevent them from doing so.

'The SOCOs have arrived. They're unloading their gear,' shouted Broadbent. He was still outside the church's main body, thankful that Jemima hadn't insisted that he accompany her to view the crime scene. He had an aversion to blood and had tried to hide his phobia for many years. Jemima was aware of it. Whenever possible, she allowed him to take a back seat in the initial examination of the crime scene. Though, as she was about to go on maternity leave, Broadbent would have to step up to the plate. He was fortunate that she was so sensitive to his needs and was prepared to cover for him. But he couldn't risk taking a chance with anyone else. It was a weakness that could be used against him, and Broadbent didn't fancy the idea of other colleagues getting wind of it. After all, he didn't want to remain a sergeant for the rest of his career. If he was going to progress, there was no way he could continue to shy away from that aspect of the job.

'Send them in when they're ready,' said Jemima.

With a limited amount of time for quiet contemplation of the scene, Jemima took a final look around, committing details to memory. Her work here was done. The SOCOs would meticulously process the scene, record and photograph everything. The body would be taken to the

University Hospital, where John Prothero would carry out a post-mortem examination. Hopefully, this collection of scientists would come up with some valuable information to help the investigation.

Jemima turned her head at the sound of muffled voices. They were too far away for her to hear what was being said. But as the voices got louder, she recognized that one of them belonged to Jeanne Ennersley, the lead SOCO. They'd encountered each other on numerous occasions over the years and had grown increasingly fond of each other.

'Here we go again.' Jeanne was marching purposefully down the aisle. 'It's our first time at this village. There's a crowd, presumably locals, gathered in the car park. A couple of them have even brought camping chairs and refreshments. They're obviously treating it as though it's live theatre. They must lead pretty boring lives if this is the highlight of their day.'

'I live about a hundred yards away, and I can categorically say that nothing much happens around here. They'll be talking about this for years to come, Jeanne. It's a wonder some of them didn't try to get selfies with you,' said Jemima.

'In fairness, most of them look as though the digital age has passed them by. I doubt there's a mobile phone between them. So, Jemima, what have we got?'

'Unidentified young female shot in the chest with what I believe is a bolt from a crossbow. Anything you're able to tell me will be helpful, as at the moment I don't have anything to go on.'

'I already know the answer but still, have to ask the question. Did you touch anything?'

'Nothing at all, Jeanne. With the size of my stomach, I wouldn't even risk trying to waddle between those pews. I've not got closer than the aisle. The priest's already told me that he didn't go near the body. And as far as I'm aware, no one else has been in here since it happened. So, any evidence found on her should be from the time of the attack.'

'Good. You know the drill by now. We'll process the body and get her shipped off to John Prothero. I'll let you know of any findings. Now get yourself out of here. Go and put your feet up. You look fit to drop.'

'Fat chance of that, there's too much to do. Are you able to give me a ballpark on the time of death?'

'Not for a few hours. I'll need ambient temperature readings to compare with the body to calculate the rate of cooling. But you'll be the first person I contact when I have the information.'

Jemima headed out of the church and found Broadbent talking with Gareth Peters. 'What did Winston Mundell have to say for himself?' she interjected.

'He initially insisted that he locked up last night. But when I pushed him on it, and one of the other villagers hinted that he might have forgotten, he reluctantly admitted that it could have been the case.'

'Which villager?' asked Jemima.

'Er . . . that'd be Ceri Jones,' confirmed Peters, reading from his notebook. 'She also attended the bell-ringing practice last night. She confirmed that they all left the church at the same time, but just as Winston was about to lock up, he got a call on his mobile. Ceri and the others headed home at that point, leaving Winston to it. And when Winston was reminded of the call, he admitted that he couldn't be certain of having locked the church.'

'Which would explain how someone was able to get inside without there being any sign of a break-in,' said Broadbent.

'For now, I'd like you to speak to the villagers. Take statements from anyone who saw or heard anything unusual from when the bell-ringers left the church to the time Father Roy discovered the body. It'll be a while until Jeanne Ennersley can narrow the time frame for when the death occurred,' Jemima said. 'I'm going to have a word with my sister. When you've finished taking statements, come and find me there.'

CHAPTER 8

Jemima headed back along the lane. Usually, she would have chosen to be the first to interview those living close to a crime scene. But the location of this particular murder made that impossible. This was a place where everyone knew everyone else. And despite being a relative newcomer to the village, she was already familiar with some of the residents. As there was a real chance that familiarity could compromise her objectivity, it was a risk Jemima was not prepared to take. She would ensure that others on the team would initially question anyone she knew, as they would be completely impartial. Though, that did not apply to Lucy.

Jemima was sure that her sister was above reproach. She would have had no involvement with the events of the previous night. So, it was safe to speak with her to get her view on the other villagers. Lucy had lived in her house for the last five years. She was a sociable person and might have seen or heard things useful to the case. Not that Lucy was a gossip — far from it. But people trusted her and she would have a feel for what the other villagers were like. And it would be helpful to have a knowledgeable inside source on any gossip or potential scandal that could shed some light on this shocking event.

It was only within the last year that Jemima and her sister had become close. Despite there being only a few years between them, they had had a fractious relationship. Lucy had been their mother's favoured child. That role would, in the majority of families, have resulted in the occasional privilege. But the Goodman family was far from typical.

To the outside world, everything at Chez Goodman was hunky-dory. And for every family member, apart from Jemima, that was indeed the case. But Celia Goodman was a narcissist, and Jemima her target. It was no wonder that, as far as Jemima was concerned, life was confusing, miserable and unfair.

It is only natural for a child to crave their parents' attention. And if one of those was a stay-at-home parent, then that is the person the child will form a closer bond with. It's the way children learn about the world and the method by which behaviour is validated. So, it was to be expected that Lucy Goodman, as the favoured child, trusted what her mother told her. She was groomed into believing that Jemima was badly behaved. It explained why Lucy was rewarded with so many treats, yet Jemima was frequently disciplined and sent to her room.

Throughout their childhood, whenever Jemima protested that it wasn't fair, Lucy just accepted that it was yet another example of her sister's bad behaviour. Despite Lucy's obvious intelligence, she turned out to be a poor judge of character. Indeed, until she overheard her mother's appalling tirade on Jemima following the rape, Lucy hadn't acknowledged her mother's abhorrent behaviour.

The awful realization had hit her as sharply as any slap across the face. Celia Goodman's behaviour was nothing short of repugnant. It troubled Lucy that she had not seen this side of her mother before and caused her to reflect on those occasions when her sister had claimed unfair treatment. It was also a wake-up call for their father.

Until that point, Donald Goodman had overlooked his wife's behaviour. He loved Celia with all his heart. Although he had witnessed occasional outbursts over the years, he had somehow airbrushed out his wife's bad behaviour towards Jemima. Celia was calm and plausible. She had a way of explaining things, which he was ready to believe. After all, Celia's truthfulness and sincerity were two of the qualities that had attracted him to her in the first place.

When his daughters were younger, Donald had spent much of his time at work. Celia had been a stay-at-home mother, so he fully believed that she knew the children far better than he did. Therefore, Donald didn't think to question his wife's judgement on any child-related matter. As far as he was concerned, her judgements were both fair and measured.

Lucy was the sibling who excelled from an early age. She was intelligent, well behaved and had an easy-going personality. Jemima was clever too but was moody and always appeared to be distant. There had been many occasions when Donald had wondered why Jemima seemed withdrawn. But whenever he raised these concerns with his wife, she always brushed them away, insisting that Jemima was just a naughty child who required firm handling. Celia was adamant that Jemima was jealous of Lucy, which was why she acted the way she did.

Donald was contented with his life and proud of his family. He never considered how the family dynamics worked. It didn't once occur to him that his wife was the root of Jemima's problems, as he wholeheartedly believed that Celia was perfect. In his opinion, she was a shining example of how other women should behave, and he thanked his lucky stars for the way his life and his family had turned out.

In recent months, Lucy realized that she had a whole lot of making up to do. Not that she had ever purposely set out to be horrible to her sister. But having witnessed her mother's offensive outburst at a time when Jemima needed kindness and understanding, Lucy had realized that her mother had hoodwinked her throughout her entire life. Over the years, Celia had dripped poison into Lucy's ear about how Jemima was such a bad person. But as Lucy had reflected on past incidents, she had begun to see things in a new light. She was sickened to realize that she had so readily bought into her mother's web of lies.

Lucy had taken a hard line with her mother, cutting her off, refusing to allow her anywhere near her grandchildren. It had also brought things to a head with Donald, as he could no longer ignore the fact that his wife's behaviour was shameful and unacceptably cruel. Celia remained unrepentant, blaming Jemima for what had happened, and Donald had been so sickened by her behaviour that he filed for divorce. He had found himself in an intolerable situation. Until the divorce went through, they were forced to continue living under the same roof, even though they were not speaking to each other. The Goodman family had fractured, and Celia had been cast adrift.

Jemima made her way towards the log cabin, where she could see that Lucy was speaking to someone on the telephone. As she opened the door, Lucy glanced up, smiled and pointed to a nearby chair before holding out the fingers of her free hand to indicate that she had almost finished the conversation.

'What's going on? Has something happened in the village?' she asked as soon as she ended the call.

'A young woman's been murdered at the church,' said Jemima.

Lucy was so surprised that her mouth hung open in disbelief. She stared at her sister for a few seconds, narrowed her eyes and gave a slight shake of the head. 'Sorry, I must've misheard. What did you just say?'

'You heard me right. There's been a murder at the church.'

'The kids! Are we in danger? Was it anyone we know?' she asked, her voice rising with each syllable. The colour had drained from her cheeks, and fear was written over her face.

'Calm down, Luce. As yet, we haven't identified the victim, and we don't have a motive. It would be sensible to take the precaution of locking doors and not leaving downstairs windows open. But if you lived in the city, you'd do that as a matter of course. You should have a word with Eloise. Tell her to keep the kids entertained with indoor activities. I think at the moment it's too risky to allow them to play outside in the garden, even if she were to supervise them.'

'But we moved to this village because it's a quiet backwater. Nothing bad ever happens here.' Lucy's voice cracked with emotion, and she hurriedly wiped her eyes on her sleeve.

'It's a nice but naive view, Luce. The truth is that bad things happen everywhere. No one knows what goes on behind closed doors. Sometimes people are even oblivious of what goes on inside their own home.'

Lucy lowered her eyes in shame. 'You know how sorry I am about—'

'Don't be silly, I'm not having a go, Luce, it's a statement of fact. No one really knows anyone. If someone's determined to hide things, then they'll find a way to do it. You've just got to hope that those closest to you are not like that.' She looked out of the window. 'With everything that's happened to me, I've not paid much attention to our neighbours. I know a few of them by sight, but I don't know their life stories.'

'Is that your way of telling me that you think one of our neighbours is a murderer?' squealed Lucy.

'No, it's not. You need to calm down. At the moment, there's no reason to suspect that any of us are in immediate danger. But given the location of the murder, I'm going to need background information on everyone living in this area. Murders are often committed by people with close links to the victim and a familiarity with the murder location. So, until I have a reason to rule them out, everyone in this village will be treated as potential suspects. It's the way things work.' She flipped open her notebook. 'Now, I need you to tell me everything you know or have heard about the people living in this village.'

CHAPTER 9

Jemima understood that her sister was freaked out by the murder. It was a natural reaction. Lucy surrounded herself with lovely things and friendly people. Even her business had positivity and wholesomeness stamped all over it. A murder committed just a hundred yards away from her home and workplace was enough to rock her world. It brought fear and uncertainty where there had been none.

There was no doubt in Jemima's mind that her sister had nothing to do with the murder. She was confident that Lucy could be trusted to tell the truth as she saw it. She had no reason to hide anything or withhold information. In other words, whatever Lucy told her, be it village gossip, intuition, or cold hard facts, could be used to verify information originating from other sources.

'Well, this isn't the way I envisaged today panning out,' sighed Lucy. 'Let me see . . . Since the murder occurred at the church, I'll start with Father Mason Roy. When he first arrived, people thought he was American. He's not. He's Canadian, previously the incumbent at a church in Ottawa. The accent's quite exotic in these parts, and you'd have to be blind not to notice that he's drop-dead gorgeous. He's breathed life into the church. Within a few weeks of his arrival, attendance rocketed

— mainly on the female front. As he's Anglican and single, he instantly became the village's most eligible bachelor. But as far as I'm aware, no matter how hard numerous women have tried, he hasn't shown any interest.'

'I had noticed he's easy on the eye.' Jemima smiled suggestively. 'Not that I'm in the market for a relationship at the moment.' She quickly qualified her throwaway statement.

'Wow, sis! Welcome back to the land of the living. I never thought I'd hear you admit to having the hots for a vicar.' Lucy's eyes twinkled with delight.

Jemima was pleased to see that her words had had the desired effect. With something to distract her, Lucy had relaxed and was more likely to speak freely. Keen to capitalise on this, she continued her questioning.

'So, do you have any idea why he came to this village? It seems such a radical move — a city church in Ottawa to a sleepy village in Wales.'

'No one seems to know. Of course, there's been plenty of speculation, but it's still a complete mystery. Personally, I think it enhances his allure. Is he your prime suspect? After all, the murder took place inside his church.'

'We're only an hour into the investigation, Luce. We've not even identified the victim, so it's way too soon to have a prime suspect. And even when I do, I won't be able to discuss it with you. Let's move on to someone else,' said Jemima.

'Well, there's Winston and Christina Mundell. They run the cattery on the far side of the village. There was some bad feeling when they first set it up. Opposition to the planning permission. Some villagers objected because of the potential noise factor, but it went ahead, and there've been no problems. I think Winston's a churchwarden, and he organizes the bell-ringing practice. You'll know already that it causes more noise than any number of cats could possibly make.'

'You're not wrong there.' Jemima nodded in agreement. It had occurred to her that the local campanologists were a collection of people with no musical ability or sense of rhythm.

'What about Christina? Does she get involved in village life?'

'No, she's quite introverted and crazily busy with the cats. As far as I understand it, she's the driving force behind that enterprise's day-to-day operation. I think Winston's taken on the admin side, which leaves him free to get involved with other things.'

'What about the people who run the pub?' asked Jemima. Despite the establishment being the hub of the village, she had only been inside on a few occasions.

'That'd be Wayne and Rosie Forbes. Can't say I've heard anything bad about them. But they've got teenage sons, Nathaniel and Curtis. From what I've heard, they're a bit of a handful. It might be worthwhile taking a closer look at them. I got the impression they might hang around with a bad crowd.'

'Do you know their age?'

'I can't be certain. Possibly sixteen or seventeen, so old enough to get into trouble,' said Lucy.

Jemima was well aware of her sister's intolerance of bad behaviour. In Lucy's mind, something as innocuous as failing to acknowledge a neighbour with a cursory wave of the hand would be enough to mark them out as someone to be wary of.

'And, of course, there's John Jones.'

'Who's he?' asked Jemima.

'He's married to Ceri Jones. She's one of the campanologists. But I'd say that John's the nearest thing this village has to a criminal. Someone said he was once arrested for poaching, but that's about it. Though, it's a huge leap to think he'd be a murderer.'

'No one knows what any of us is capable of, Luce. So, who else is there?' Jemima had a sinking feeling that this fact-finding mission was getting her nowhere.

'Let me think . . . Well, there are Valerie and Max Cheedle. She's a teacher, and he's a writer. I don't know anything about them. Then there's the Bhatts. Deepak's a radiographer, and Sarah works in a bank. They've a teenage son, Krish. That lad comes across as being quite introverted, nothing like the Forbes twins. But they're all just regular hardworking families.'

'Do any of these families live in that property just about visible from my bedroom window?' asked Jemima.

'You mean West Winds?'

'Yes, if that's the one on the hill. I've never been up that way, but it looks as though it's at least a quarter of a mile away.' Jemima had often wondered what it would be like to live in such an isolated spot.

'No. That's not part of the village. It's the Johnsons' place. Gabrielle and her husband own it. They've twin girls, Blythe and Roslyn, cute little things. They're primary-school age.'

'So how do you know them?'

'Gabrielle's a leading light in the local chamber of commerce. She's quite a force to be reckoned with. Got her fingers in a lot of pies,' said Lucy.

'Is that a bad thing? Do you mean she's dodgy?'

'Oh no, nothing like that, it's just sour grapes on my part. I suppose I'm just a little envious. Gabrielle just seems to have it all. Their house is huge, and they've got a lot of land. It's definitely a sign of success. It must be worth a fortune.'

'You're so funny, Luce,' interjected Jemima. 'You're successful in your own right. Yet you're still not satisfied with what you've achieved.'

'I find it motivates me. I like having something to aspire to. It keeps me focused. Anyway, getting back to the Johnsons, I don't think there's any money shortage there. They own Chesrielle Haulage,' said Lucy.

'I think I've noticed that particular fleet out and about. Are the vehicles kept on their land?'

'No. There'd be an outcry if anyone tried to run that sort of business from around here. The last thing any of us would want would be HGVs coming and going at all hours. Apart from the noise, it wouldn't be safe to have vehicles of that size regularly using these lanes. I'm sure Gabrielle said that the business is located somewhere in Cardiff. Possibly off Rover Way? At least, I think that's where their haulage yard is.' She frowned. 'Come to think of it, I haven't seen the Johnsons for quite a while. I hope they're all right. I'll ask Eloise if she's heard anything. The Johnsons used to have a nanny too, so I'm sure Eloise will know her. They'll undoubtedly have met up at a playgroup and kept in touch.'

'What's Gabrielle's husband's name?'

'I believe it's Chester,' said Lucy. 'Hence the name of their company. Chesrielle Haulage. Far too sickly sweet if you ask me.'

Before Jemima had a chance to ask anything else, there was a knock on the door. It opened immediately as Broadbent stuck his head around and smiled at Lucy. 'Fin and Gareth are on their way back to the station. You ready to go yet?'

'Yeah. We'll catch up this evening, Luce.' Jemima shuffled forward in the seat and placed her hands on the arms of the chair as she struggled to her feet. Simple movements that she had once taken for granted were becoming more problematic as the baby continued to grow.

* * *

Back at the station, the team sat down to pool the small amount of information they had gathered. They were keen to get going, but John Prothero had informed them that he could not start on the post-mortem until the following day. He was already fully committed until then. Adannaya Okoro, who worked alongside John, was on holiday, so there was no chance of her picking up the slack. It was frustrating, but there was nothing anyone could do about it.

'What have we got so far?' asked Jemima.

Ashton grabbed a marker pen and headed towards the whiteboard. Jemima was usually the one to record things on there, but the rest of the team knew she was finding things more difficult these days. Everyone agreed that Ashton had the most legible handwriting, so it made sense for him to take on the task.

'I took Father Roy's statement, which was exactly what he told us when we spoke to him at the church. I got the impression that he was telling the truth, and I don't think he was holding anything back. I asked him if he would fill me in on his parishioners. Unsurprisingly, given his profession, he refused. He said he wasn't trying to be obstructive. It was just that talking about his parishioners would be a betrayal of trust, as he encourages them to open up and speak to him in confidence. But he did tell me that in his opinion, none of the parishioners would be capable of taking a life in such a brutal manner.'

'That's all very well, but Father Roy's outlook on the world might very well be coloured by a desire to always see the best in people,' said Jemima. 'I doubt he's ever been this close to a murder scene. So, I don't think we should pay any attention to whatever instincts he has towards his parishioners' capabilities. I can guarantee his assessments won't be evidence-based. They'll be purely intuitive.'

'There were a few properties where no one appeared to be at home,' said Broadbent. He listed those addresses.

Jemima nodded. 'They were most likely at work. As I don't know those people, I'll make the rounds this evening and take statements from anyone who thinks they might have seen or heard anything.'

'I spoke to someone named Max Cheedle. He was a right pompous git. Went on about how I'd interrupted his creative flow. I don't know who he thinks he is. He reckoned that he wasn't able to help, but I think he was hiding something. So I think it might be worth doing a bit of digging there,' said Broadbent.

'Did you speak to his wife?' asked Jemima.

'No, he said she was out at work.'

'In that case, I'll call there this evening. Any updates, Gareth?'

'I spoke to the couple at the pub, Rosie and Wayne Forbes. Neither of them witnessed anything out of the ordinary. But apparently, she's a light sleeper, and she reckons that she was woken by a vehicle driving past around two in the morning. She said the engine sounded too deep and loud to be a car. It was more like an HGV. Apparently, it's happened a few times over the last couple of months.'

'Is that all we have?' asked Jemima. The question was rhetorical, reflecting the sinking feeling that this case wasn't about to be wrapped up quickly. It was a worrying thought that the killer was out there somewhere, possibly even eyeing up their next victim. And given the proximity to where Jemima lived, it was particularly perturbing.

Apart from the fracas with Nick, shortly before he walked out on them, Jemima had always considered her home to be a safe space. This murder brought ugliness and fear far too close to home. It meant that there was a potential threat to people she loved, and it had come at a time when, because of the pregnancy, Jemima knew she wasn't up to protecting them.

Her email account pinged, announcing the arrival of a message. Jemima glanced at the screen and saw that it was from Jeanne Ennersley. There was also an attachment. The message was short and to the point.

Thought this might be useful.

And it certainly was. Jeanne had attached a photograph of the dead woman's face.

Jemima set to work. 'Get this out to the media outlets, Gareth. You never know, we might get lucky and be able to ID the victim. While you're at it, print off copies for each of us. Dan, organize people to man the phones this evening. Even if this doesn't result in a positive ID, it's guaranteed that there'll be the usual round of timewasters and attention-seekers clogging up the phone lines.'

She turned to Finlay. 'Make a start on trawling through the missing persons database. You may get a hit. After all, it worked on the Llys Faen Hall murders. You two can give him a hand when you've finished,' she said to Dan and Gareth. 'In the meantime, I'll go and update Kennedy.' Jemima struggled to her feet.

CHAPTER 10

Later that afternoon, Jemima set off back to the village. Broadbent had insisted that he accompany her. As it was getting late, he had taken his own car so that he could head home after they'd interviewed the villagers. These days he seemed to stick to her like glue. Deep down, Jemima was grateful for his concern. Though, at times, his overprotectiveness was a little claustrophobic.

Back at the station, Ashton and Peters were still hard at it. Jemima had insisted that they should not stay longer than the end of their shift. There were always budget constraints to worry about, and at the moment, it wasn't as if there was much they could do. The pace would inevitably pick up when they received the SOCO team's findings, and any evidence revealed by the post-mortem.

The night shift would have the phone lines covered. Those officers were more than capable of dealing with an influx of calls. She'd left instructions for them to contact her should any useful information come in as a result of the victim's face being shown by the media.

Jemima pulled up outside the Bhatts' home, and Broadbent tucked his car in behind hers. Apart from its thatched roof, it was a property largely obscured from sight by a perfectly manicured privet hedge. And as she opened the full-height, solid, wooden gate and stepped into the front garden, her breath caught in her throat, and she stopped to stare. The property was stunning. It was precisely how Jemima had imagined her dream home to be, even down to the plants in the garden.

'Hello, can I help you?' asked a woman who was on her knees, tending to one of the flower beds.

Jemima felt her heart miss a beat and her hand reflexively jerked towards her chest. She had been so captivated by the property that she'd failed to spot that anyone else was there.

'Sorry, I didn't mean to scare you. Was there something you wanted?' The woman stood up and brushed her clothes down.

'No, I'm the one who should apologize. I didn't see you there. I was just blown away by the beauty of your home and garden. Sorry, I'm not usually like this. It's been a long day. I'm Detective Inspector Jemima Huxley, and this is Sergeant Broadbent.'

'I thought I recognized you. You're Lucy's sister, aren't you?' She walked towards them, extending her arm to shake their hands. 'I'm Sarah Bhatt, but you obviously know that since you're standing in my garden. I heard what happened up at the church. It's shocking. Absolutely terrifying. Come through to the rear garden. We can sit down while we talk.'

Jemima was amazed to discover that the rear of the property was even nicer than the front. The Bhatts certainly took pride in their home, and Sarah Bhatt was obviously a keen gardener. The woman appeared to be in her early forties, with short hair styled to emphasize her cheekbones. Her complexion was flawless, even though she appeared to be wearing no cosmetics.

'You're right. We're here about what happened last night,' said Jemima. She and Broadbent sat on a wicker sofa plumped up with a colourful array of cushions. A sizeable striped awning shaded the area from the sun's rays, while allowing an uninterrupted view of the garden. 'Did you see or hear anything out of the ordinary last night?'

'Around here? No. But then again, I spent a few hours with my headphones on, propped up on the sofa listening to an audiobook. To be honest, I was so engrossed in the story that a bomb could have gone off, and I wouldn't have noticed. I'd also had a couple of glasses of wine, which made me feel sleepy. I was in bed by about ten thirty and didn't wake up until the alarm went off at about seven this morning.'

'And what about your husband?' asked Jemima.

At that moment, a teenage boy sauntered into the garden. He was holding a large textbook under his arm and carrying a can of soda in one hand and a banana in the other. 'Mum, have you se—' He stopped abruptly when he spotted that his mother had company.

'This is my son, Krish. Krish, darling, this is Detective Inspector Huxley and Sergeant Broadbent,' said Sarah.

'H-hello,' said Krish. His voice was suddenly barely audible, and his cheeks burned with embarrassment as he mumbled the greeting. The lad was as thin and gangly as a newborn foal. His limbs appeared disproportionately long for his slender frame, making his movements appear jerky and awkward. It gave the impression that he wasn't quite in control of his own body.

'Hi, Krish. Did you see or hear anything unusual last night?' asked Jemima.

The boy shook his head.

'Be a love and ask your father to join us,' said Sarah. As her son headed back inside the house, she turned to them and whispered, 'Krish is incredibly shy. He's at that awkward age — no longer a boy, but not yet a man. And he just keeps on growing. It seems as though he goes to bed only to get up the following morning a few inches taller. He's eating us out of house and home.'

When Deepak Bhatt appeared a few moments later, he was dressed in running gear and carrying a pair of brightly coloured running shoes. With the introductions out of the way, he sat down and proceeded to change his footwear.

'Deepak's training for the London Marathon,' said Sarah.

'That takes a serious amount of commitment,' said Broadbent.

'It does. I try to do at least ten miles a day, no matter the weather. Have you got the running bug, too?'

'Me? No. Though, I should make the effort. Do you stick to the same time each day?'

'No, it varies. A lot depends on what time I manage to get home from work. Sometimes it's quite late, and I've lost the light. It happens a lot in the winter, so on those occasions, I use the running machine in the garage.'

'Did you notice anything unusual when you went for your run yesterday?' asked Jemima.

'As a matter of fact, I did. I'd set off later than I'd hoped and followed part of my usual route. I knew I only had time for about five miles before I'd lose the light, but I thought I'd do that first, then make up the distance on the running machine. Anyway, I was on the footpath that crosses the field above the church, and I saw some movement in the church-yard. It was strange. In all the years I've been following that route, it's the first time I've seen anyone there.'

'What exactly did you see?'

'There were two people. I think, but I can't be certain, that it was a man and a woman. They were quite animated, but I was too far away to see them clearly. I certainly couldn't tell who they were. But I got the impression they were hav-ing an argument. Do you think it could be related to what happened inside the church?'

'Quite possibly. It's definitely something we'll follow up. What time would this have been?'

'Best guess, I'd say approximately eight thirtyish to nine.'

Given the estimated timing, Jemima knew that it was almost an hour after the bell-ringers would have left the church and gone home. Throughout her time at the village, she'd come to know the churchyard as a quiet place. Except for funerals, Christmas, Mothering Sunday, birthdays or anniversaries, people rarely visited the graves.

Despite her aversion to religious gatherings, Jemima enjoyed wandering through the churchyard. Gravestones fascinated her. She'd been drawn to them ever since childhood. She'd stop to read the inscriptions and wonder what the dead had been like in life. But the ultimate attraction of the place was that she had not once come across anyone else. She loved the peace. It gave her time to think without having to worry about anyone else. It was a welcome change. Something she was unable to do either at work or at home with Lucy and the children.

The village had somehow also avoided attracting unwanted attention from groups of teenagers, though there were a few of that age group living in the area. It seemed that whatever socializing occurred either went on behind closed doors or else out of the immediate area. Not that there was anything of interest, apart from a village green and a small duck pond. The village seemed idyllically tranquil. That was, until the horrendous events of the previous night.

'Can you recall exactly where you saw them?' asked Jemima. The graveyard wasn't large, but it was still a big area to cover.

'It was towards the top end, near a tree on the far side of the churchyard. I remember thinking it was an ideal spot for a clandestine meeting as it was far enough away from the church and obscured to a large extent from the road. If I hadn't been running across that particular footpath, it's possible that no one would have seen them.'

'There's always the chance a dog walker would have spotted them,' interjected Sarah.

'They don't tend to head up that way. Most of them favour the village green and take the path by the stream,' said Deepak.

'Would the majority of locals know that?' asked Jemima.

'I'd say so. Sarah wouldn't. She doesn't come running with me, and we don't have a pet. Dog walkers tend to favour that route as they've got several pet-waste disposal bins along that way. It's ideal as the owners don't have to carry the poo bags too far once they've picked it up after their dog.'

'Thanks, that's been helpful. One final question before I go, did you hear a large vehicle going past sometime in the night?' asked Jemima.

'I did. I think it was about two thirtyish. I know she won't appreciate me saying this, but Sarah's snoring woke me up shortly before.'

'I don't snore!'

'Believe me, you do. Not that I'm complaining,' said Deepak. He gave his wife a mischievous grin.

'And is it unusual for a large vehicle to travel along this road at that time?' asked Jemima.

'In the last few months, I've noticed a few, though it's not a regular occurrence. Before that, I don't recall hearing any.'

CHAPTER 11

Having left the Bhatts, they headed back towards the church. Jemima spotted the SOCO vehicles were still in the small parking area and breathed a sigh of relief. At least there would be people to help them scour the far end of the churchyard. She wasn't holding out much hope of finding anything, but could it be coincidental that a couple had been spotted arguing only a few hundred yards from where a brutal murder was committed? Chances were that it had nothing to do with the murder, but it had to be looked into, if only to be able to rule it out.

Jeanne Ennersley was standing outside the church, gazing skyward as though seeking divine intervention. From a distance, she appeared to be deep in thought, but as Jemima approached, she dropped her gaze and turned to greet her. 'You've just caught me taking a breather. All that incense gives me a headache, and those pews are so close together, it makes it difficult to work. Can't see why they don't space them out a bit. I doubt they get many through the doors, even though someone's said that the vicar's a bit of a dish. So, is this place Anglican or Catholic?'

'Anglican, but for some reason, Father Roy doesn't want to be referred to as a vicar,' said Jemima.

'You seem to be in the know.'

'Not really, it was something my sister told me. I'd not met him until today. You're right though, he is quite attractive, and he's single. Not that I'm in the market for a relationship.' Jemima gently rubbed her abdomen.

'Who knows, eh? Give it a month or two, when you've got your figure back.' Jeanne tilted her head and gave Broadbent a theatrical wink.

Broadbent gave a weak smile. He didn't want to offend Jeanne, but he didn't know how Jemima would feel about such a comment, and she was his primary concern.

Unperturbed by her suggestion apparently falling flat, Jeanne turned her attention back to Jemima. 'Anyway, what are you doing here at this time of the evening? Shouldn't you be putting your feet up? Isn't that what pregnant women do?'

'Chance would be a fine thing,' laughed Jemima. 'I've just been told by one of the villagers that some sort of altercation might have occurred in the churchyard last night, possibly by that tree.' She pointed in the general direction.

'And you want to take a look as you're wondering whether it's linked to the murder and there's any potential evidence left behind?'

At that moment, Broadbent's phone rang. 'I've got to take this,' he said. He turned away and slowly walked down the path, gravel crunched beneath his shoes.

'Exactly. I know it's an imposition but do you fancy accompanying me?' asked Jemima. 'Goodness knows how long Dan will be. His calls often take quite a while.'

'Well, in the spirit of female solidarity, I feel compelled to accompany you. After all, we must ensure that that little one of yours remains safe and sound. Let's face it, you could easily turn your ankle on this ground.'

'Thanks, Jeanne, I owe you one.'

'No thanks necessary. Truth is, I'd agree to almost anything to delay going back inside there. It's good to be able to walk around for a while and not have to worry about doing my back in or hitting my head on a wooden bench.'

They strolled along at a leisurely pace, listening to the sounds of livestock in a nearby field.

'Seems like a nice village. You planning on staying here once the baby's born?' asked Jeanne.

'At least for the foreseeable. My sister has a live-in nanny. She's agreed to look after this little one and see to the school runs with James.'

'So, it's worked out OK in the end. I take it you're returning to the job?'

'I want to and have to. I don't have any other way of supporting us, and I'm good at what I do. I know everyone's different, but it would drive me insane if I was a stay-at-home parent. I want the best of both worlds.'

'And there's no reason you shouldn't have it,' said Jeanne.

There would be another hour before the sun was due to set. The sky was clear with no sign of rain. It had been that way for a few weeks, with daytime temperatures pleasantly warm. The landscape was parched as the sun had baked the ground, reducing the grass to patchy withered blades. Any potential evidence would not include helpful footprints in moist soil.

'The girth of this trunk is certainly large enough to hide anyone from sight,' Jemima said. 'Anyone walking at road level wouldn't see someone up here, and if you were in a vehicle, you wouldn't have much time to stare.'

'Perhaps an ideal location for a romantic tryst?' suggested Jeanne.

'Could be. Hey, what's that?' Jemima pointed at a small object close to the base of the tree. The blades of grass were longer and more plentiful there as they were sheltered from the sun's direct rays by the thick foliage on the branches above. Jemima moved her legs apart as she spoke to enable herself to crouch.

When Jeanne saw what she was about to do, she interjected. 'Oh no, you don't, not in your condition. Stay where you are. I'll take a look.' Taking a glove from her pocket, she blew into it to allow her hand to easily slip inside. 'Well, I never!' She stood up to reveal an earring. 'Looks like your source was right — someone was here. Though, of course, we've no way of knowing if this was dropped there last night.'

'Did the corpse have a similar earring?' asked Jemima. She knew the answer before she'd even asked the question.

'No, I'm afraid not.'

'I s'pose that would have been too easy. Bag it up anyway. If I can find out who it belongs to, there's a chance they might have seen something relevant to the case. I'm not ready to discount it yet. Let's face it, it could even belong to the murderer.'

Jemima suddenly felt deflated. The excitement of finding something only to discover that it wasn't linked to the victim was so disappointing. Usually, this wouldn't have had such a profound effect on her. She had been a detective for long enough to know that most potential evidence turned out to be irrelevant to the case you were investigating. But as the pregnancy was progressing, her moods yo-yoed, and weariness compelled her to clutch at straws.

CHAPTER 12

Having finished at the church, they headed towards their respective vehicles. 'Where next?' asked Broadbent.

'The Cheedles, since you didn't get to speak to his wife. I'll talk to her. You can question him again.'

'Great. Bet you anything, he'll still be an obnoxious git,' muttered Broadbent.

After only a few moments spent in Max Cheedle's presence, Jemima had to agree with Broadbent's initial assessment of the man. He had the swagger and confidence of someone who believed his own hype.

'Oh, it's you again.' He sighed. He opened the door to its full extent, folded his arms and leaned against the frame. 'What do you want this time?' His lip curled contemptuously. He made a point of looking Jemima up and down, and it was apparent that he found her wanting.

'We've come to speak with your wife,' said Jemima.

'What's this — work experience for the junior officers?' He directed the question at Broadbent, nodding towards Jemima. It was clearly meant as a put-down, yet the man seemed unaware of how stupid it made him sound.

'I'm sorry, I should have introduced myself. I'm Detective Inspector Huxley, and I'd like to speak with your wife. Is she at home?'

Jemima had no sooner finished asking the question than a harried-looking woman walked down the hallway, wiping her hands on a tea towel. Her hair was greying and somewhat unkempt. Her pale complexion emphasized dark shadows beneath heavily hooded eyes, with crows' feet so pronounced they were on the verge of becoming crevices. Nevertheless, even in the dim light of the hallway, her eyes were unmistakably bright. When she spoke, Jemima realized that the woman was far younger than she appeared. It led her to believe that Valerie Cheedle was either ill, suffering from stress, or both.

'Did I hear you say that you wanted to speak to me?'

'That's right. May we come in?' said Jemima.

'Of course. Step aside, Max. You'll have to excuse my husband. He's not much of a people person. It comes from spending far too much time with only fictional characters for company.'

Jemima suppressed a smile. She liked this woman already.

Max Cheedle snorted but stepped aside without uttering another word, bizarrely waving them in as though he were directing traffic.

Valerie shook her head despairingly. 'Come through to the conservatory. Excuse the mess in the kitchen. We've only just eaten, and I haven't finished clearing up yet.'

'I've got work to do, so keep the noise down,' said Max. His words were uttered in a self-important manner. It was meant to impress yet succeeded only to irritate.

'Actually, I need to ask you some more questions first,' said Broadbent. Deepak's assertion of having seen two people in the churchyard and hearing a large vehicle in the early hours of the morning were things they intended to ask the other villagers about.

'Oh, for God's sake . . . Fine, let's get on with it. I suppose I can spare a few minutes,' said Max.

Jemima followed Valerie through the kitchen, while Broadbent went into a separate room with Max. She took a seat opposite Valerie, who obsessively played with her wedding ring, twisting it around her finger as she forced herself to sit back in the seat and smile as though she didn't have a care in the world.

'I take it that you're here about the murder?' she asked.

'That's right. Did you see or hear anything unusual last night?'

'No, I have medication to help me sleep. It knocked me out. I'm not going to be able to tell you anything useful. It was just a typical evening for me. I got home from work, prepared dinner, cleaned up and watched TV by myself. I went to bed at about ten thirty. I remember looking at the clock, because I heard Max come back.'

'Your husband was out that evening?'

'He goes out most nights — claims he needs a walk to clear his head.'

'You sound sceptical?'

'It's another one of his pathetic cover stories. My husband's a serial philanderer. We've been married for almost sixteen years, and it's been going on before we got married. I caught him at it on our wedding day with one of my bridesmaids. They were in the bathroom of the honeymoon suite. If I'd had any self-respect, I would have told him it was over and shamed him in front of our guests. But I was pregnant, and he was so apologetic.'

'You have a child?'

'Had. H-he died three years ago. H-hit and run.' Valerie's voice cracked with emotion, and her eyes filled with tears.

'I'm sorry to hear that,' said Jemima. She felt a lump rise in her throat and swallowed hard. These days her hormones were playing havoc with her emotions. Hearing about a child's death and witnessing his mother's all too apparent distress made Jemima want to place her hands protectively over the life inside her. Instead, she discreetly bit her bottom lip as she battled the urge to do so, appreciating it would be a crass and inappropriate gesture.

'Max's latest must be local,' Valerie continued. 'It's easier to overlook his indiscretions when it's someone I don't know. But as he sets out on foot, it's got to be one of the villagers. Though God only knows what she must see in him — an arrogant, mediocre writer who's failed to make it big.' She laughed mirthlessly. 'I'm on the verge of kicking him out. I really don't think I can take it anymore. He's got more to lose than I have. You see, I don't love him. I haven't for a long while. We hardly speak to each other and sleep in separate bedrooms. He's a leech and a letch. I'm the breadwinner in this relationship, whereas his royalties are pitiful. But I don't care anymore. The house is in my name. It's the only way we could get a mortgage. Anyway, you're not here to listen to me drone on about my sham of a marriage.'

Jemima held out the photograph of the dead woman's face. 'Do you recognize this woman?'

'Is she the victim?'

Jemima nodded.

'Can't say I do. She looks very young, but she's not from around here, and I don't recall having seen her at school.'

'Thank you for your time.' Jemima edged forward in the seat, pressing down on its arms to help raise herself up. 'I'm just going to join my colleague as there are a few things I need to check out with your husband.'

'Be my guest, but don't expect him to tell you the truth. He spends most of his time in whichever fictional world he's working on. He's lost the ability to know the difference between the truth and a lie.'

As Jemima headed back towards the front of the house, Broadbent was coming out of Max Cheedle's study. He'd already shut the door behind him, and so Jemima spoke to him in a voice quiet enough so that the writer would be unable to make out what they were saying.

'Did he recognize the woman?'

'Claims he hasn't seen her before.'

'Did he tell you that he was out last night?'

'No, he said he stayed in.'

'Well, he didn't. I think it's time I spoke to him.'

Jemima opened the door and stepped inside. Max Cheedle abruptly spun around in his swivel chair. There was no mistaking the look of annoyance on his face. 'What is it this time?' he growled. His eyebrows were almost knitted together as he scowled at both officers.

'We're investigating a murder, Mr Cheedle, and you've lied to my sergeant.'

'I have n—'

'Enough! Don't test my patience, Mr Cheedle. I'm tired. I'm hungry, and I want to put my feet up. So don't think of lying to me because if you don't tell me the truth, I'll arrest you for wasting police time, and Sergeant Broadbent will take you back to the station, where you can spend the night in a cell.'

The man's eyes widened, and his complexion paled. Having spoken to his wife, Jemima knew that he lived his life as an arrogant bully who did whatever he liked. He clearly thought he was a cut above everyone else and would never have his pseudo-authority questioned. But Max Cheedle was soon going to realize that he had met his match in her. Jemima had no intention of putting up with any of his nonsense.

'You told my sergeant that you didn't leave the house last night. I know that's a lie, so tell me where you went and who you were with.'

'It's none of your bu—'

'Cuff him and read him his rights.' She had no desire to arrest the man, but he was testing her patience.

Broadbent extracted a set of handcuffs, and Max Cheedle's resolve crumbled.

'There's no need for that. I'll tell you everything.' The cadence of his voice had changed. It was noticeably a few tones higher as the words spilled from his lips in quick succession. 'I was with a friend.'

'Not good enough. Which friend? I need a name.'

'Christina. Christina Mundell. She owns the cattery at the other end of the village. We're seeing each other, but don't tell my wife.'

'I need details about the time and place.'

'Seriously? It's just an affair. I've nothing to do with that awful murder. It makes me feel queasy just thinking about it.'

'Stop wasting my time.' Jemima placed her hands on Max's desk and leaned towards him, intent on invading his personal space. 'Tell me what I need to know, and we'll check it out.'

'OK, fine!' Max used his feet to push his chair away from her. 'We met at about eight thirty at the far end of the churchyard.'

'That was you?'

'Did you see us?' he asked.

'No, someone else did. What time did you leave?'

'About nine fifteen. We can't stay too long. Her husband would get suspicious.'

'Did you see or hear anything unusual while you were there?'

'Nothing. Then again, we weren't exactly paying much attention.'

* * *

'His wife should throw him out,' said Jemima, as the door of the Cheedles' house closed behind them.

'He's despicable,' agreed Broadbent. 'Where now, the cattery?'

'Yeah. Let's check out Christina's version of events.'

CHAPTER 13

In recent months, Jemima had driven past the lane leading to the cattery at least twice a day. Yet throughout that time, she hadn't had any cause to visit the property. A large wooden sign highlighted the entrance to Bluebell Cat's Hotel. Jemima shook her head in despair as she read the establishment's claim to offer a '*home-from-home experience for your feline family member, in a top-of-the-range cat chalet*'. The first glimpse of the rows of enclosures proved her scepticism to have been valid, as the structures were nothing more than a combination of UPVC and wire cages.

Broadbent followed her up the path towards the reception building. The sound of piped music floated on the air, designed to keep the feline guests calm, Jemima guessed. As they approached, an attractive woman strode out to meet them.

'Dropping off or collecting?' she enquired.

'Neither.' Jemima held out her warrant card and introduced herself and Broadbent.

'I heard what happened. It's terrifying to think it took place virtually on our doorstep.'

'What can you tell us about events up at the church last night?' asked Jemima.

'I wouldn't know. I'm not part of the campanology set. You'd need to speak to Winston about that.'

'You know that's not what I'm referring to.' Jemima raised her eyebrows and held the woman's gaze.

Christina Mundell would not have made a good poker player. It was immediately apparent that she knew what was being alluded to. At first, she attempted to deny it, but embarrassment won out, and a blush rose from somewhere beneath her neckline. In a matter of seconds, she looked as though she had stepped into a sauna, yet she still tried to bluff it out. 'I-I've no idea what you're talking about.'

'Max has told us everything,' said Jemima.

At the mention of his name, the woman lost what little composure she had so far managed to retain. Her chin dropped to meet her chest, and her shoulders shook as she sobbed inconsolably. It would have been easy to mistake her sense of guilt for someone grieving for a loved one, such was the level of her display of emotion.

'Don't say anything to my husband. Please, *please*, I'm begging you. Winston doesn't know anything. It'd break his heart if he ever found out I'd cheated on him. I don't even know why I'm doing it. It's not as if I like Max. He's a self-obsessed shit, but I just got drawn in. I haven't got the most glamorous of lives here, looking after other people's cats and cleaning up after them. I just wanted some excitement. But I'll end it now, I promise. Right now, just don't say anything to Winston. I love him too much to break his heart over a stupid fling that means absolutely nothing.'

'We're not interested in your morals, Mrs Mundell. We're investigating a murder. Since you were in the vicinity of the crime last night, we just want to know what time you were there and whether or not you saw or heard anything suspicious. How you choose to live your life is down to you. Though, I can't guarantee that the fact that you were in the churchyard last night won't come out as a result of our investigation, if it's deemed to be pertinent to the woman's death.'

'You mean you won't tell my husband?' Christina was clearly clutching at straws, hoping that her life wouldn't suddenly blow up in her face.

'There are no guarantees, Mrs Mundell. But everything you tell us will remain confidential unless it becomes relevant to a prosecution for the murder,' reassured Jemima. As she spoke, she did her best to keep a rising sense of irritation out of her voice. The woman clearly wasn't the brightest. Her overwhelming self-pity seemed inappropriately selfish. A young woman had been viciously murdered and all she could think about was herself.

'Have you lost an earring?' asked Jemima.

'Yes, it has three blue beads.'

'We've just found it in the churchyard.'

'Could I have it back?'

'Not until we've completed the investigation.'

Christina sighed and swallowed hard. 'Winston gave me those earrings last Christmas,' she said, touching her bare earlobes. 'I suppose that I'd better tell you everything.'

In the end, Christina's version of events matched her lover's.

'Poor Winston, having a wife like that,' said Broadbent as they walked away.

'I can't believe that she was happy to meet Max Cheedle in the churchyard, so soon after the bell-ringing practice. Her husband organizes that. It's almost as though she wanted him to find out what she was up to.'

'Do you want to interview any of the other villagers tonight?' asked Broadbent.

Jemima was left in no doubt that he wanted to go home, as he made a show of looking at his watch. 'No, we've done enough. There's always tomorrow. I'm done in. I need to get home to put my feet up. Thanks for coming out here this evening. I really appreciate it.'

Broadbent opened the driver's door of his car. 'You're welcome. Now go home and get some rest.'

Jemima didn't need telling twice. With each passing day, her energy levels seemed to deplete more quickly. She had wanted to speak with far more villagers that evening, but it would have to wait until tomorrow. Her body was telling her that she needed to slow down, and the baby came first.

CHAPTER 14

The following morning, Jemima arrived at the station to find the others already hard at it. She had set off from home at a reasonable time, but the unexpected appearance of road-works near the Culverhouse Cross roundabout had caused tailbacks. It was an annoying delay.

She draped her jacket over the back of her chair. 'Sorry I'm late.'

'No probs. We've just continued with yesterday's tasks,' said Broadbent. As the only other parent on the team, he appreciated Jemima's difficulties as the pregnancy progressed. His wife, Caroline, had struggled throughout her pregnancy, especially so in the last trimester.

'What was the public response like from the photo head-shot?' asked Jemima.

'Ahh . . . about that. None of the media ran it last night,' said Gareth. He looked at the floor as he spoke, unable to meet Jemima's gaze.

'Seriously? You submitted it in plenty of time for them to use it?'

'I did. I walked it round to the press office and handed it to Fran Witchard. She's the designated liaison officer. It was unusually quiet there. In fact, she was the only one in the room. I talked her through what had happened, and she promised me that it would be sent out to the usual media outlets in time for them to run it. But it turns out that she didn't do it . . .' The last few words trailed off, and Gareth's body tensed as he waited for the almost inevitable reaction.

'So what happened?' In normal circumstances, Jemima would have been incandescent with rage. Not with Gareth. He had followed the procedure to the letter. The failure was with the press officer who had let them down and caused an unnecessary delay, which might have a knock-on effect further down the line.

'I didn't realize until this morning that it hadn't been released to the press. None of us watched the news last night. I came in early to find out what sort of response they'd had, only to be told that there hadn't been a single call. So, I legged it over to the press office. Fran hadn't done anything. Apparently, she got a call about her father being rushed into hospital shortly after I'd spoken to her. It was unexpected — a heart attack, I think. Anyway, she raced out of work without telling anyone. The photograph was left on her desk overnight. She hasn't come into work today, which isn't surprising given the circumstances, and no one had thought to take a look at the paperwork on her desk.'

'Wonderful!' Jemima shook her head in despair. She couldn't even muster the energy to display her anger. The pregnancy was definitely mellowing her. It was barely nine o'clock, and she was already feeling weary. There would be nothing to gain in going off on one. As for Fran Witchard neglecting her duties — well, Jemima thought she might have done the same if her own father had suffered such a severe health scare. Though she liked to think she would have had the fortitude to tie up any professional loose ends first. But when emotions came into play, they could impact even the most professionally conscientious person.

'I've spoken with Aled Jenkins this morning,' said Gareth. 'He's the other press officer. He assured me that he'll assume responsibility for it and get everything off to them by ten o'clock at the latest. The headshot will be out there for everyone to see later this morning.'

'In that case, I'd like you to organize for a handful of people to man the telephones today, and you should be one of them. At least that way, you can ensure that it's running efficiently, and you can chase up any possible leads.'

'Sure, I'm on it.' He headed towards the door.

Jemima turned her attention to Ashton. 'How's it going with the missing persons database?'

'Twenty-three potentials so far, but I'm still working my way through it. It helps that we've got the headshot, but I really need more information. If I knew things such as the height and eye colour of the victim, I'd be able to rule out quite a few of them. As it is, we'll soon be drowning in possibilities.'

'Dan and I will be heading over to the University Hospital shortly. John Prothero's due to begin the post-mortem. I'll ask him to confirm height and eye colour straight off and get Dan to give you a ring.'

'Thanks, guv. Appreciate it.' Ashton turned back to the screen.

'John Prothero called to say that he's ready to start. I told him we'd be there within the hour,' said Broadbent.

'In that case, we'd better head straight there. We can't keep him waiting. We'll take a look at the personal effects later.'

Jemima looked for and subsequently spotted the tell-tale sign that Dan Broadbent was psyching himself up for attending the post-mortem. Throughout their time together, she'd kept his secret about having a weak stomach and an aversion to blood. Given the things they encountered on an almost daily basis, it was an inconvenient phobia. They both knew that if the other officers found out about this particular weakness, it would set him up for a lot of ribbing. But at least that would just be his pride taking a hit. A far more serious implication was that it could go against him as far as career progression was concerned.

Broadbent nearly always accompanied Jemima to post-mortems. He dreaded it but believed her when she told him that it was a form of exposure therapy. And he had to admit that the more post-mortems he attended, the less queasy he became. It helped to know that he was no longer going to see something new. He'd even stopped fixing his gaze at some elusive spot on the ceiling, occasionally daring to look down on the corpse on a few occasions, when Jemima unceremoniously dug her elbow into his ribs.

He knew that it was ultimately for his own benefit. But knowing something and actually doing it were two very different things. And when Jemima took time off on maternity leave, Dan was going to have to step up to the plate. If he fell apart or bottled it, the truth would be out there, and there'd be no second chance. The proverbial clock was ticking. It was make-or-break time.

'Ah, it's my favourite detectives. Jemima! Daniel! Come in, come in.' John Prothero opened his arms wide as he greeted them theatrically. No matter how horrendous the case, he always appeared to be pleased to see them.

'Here we go again, John.' Jemima smiled warmly at him. It was impossible not to like John Prothero. With a wicked sense of humour and a twinkle in his eye, he was an accomplished raconteur. When you first observed him at work, it would be easy to mistake his genial demeanour for lack of competency. Yet that was far from the truth. In all the years she'd known him, John Prothero had never missed a thing. He was at the top of his profession, with a laser-sharp intellect. To top it off, he was one of the nicest people Jemima had ever met.

'As I knew you were coming, I got someone to bring a chair in for you. After all, I can't allow the mother of my future godchild to stand.'

Jemima's eyes widened in surprise.

'Gotcha!' Prothero slapped his thigh and doubled up with laughter.

Broadbent grinned.

'I don't know what you're smiling at, lad. You're going to have to stand through this. You're just the hired help, not actual police royalty. Have you thought of names yet, Jemima?'

'I haven't, John.'

'Well, as you know, I was an avid fan of *Game of Thrones*, so I'd like to suggest that you consider calling him Jon if it's a boy. I've no idea if you watched it yourself. Still, Jon Snow was an exemplary character, and of course, there's the fact that it also happens to be a variant spelling of my name. What a coincidence, eh?' He winked. 'Now, if it's a girl, I thought you could name her Daenerys. She was the so-called Mother of Dragons — possible Welsh connection there, perhaps? Also, there's the fact that Nerys forms part of the name, which of course, is another Welsh connection. I'm thinking of the wonderful actress Nerys Hughes — though perhaps that's a bit before your time. Anyway, I've given you food for thought, but it's not the appropriate time to dwell on such matters. Come on, chop-chop, there's work to be done. She's been tucked up in the cooler overnight. I haven't even set eyes on her yet.' He addressed one of his assistants. 'Let's open this zipper and get her out.'

'I'd like height and eye colour straight off,' Jemima said. 'It'll help my team eliminate some potential missing persons.'

'Let me see . . . 163 centimetres. So, approximately five feet four inches. Eye colour, blue.'

'I'll give Ashton a call.' Broadbent headed out of the room. It was the ideal opportunity to make a quick exit. His eagerness to get out of there was noticeable, as he walked far faster than his usual pace.

'Make it quick, lad. I've no intention of doing anything until you come back,' shouted Prothero.

Broadbent held up a hand to indicate that he had heard.

'I bet he's hoping for a quiet time while you're off on maternity leave. One thing's for sure, he won't want to come here with anyone else. He'd be the butt of their jokes for the remainder of his career.' His gaze fell on to the body. 'I'll save the cutting until he returns, but I've already noticed something interesting.'

'What's that?' asked Jemima. In a case like this, interesting was good, as it would inevitably give some insight into the victim. Possibly even help to identify her.

'Her eyes are sunken.'

'What does that mean?'

'Hold on for a second, and I'll tell you if my suspicion's correct.' Prothero pressed his fingers into the victim's flesh. 'Thought so — she's severely dehydrated. Do you see that? When I apply pressure, the skin slowly rises back into position. Now, if I were to do that to any of us, it would return to normal almost immediately.'

'What causes it?' asked Jemima.

'Best guess is hypertonic dehydration. I'll know for sure when I open her up. Look at the state of her. Her skin's filthy, and her hair matted. I'd hazard a guess that there are three possibilities. She could have been living rough. It's also possible she was kept somewhere. Though there are no ligature marks to suggest she was restrained. Or, of course, she could have been hiding.'

Broadbent strode into the room. 'What have I missed?'

'Nothing important, lad. I was determined not to start without you. But I can tell you immediately that the crossbow bolt was the most likely cause of death. Then again, you could have worked that out for yourself. There's no doubt in my mind that she would have bled out pretty quickly.'

Broadbent steadied himself against the back of Jemima's chair. 'Any sign of sexual assault?'

'Patience, lad. I know I'm good, but even I can't be expected to do everything at once. I'll get to that further down the line.'

Broadbent blushed. The only reason he'd asked the question in the first place was that he knew that it was something they routinely looked for in the post-mortems he had attended. It was the little boy in him, desperate to please and demonstrate that he was up to the task. It seemed all the more critical at the moment since Jemima would be leaving them for a while. He needed her to have confidence in his abilities, as he didn't want her to worry about the squad while she was on maternity leave.

With his hands still on the back of the chair, Jemima was aware of Broadbent shifting his weight from foot to foot as he continued to watch Prothero work. It was a slow yet fascinating process, though neither could understand why anyone would choose to do this day in, day out.

Prothero's examination of the body had been going on for quite a while before he next spoke. 'Right, let's begin with the Y incision. Ah, now this is interesting. The stomach's empty. She hadn't eaten anything for quite a while, but doesn't appear to be malnourished.'

'Which suggests that she wasn't a regular rough sleeper,' said Jemima.

'Exactly and take a look at her hands.' He slipped a hand under the wrist to enable Jemima to take a closer look without having to bend over.

'They're acrylic nails,' said Jemima. They were dirty and jagged, but it was still evident that they were the work of a professional manicurist. 'This woman cared about her appearance. She also had disposable income, which means she had a life where someone should have missed her.'

'That'd be my reading of the situation. Let's take a look at her feet.' Prothero moved down the cadaver. 'Ah, now this is interesting. There's a marked difference between the soles of the feet. Take a look at this. One is relatively clean, but the other's dirty. There are cuts and abrasions. Now, if I was a betting man, I'd put money on the likelihood that our young Cinderella was only wearing one shoe.'

Jemima's heart skipped a beat as she felt a small glimmer of hope. 'Stay here, Dan. I'm just popping outside to ring Ashton and ask him to find out if we've got both of her shoes in the evidence locker. I won't be long.'

Jemima could tell from Broadbent's expression that he was disappointed not to be the one to get to leave the room.

As the door closed behind her, she selected Ashton's number and pressed speed dial. He answered almost immediately, and she stayed on the line as he headed down to the evidence locker.

'There's just one shoe,' he confirmed.

'In that case, take a photograph of it and print copies. I want you to organize a search party. We need to locate that other shoe. If we find it, we'll know which direction the victim came from. Get the team to start with the lane at the entrance of the church. They need to spread out in both directions, paying particular attention to the hedgerows if it's not on the carriageway. I want them out there immediately. There's a big area to cover, and right now, we've got nothing to go on.'

'And if they don't find it?' asked Ashton.

'Then they'll have to search the surrounding fields. Let's just hope that it doesn't come to that. Broadbent and I will stay for the rest of the post-mortem. Give the team leader my number and tell them to call me if they find anything. Other than that, I'll see you back at the station.'

Jemima returned to the post-mortem. 'Have I missed anything?'

'Nothing of interest, apart from the fact that the hymen's ruptured, so odds on she wasn't a virgin. Though, as far as I can tell, there's no evidence of sexual activity having occurred close to death. So at least you can rule that out as a motive.'

'What are her teeth like?' she asked.

'Oh, I can tell you've been watching and learning. You'll be doing my job soon. Let's see, shall we?' Prothero pulled the jaw downwards and shone a light into the mouth. He squinted and prodded a tooth with a probe. 'I'd say she's looked after her teeth, but if you take a close look at this upper incisor, it looks to me as though it was chipped, and she's had it repaired. It's an excellent piece of work, which in my opinion wouldn't have come cheap.'

'Everything appears to point to the victim not being short of money,' Jemima said. 'Which suggests that sooner or later, someone somewhere will notice she's missing.'

CHAPTER 15

They arrived back at the station just as Jemima's phone rang. It was the officer in charge of the search teams. 'We've completed a thorough search a quarter of a mile in each direction. Found nothing. Do we keep going? Or do you want us to make a start on the fields?'

'Stay on the lane for now. Quarter of a mile's hardly any distance at all. She could have travelled on foot from further out. There's no guarantee you'll find anything, but if I was running in the dark, I'd stick to the lanes. The fields are uneven. There'd be more chance of turning your ankle, and then you're done for.'

'But if the killer had a vehicle, they'd be more likely to catch up with her along the lane,' countered the officer.

'I agree, but something tells me you should keep searching those lanes. It's my call. If I'm wrong, it's on me,' said Jemima. She hung up before he had a chance to respond.

An hour later, a call came through to say that the missing shoe had been located. When the officer explained where it had been discarded, Jemima swallowed hard. She blindly reached for the nearby chair and slumped on to it as her legs threatened to give way. The victim's shoe had been found on the lane that led directly past Lucy's house.

Sometime during the hours of darkness, the young victim must have fled past where Jemima was sleeping. She must have been terrified, most likely running for her life. If only Jemima had realized what was happening, she could perhaps have saved the young woman's life. But she hadn't, and the victim had been hunted down and slaughtered inside the church.

'Did you find anything else when you searched the area?' pressed Jemima.

'Nothing. It's been a dry spell, so there were no tyre tracks or footprints. There wasn't even any litter. It's so different to the city. There was hardly any traffic.'

While Jemima was on the phone, Gareth Peters' extension rang. He spoke briefly, then headed out of the room. A few minutes later, he returned with Jeanne Ennersley in tow.

Jemima was surprised to see the woman walk into the incident room. She opened her bag, extracted some photographs and set them out on the table. They all gathered around to hear what she had to say.

'As you can see from the photographs at the crime scene, there was a single point of impact from an eighteen-inch carbon crossbow bolt. They don't come cheap. We're talking about ten pounds for a single bolt. Of course, in most cases, they can be reused.' Jeanne was talking in her usual matter-of-fact way, unaware of the inner turmoil she had inadvertently whipped up in Jemima.

The discovery of the victim's shoe discarded so close to Lucy's house had shaken Jemima. She knew it was an irrational thought, but she couldn't shake the idea that she had let this young woman down. If only she'd looked out of the window and seen her running past. She could have called out to her, gone downstairs to let her in. But instead, she'd been asleep. Oblivious to this young woman's plight. And this stranger had died because no one had been there to save her.

'Is there any legislation in place for the sale of crossbows?' asked Broadbent.

The sound of his voice brought Jemima back to the here and now.

'Put it this way, it's woefully inadequate. You can buy one on the internet, and as you've already seen, it's a lethal weapon. The legislation doesn't reflect the impact these weapons have if they get into the wrong hands. For some reason, they're classed as more sports equipment than a weapon, frequently sold under the guise of target practice. The only legal aspect is that it must not be sold to, owned by, or used by anyone under the age of eighteen and can only be fired on private land,' said Jeanne.

Broadbent shook his head. 'That's ridiculous.'

'Well, that's our wonderful country all over,' said Jemima. 'Most of our laws are archaic and no longer fit for purpose. But hey, we should just stop moaning and get on with picking up the pieces.'

Jeanne ignored the interruption. 'Given the trajectory of the bolt, I'd say it was fired from the aisle by someone who was anywhere between five feet eight to five ten. Poor thing didn't stand a chance. It was basically point-blank. The killer sighted her up, and she had nowhere to go.'

Jemima shivered at the thought of it. Like many officers, she'd seen her fair share of awful deaths. But this was so close to home that it seemed virtually unbearable. Since her initial visit to Lucy's house, all those years ago, she'd always thought of Leighton Meadow as a rural idyll. It was peaceful, so far removed from life in the city, and the villagers were friendly. But she'd been fooled into believing that it was a safe place to live. And given her chosen career, she should have known better. She folded her arms across her abdomen, subconsciously protecting the life growing inside her.

'What were her clothes like?' she asked in an effort not to dwell on her fears.

Jeanne set out a series of photographs that had been taken of the victim's clothing. 'They're not cheap chain-store ones. In fact, they're not British labels. Though, I've no idea which country they're from.'

'So she might not be from this country?' said Broadbent.

'It's a possibility, but these days, it's easy to purchase things from virtually anywhere in the world,' said Jemima. 'We'll take a look at the labels and see where that leads us.

'I don't suppose she had a phone or any other personal effects which could help identify her?'

'No. I'd have let you know immediately if I'd found anything like that. I've a feeling that unless someone recognizes her face, it's not going to be easy for you to find out who she is. But I think Daniel could be right. Take a look at her jewellery. There's not much, but her necklace and earrings are quite unusual. They appear to be made from a greenish crystal. I've not come across anything like them.'

* * *

Broadbent had only just returned to the room, having escorted Jeanne out of the building, when the phones in a nearby room started ringing. Gareth Peters appeared in the doorway. 'Guv, I thought you'd want to know that the victim's photograph was just shown on the latest local news bulletin. As you've no doubt heard, we're starting to get a response. Fingers crossed we get at least one viable lead out of this.'

'Keep me updated.' Jemima barely raised her head as she spoke. She was focused on scouring the internet in her quest to identify the country of origin of the victim's clothes and jewellery. The necklace and earrings were quite striking. When Jemima typed in a search for a green crystal, it threw up several possibilities. Thankfully, each of them also had an image. Jemima continued to search until she came across a photograph of a crystal called moldavite.

Confident that this was what the victim's jewellery was made from, Jemima did a more specific search on the crystal. She discovered it was a natural glass element, formed most likely when an asteroid collided with the earth. And as she continued to read, she found that most moldavite deposits were located in the Czech Republic.

Jemima had a feeling she could be on to something. The victim's clothes were unavailable as they were being tested at the lab. Still, Jeanne had photographed them, including any labels or logos she had come across. A couple were easily recognizable brands. But when she typed in two unfamiliar ones, they both came back with the Czech Republic as their place of origin.

It was unlikely to be a coincidence that the jewellery and the clothing were both linked to the Czech Republic. The victim was likely to be linked to the area too. When you put that information together with the post-mortem findings, the most obvious conclusion was that the young woman had escaped from a trafficking operation.

Despite having no direct experience of investigating human traffickers, Jemima knew it was improbable that the dead woman would have been the only trafficked person brought over by a gang. As they were taking the risk, they would have wanted to maximize their profit. There had to be others, either waiting to be sold and moved on or else put to work somewhere nearby.

Even for someone such as Jemima, who had spent her entire working life encountering the worst of human depravity, this was a shocking and unthinkable realization. Everyone knew that human trafficking was a genuine problem. There hardly seemed to be many weeks that went by without some case being reported in the media. Yet somehow, the knowledge got pushed to the back of people's minds. No one wanted to believe that it went on within a stone's throw of where they lived. People they regularly passed in the street, perhaps those they exchanged pleasantries with, could be engaged in such evil, contemptible exploitation. And it was that very same subconscious denial that allowed the deed to flourish.

The squad was well equipped to investigate the murder. Still, Jemima knew they would need specialist help to investigate whether or not this had occurred due to human trafficking. She went to speak to DCI Kennedy, who agreed that Jemima should contact Charlie Morgan. He headed up the locally based human trafficking unit in the National Crime Agency.

It was approximately a year ago when the squad had had their first encounter with Charlie. But it had nothing to do with trafficking. Charlie's wife, Violet, had been abducted. He'd feared for her safety at the hands of a man named Byron Toombes. The investigation had led to Jemima and Broadbent being hospitalized. The ramifications of that day had sent shockwaves across many lives.

That afternoon, Jemima tried but failed to get hold of Charlie Morgan. In the end, she left a message on his machine, telling him what she suspected and asking him to call her as soon as he was able.

CHAPTER 16

Jemima knew the value of having regular downtime, especially now that she was in the third trimester of her pregnancy. She'd scoured every available piece of literature on the subject. They all mentioned the importance of maintaining a normal blood-pressure level. However, that evening, despite her determination to forget about the case, she found it impossible to put it out of her mind.

Lucy spoke fondly about each of her pregnancies. She was forever telling her sister that it was important to rest. She also advocated the use of scented candles and listening to relaxation tapes. But for Jemima, the idea was nothing more than a pipe dream. She had known from the outset of her pregnancy that her lifestyle wouldn't allow things to pan out that way.

Jemima's circumstances were far from ideal. After all, she was a single parent, living in her sister's house. At work, she dealt with highly stressful situations that required her to lead by example. She was sure that the others on her team would willingly cut her some slack. But that was not the way she intended to operate. Having fought hard to carve out a successful career in a male-dominated environment, she had no intention of asking anyone to do something she wasn't prepared to do herself.

Jemima didn't want to admit it to herself, but she was on tenterhooks waiting for Charlie Morgan to call her back. They hadn't spoken in many months. The awkwardness of what had brought them together last year still hung about in the far reaches of her thoughts. On the few occasions when Jemima's phone rang, she felt her heart miss a beat. But each time she glanced at her screen, it turned out to be someone else altogether.

By the time Jemima arrived home, Lucy's three little ones were already asleep, and James was sitting at the kitchen table, hunched over a book as he busied himself with his homework. He glanced up and rushed over to give her a hug. Jemima wrapped her arms around him, ruffled his hair and bent down to kiss the top of his head. 'Want some help, bud?' she asked.

'Yeah!' He grabbed her hand and led her towards the table.

Jemima knew the boy didn't really need her help. He was more than capable of mastering any task his teacher set him. She glanced at her sister, silently asking if she minded her not helping with the food preparations.

Lucy gave her the thumbs up and continued to effort-lessly float around, preparing dinner for herself and her sister. She was humming to herself, looking serene, a picture of perfection without a hair out of place.

Until Jemima had moved in with her sister, she had failed to fully appreciate just how impressive Lucy was. She was quite literally a human dynamo, with seemingly bound-less energy and enthusiasm. Nine times out of ten, Lucy pre-pared their meals, and Jemima felt guilty about allowing her to do so much. After all, despite Lucy having the luxury of working from her plush home office in the log cabin, she worked incredibly hard. But Jemima's hours were unpredict-able. While investigating a case, she sometimes found herself unable to get home for hours on end. However, it was coun-tered with the occasional slower period.

As for Lucy, it didn't seem unusual for her to be at it twenty-four seven. Her phone frequently pinged with the arrival of emails for orders that had to be sourced, delivered, and turned around to meet tight deadlines. It seemed that Lucy was becoming a victim of her own success. The more word got around, the greater her customer base became, and the more work came her way. Jemima marvelled at how her sister dealt with everything in a calm and organized manner. There was no doubt in Jemima's mind that her sister deserved the level of success she had achieved.

James was in bed reading a chapter of his book when Jemima and Lucy sat down to eat.

'What's the latest?' Lucy asked.

'You know I can't talk about it, Luce. But it's bad. We all need to be vigilant. The kids mustn't go into the garden and always ensure that the doors and windows are locked. That includes your office. You're vulnerable out there on your own. We don't know who's behind this. Until we've taken the person responsible out of circulation, we all have to be mindful of the threat.'

'I can't believe that a murder occurred a few hundred yards from this house.'

'I know. It's too close for comfort.' Jemima put her fork down and reached out for her sister's arm, squeezing it gently to reinforce the seriousness of what she was about to say. 'You need to realize that you can never fully trust anyone, Luce. People only show you the side of themselves that they want you to see. It's not only strangers you need to be wary of. It's dangerous to presume that just because you've known someone for a long time, they're incapable of doing something bad.'

'That's such a cynical attitude, Jem.' Lucy shook her head and sighed.

'I know, but at the moment, it's the way you need to be. I'm not trying to scare you, Luce. Right now, we've no idea what we're up against, and I just want all of us to be out of harm's way. Yesterday, when I got the call, and I realized where it was, it knocked me for six.' She looked past her sister's face into a vague spot in the distance. 'I've always thought of this place as being safe. I know it's foolish, but in my mind, I've set it apart from all the awful things I've seen people do to one another.

'I'll be having this baby in a matter of weeks, and it scares the hell out of me that something rotten might be going on in this village. It's not what I want for any of us, let alone the baby. I deal with more than enough shit in my life, Luce. I need this to be a safe space, somewhere I don't have to keep looking over my shoulder wondering if some unstoppable calamity is heading our way.'

'This paranoia is down to your hormones, Jem. Once the baby's here, you'll soon get back to your old self.'

'Ummm, if you say so.' She directed the conversation back to a subject that felt less personal. The last thing she needed at the moment was to be reminded of how vulnerable she felt. 'A few villagers said that they heard a large vehicle being driven through the village on the night of the murder. Did you happen to hear anything?'

'Can't say I did, but that's hardly surprising. By the time I get to bed, I'm so tired that I'm virtually asleep as soon as my head hits the pillow. The house could fall down around me, and I wouldn't know about it. Surely you would have heard something if it came along the lane? You must be up and down all night, needing to pee.'

Jemima winced. Her sister's words were an unwelcome reminder that she had been fast asleep and oblivious to the events that had taken place only a matter of yards away. Events that had led to the violent death of a stranger. 'I didn't hear anything either. I had heartburn, so it took me a long time to get to sleep, but when I eventually dropped off, I didn't wake up until the alarm sounded.'

'Did this vehicle have anything to do with the murder?'

'I honestly don't know, Luce. I was just wondering if it had headed up this way.'

The conversation got Jemima thinking that even though the Johnson property was not part of the village, it would still be worth speaking to the family. If the murder was linked to people trafficking, then the most likely way for someone to be smuggled into the country was in a lorry. And West Winds was remote enough for an illegal operation to be run from there without raising anyone's suspicions. It was set far enough back from the public highway to prevent anyone from getting a clear view of whatever went on up there. And as far as Jemima knew, there were no other haulage companies directly linked to the area.

That night, instead of turning back the duvet and snuggling down for some much-needed sleep, Jemima took some binoculars from the top shelf of her wardrobe and sat by the bedroom window. During daylight hours, this window was perfectly positioned to allow her a view of West Winds. But night-time in the countryside was absolute darkness, with hardly any light pollution spilling into the surroundings. There would be little chance of seeing anything, but she had to try. She pointed the binoculars in the general direction of West Winds and adjusted the focus.

After a few minutes of seeing nothing, she finally gave up and decided to go to bed. She lay in the darkness, unable to shake the thought of the young woman running past the house in fear of her life. Refusing to submit to exhaustion, she flicked on the bedside light and reached for her laptop. Propped up against a mountain of pillows and cushions to make herself more comfortable, she researched the Johnsons and Chesrielle Haulage. Jemima was determined to be prepared when she spoke to Charlie Morgan.

As yet, there was nothing to link the Johnsons to the murder. But the couple's home was located further along the lane where the victim's shoe was found. The Johnsons also owned a fleet of trucks, which would allow them to undertake a people-trafficking operation. However, it made no sense that the Johnsons would choose to bring criminal activities to their own doorstep. It was a hell of an unnecessary risk to take, especially since their fleet was housed on an industrial site on the outskirts of the city. That would have been a far more suitable location from which to coordinate such activities. It was a purpose-built haulage site. No one would think twice about trucks turning up at all sorts of hours. Or pay attention to the cargo they carried.

From what Lucy had said, it seemed that Gabrielle Johnson was admired by many for being an outstanding businesswoman. But that very adulation could create a perfect cover. Jemima knew that her sister had a tendency always to see the best in people, which in this instance, possibly made her an unreliable judge of character. It was not unusual for seemingly squeaky-clean people to have a well-hidden dark side. After all, no one was entirely good.

CHAPTER 17

Jemima's phone's ringtone shattered the silence and broke her train of thought. She was so uptight that she felt her heart miss a beat. It didn't help that she'd had little sleep and was now on her way into work, having to negotiate the roadworks. The upgrade was long overdue, but it made life difficult for drivers who had no choice but to use that particular route.

It was one of those mornings when everything felt like far too much effort. Jemima was tired, uncomfortable and on edge. She accepted the call and put it on speakerphone. It was Charlie Morgan.

'Sorry I didn't get back to you yesterday. Things were a bit fraught at this end. What makes you think your investigation could be linked to people trafficking?'

Charlie was treating this purely as a professional call. There had been no personal greeting or attempted pleasantries. It was as though they had no previous connection. Which, given the fact that Jemima had been hospitalized as a result of their only other encounter, seemed rather offhand. She hadn't expected an effusive display of gratitude. Still, a cursory 'How are things?' or another banal icebreaker wouldn't have gone amiss. After all, they'd pulled out all the stops to find his wife. Yet Charlie Morgan was speaking to Jemima as though she was a complete stranger.

If that's the way he wants to play it, thought Jemima, before she filled him in on what they had so far established, including the possible link to the Czech Republic.

'I'll call at the station later this morning,' Charlie said. 'I've a few things to take care of first. In the meantime, forward the victim's photograph to me, and I'll run it by Interpol. With a bit of luck, we might get a hit.'

'Thanks. How's Vi—' began Jemima. Her eyes widened in surprise when she realized that Charlie had cut her off. 'Rude, rude, rude!' she shouted, to no one in particular. It was unbelievable that their conversation had ended without so much as a goodbye.

Despite arriving at the police station a few minutes before the shift was due to start, the others were already hard at work. It wasn't so long ago that Jemima had had to keep pushing them to think for themselves and take more responsibility. It was now apparent they'd heeded her advice. Instead of feeling a sense of achievement, it made her feel redundant, though, deep down, she knew it was for the best. In a matter of weeks, she'd be out of the picture until she returned from maternity leave. Yet it hurt a little to think that while she was gone they'd manage perfectly well without her.

Jemima had a fleeting thought that this was what it would be like to watch your children grow up and become independent. She knew she should be pleased as she had helped each of these officers flourish. But a tiny part of her felt a sense of loss, which she acknowledged was unreasonable. After all, this was a work situation, not a family unit.

She dropped her bag beside the desk. 'What's the latest?'

'We had the usual level of response from the saddos and the cranks. I'm sure they live for these appeals. It's the only way they're able to feel part of something. I s'pose we should feel sorry for them, but it really winds me up that there are so many people out there who think nothing of wasting our time and resources,' said Peters.

'So no real leads?'

'There are a few possible sightings which are being followed up, but I've a feeling they're going to fizzle out.'

'How's it going with the missing persons, Fin?'

'I'm still trawling through, but nothing so far. It's soul-destroying. I feel I should be out there doing something instead of wasting my time on this.' He sighed loudly, articulating the frustration each of them was feeling.

'Well, I managed to speak with Charlie Morgan this morning. He's going to come over later. If our victim was trafficked, it would explain why no one seems to know her.'

'I've made a start on searching for incidents involving crossbows. See if it throws up any potential suspects,' said Broadbent.

'Excellent,' said Jemima. As she spoke, she realized that perhaps the word had come out a little too forcefully. She was pleased that Broadbent was using his own initiative, but a small part of her was miffed, as it was a task she had been about to ask him to undertake.

Jemima forwarded Charlie the victim's photograph, then settled down to undertake some research on human trafficking in Wales. It was a subject that was often on the news. Over the years, cases had come to light with increasing regularity. Though, as yet, Jemima had not had the first-hand experience of having worked on one. Charlie and his team were the experts in these matters. And if it did turn out that their victim had been trafficked into the country, then it would be his team who would take the lead. Jemima's team would only provide assistance as and when necessary. But whether the victim was a British citizen, a visitor, or had been trafficked into the country, Jemima and her team had responsibility for finding out who had murdered the young woman.

There was a worryingly large number of reported cases of human trafficking, which would undoubtedly be just the tip of the iceberg. There was a lot of money to be made from the sale of drugs, weapons and people. Those trades

profited from human misery, and plenty of people were prepared to make money this way. Numerous organized-crime
gangs operated throughout the country, ruthless, vicious and
unrepentant, ruling by fear of the consequences should any
of their foot soldiers dare to step out of line.

It was rare that an individual heading up a gang ever
got caught. They were careful, savvy, well connected and
wealthy. Individuals in all sorts of powerful positions were
sucked in, whether willingly or unknowingly, to oil the
wheels of these revolting enterprises. Some of the worst criminals hid behind a veneer of respectability. Their reach went
a long way, and their funds were extensive. They laundered
money. They gave bungs to those who could directly help or
influence. The rich continued to amass wealth, and ordinary
people remained oblivious of what was going on right in
front of their noses.

The phone sounded, and Broadbent picked it up. 'That
was the front desk. Charlie Morgan's downstairs. Shall I go
and get him?'

'Thanks, Dan. I'll let everyone know. I think we all need
to hear what he has to say,' said Jemima.

A few minutes later Broadbent entered the incident room
with Charlie in tow, and a frosty atmosphere descended.
From the scowl on his face, it was immediately apparent that
Dan was annoyed. Which was surprising as he was usually
a genial, easy-going individual. Yet Gareth seemed oblivious
to the obvious animosity between the two men and began to
ask how Violet was doing.

Having already experienced Charlie's rudeness during
their earlier conversation, Jemima interjected before the constable had a chance to mention the man's wife by name,
speaking loudly to drown out his voice. Gareth looked surprised by the interruption, but as he glanced at Broadbent
and Ashton, he noticed their stern looks. Broadbent gave
him a swift shake of the head, indicating that he should just
say nothing.

'Has your team found anything out?' asked Jemima.

'We've established the identity of your victim. Interpol confirmed that she was reported missing from Prague. She's a nineteen-year-old student studying at the university there. Her name's Dominika Jelinková. She went missing four nights ago along with four other female students. They were all studying the same course at Charles University. They had been celebrating a birthday with a night on the town in Wenceslas Square.'

'So there are another four girls out there?' Jemima was unable to disguise her incredulity. From the moment that the possibility of human trafficking had been raised, she had known that it was unlikely to involve only a single victim. But having that premise confirmed was a shocking reality check.

'It's a possibility. At this stage, the only thing we know for sure is that Dominika managed to escape. What we haven't established is whether that happened while the vehicle was still travelling or whether she legged it once it had reached its destination. Some or all of the other girls could have been dropped off along the way. Though, in my experience, I'd say that was unlikely, as it would increase the risk the traffickers face. Every time those vehicle doors open, there's a chance that someone could make a run for it. Or cause a commotion that would draw attention to what was going on.'

He stuck some photographs to the whiteboard and wrote a name beneath each of them. 'Anyway, these are the other missing girls,' he continued. 'We have Pavla Coufalová, Agata Rosolová, Darja Kozová and Eliska Adamcová. All aged between nineteen and twenty, from well-to-do middle-class families. It's unusual as these are not typical trafficking victims. These are girls who were always going to be missed. If anything, it gives us a head start because at least we know who we're looking for.'

He looked around at the officers. 'It's sad that in most of these trafficking cases, we have no idea who the victims are. Even if we come face-to-face with them, many of them are unlikely to speak to us, especially if they've willingly entered the country illegally. A significant proportion of these people are not reported missing, sometimes because they had no one looking out for them in the first place. Where families are involved, they usually would have paid the traffickers to smuggle a child into the country. It's the only hope some of them have, borne out of a sense of desperation. They're brainwashed into thinking that there's a better life waiting for them in a western nation. Others are fleeing war zones or equally desperate situations. In general, the traffickers are the only winners. There's no altruism involved, just greed. They don't give a damn about the desperate plight of these people, only how they can monetize the situation.'

'It's the modern slave trade,' said Ashton.

'That's exactly what it is, and it needs to be stopped. I appreciate that this is early days, and it puts a whole new slant on your murder investigation. Still, I'd like you to talk me through what you've established so far,' said Charlie.

'A few of the villagers reported hearing a large vehicle being driven through the village in the early hours of the morning that Dominika was killed. Somewhere around two thirty,' said Jemima.

'And that's unusual?'

'Yes. I live in the village, and it's normally a quiet place. There's not even much traffic throughout the day. Someone said that recently they've heard a similar-sized vehicle during the night. But he didn't say it was a regular occurrence.'

'Are you aware of any trafficking gang operating close to that particular locality?' asked Ashton.

'No, but that doesn't mean to say that there isn't an established operation already in existence there. Most of our intel comes from tip-offs by concerned members of the public. We very much rely on people keeping their eyes and ears open. Even so, much of it goes on unnoticed, or at least it's not reported to us. People either don't want to get drawn into reporting their suspicions, or else they convince themselves that they've misread the signs. But your victim and her missing friends were definitely brought into the country against their will. And at some stage of that journey, Dominika Jelinková escaped.' He perched himself on the edge of the nearest desk. His long legs stretched out, comfortably reaching the floor.

'I don't know whether it's linked to the case, but a couple living in a remote property further along that lane are the owners of a haulage company,' said Jemima.

The statement got Charlie Morgan's attention. 'And you left it until now to share that information?' The aggression was back full force. His expression had darkened, and the words dripped with incredulity.

'That's enough!' Broadbent stepped forward. It shocked and annoyed him that Charlie Morgan seemed to think it was acceptable to speak to Jemima in such a fashion. It was both demeaning and unprofessional.

'Its fine, Dan.' Jemima squeezed his arm gently. 'The information only recently came to my attention. As yet, I've no reason to suspect that this family have anything to do with *our* murder victim.' The emphasis she placed on the word would hopefully make the NCA officer think twice about turning this into a pissing contest. 'I appreciate that this morning's identification of the victim means that we will have to work together, as it's possible our case could be part of something bigger. But for everyone's sake, it would be advisable to maintain a level of professional courtesy to enable our respective teams to work together, not against each other. For the time being, I suggest you put whatever gripe you have against us to one side. What's important now is that *we* have one dead woman, and *you* potentially have four other victims that could end up that way. Anything else is just an unnecessary distraction.'

With all eyes on him, Charlie Morgan was boxed in. 'Fine,' he hissed. His lips barely moved as he spoke. If looks could have killed, Jemima would have been struck dead.

The conversation eventually moved on to the use of drones. In recent years, advances in modern technologies had made it easier for law enforcement agencies to carry out surveillance operations. Drones were all too commonly in use. Unfortunately, the devices were not just used for good purposes, as criminal elements of society had realized the advantage they could bring to their operations. Packages could be attached, drugs and other contraband delivered. It made catching criminals red-handed far more complex. It wasn't so much a problem with small-time opportunistic criminals. But organized gangs, with extensive funds behind them, had embraced this new technology. It had opened up a whole new world of opportunities. And if the devices were operated sensibly, it significantly reduced their chances of getting caught.

'We need to get eyes up there,' said Charlie. There was an implicit expectation in his statement.

'Although I live there, it's not my house. It's my sister's,' said Jemima. She was determined not to make it easy for him. If he wanted to use Lucy's property as a base from which his team could operate, he would have to directly ask the question.

Charlie sighed resignedly. 'Fine, I can see that you're not going to make this easy for me. To undertake surveillance work, we'll need to be close to the target. Otherwise, it's a no go. Will your sister agree to us using her place for a couple of days?'

'I'll ask and get back to you later today,' said Jemima. She experienced a slight sense of satisfaction in making Charlie Morgan realize that consent wasn't necessarily a given.

'If she agrees, she won't be able to tell anyone what we're up to. Otherwise, it'll blow our cover,' said Charlie.

'I can't guarantee Lucy will go for it. If she does, there's a log cabin she uses as her office, which could be utilized by your team, at least through the night. That way you wouldn't disturb us. Though, I don't think she'd be agreeable about giving up that space during the day. But given the circumstances, I'm sure we can work something out. If our neighbours are people traffickers, then Lucy will want to do everything possible to bring them down. And you don't need to worry about her being discreet. I'll personally vouch for my sister,' said Jemima.

To have eyes on West Winds, Charlie would have to use a drone. The murder of one of the missing girls had placed the others in far more immediate danger. It was highly likely their captors would panic. At the very least, they would be compelled to act quickly. A murder investigation would inevitably result in police visits and questions. And as the Johnsons owned a haulage company, they would know it wouldn't be long before the investigation honed in on them. To avoid detection, it would become essential to get rid of the others quickly. Whether the plan was to sell them on or dispose of their bodies was something only the traffickers knew. But holding on to them at the moment would not be a viable option.

Charlie knew that it wouldn't be wise to use a drone during daylight hours. Although small, it would be easy to spot, and that would be counterproductive. But at night, it would be possible to fly the drone close to the property and take a good look around. It also seemed more likely that if the trafficked girls were at West Winds, they would be moved out of there under cover of darkness. It would reduce the risk of nosy neighbours curtain-twitching if it was done while most of them were tucked up in bed and fast asleep.

'Right, I must go. I don't have time to waste,' said Charlie, as he stood and turned towards the door.

'I'll walk you down,' said Jemima.

'No need for that. I'm more than capable of finding my own way out.'

'Believe me, there's every need. This isn't your station.' It was implicit in Jemima's stern tone that this wasn't up for discussion. She had no idea why Morgan was acting in such a hostile and disrespectful manner, but she was determined that the man wasn't going to walk out of there before he had provided an explanation.

As Charlie harrumphed, everyone present spotted him clench his fists then slowly release them. There was a moment when it appeared that he might kick off. Instead, common sense prevailed, and he narrowed his eyes as he glared defiantly at Jemima. 'Very well, after you.' His voice dripped with contempt.

Once outside the room, Jemima confronted him. Her voice was low and level. She had no wish to argue with the man. But she did want to know why he was being so antagonistic and downright rude. 'For the sake of our respective cases, we need to clear the air, Charlie. Something's clearly upset you, but I've no idea what that might be.'

'No idea?' hissed Charlie. His eyebrows arched in mock surprise. 'You've seriously no idea? You should have done your job seven years ago. That's what's wrong with me. If you'd got Toombes back then, Violet would never have been abducted last year.'

'We did everything we could.'

'Yeah? Well, it obviously wasn't enough. Violet's a wreck. My marriage is over. That's on you!'

Jemima was speechless. On both occasions, she and Broadbent had given their all to save Violet. They had sustained considerable injuries in the process. Whatever had subsequently gone wrong with Charlie's marriage was nothing to do with Jemima or any other officer who had worked those cases.

CHAPTER 18

As a result of their discussion, Jemima and Broadbent were to visit West Winds later that morning. They would speak with the Johnsons, just as they had with the other villagers. Ideally, Charlie Morgan wanted them to postpone any contact with the couple until his team at the NCA had a chance to find out more about them. But as Jemima had pointed out, they were investigating a murder. Should the Johnsons discover that there had been an excessive delay in the police approaching them, it could cause them to speculate on the motive behind such a postponement.

In the meantime, the NCA would set up a small surveillance operation at the Chesrielle Haulage yard. Another of their teams would check with the port authorities to establish routes and the regularity with which Chesrielle trucks passed between Europe and the UK. Until they had proof, their theories were entirely based on supposition. They could be way off the mark.

Other NCA officers would be tasked with gathering and forensically combing through financial and other records filed by the company. It was painstaking but necessary work, which would be invaluable further down the line should a case be brought against the Johnsons.

Using Ordnance Survey maps and aerial images readily available on the internet helped them get the lie of the land. The property was remote enough for illicit activities to occur without attracting unwanted attention. There were also various outbuildings, any of which could be being used to house the young women.

Jemima spoke to Lucy and explained the situation. The latter was surprisingly amenable to the NCA using her property to run a surveillance operation. She already knew Charlie Morgan as he was married to her friend Violet. Though she and Violet had drifted apart in recent years, given the connection to his wife she trusted that Charlie would not do anything that put them in danger.

Lucy's house was closest to West Winds, yet it was far away enough that there was no chance of overhearing or seeing any suspicious activity at the other property. Anything could happen at the Johnsons' place, and no one would be any the wiser.

Throughout the time she had lived at her sister's house, Jemima had not ventured in the direction of West Winds. It wasn't that she was unadventurous. It was merely because there seemed little point, as the lane was a dead end. Only those who wished to visit West Winds travelled along that section of the road. There was no other property in that direction and nothing of interest to entice anyone to head that way.

As things stood, two pieces of circumstantial evidence suggested the possibility that the Johnsons could be linked to the murder. Firstly, the victim's shoe had been found on the lane between Lucy's house and West Winds. It was a section of road that was rarely used, and it was unlikely the victim would have come across it by chance. Secondly, as it seemed likely that the young woman had been trafficked, and the Johnsons operated a haulage company, they had the means to smuggle people into the country. Jemima knew that the couple warranted investigation. If only to end up ruling them out.

This was a delicate fact-finding mission that could have far-reaching consequences should they inadvertently tip off potential people traffickers. The murder investigation could quite feasibly be part of a more significant problem. The NCA's involvement added another layer of complexity to everything they did from this point forward, and it meant that the investigation was not entirely under her control.

Charlie Morgan had made it clear that he expected complete transparency from Jemima and her team. She somehow doubted that the NCA would return the favour. The police were effectively expected to operate with one hand tied behind their backs.

As they had no idea what they would encounter at West Winds, Charlie had insisted that a small team of NCA officers assemble at Lucy's house to be on hand should they be needed. If Jemima contacted him to say that it was likely the missing girls were on the property, they could respond within minutes and hopefully control the situation before events escalated and anyone got hurt.

They approached the far end of the lane, which widened into a large turning circle. The turn-off towards West Winds was shortly before that, at a point where a sign stated that this was a private driveway and that trespassers would be prosecuted.

'Remind you of anywhere?' asked Broadbent, as he steered the car through the narrow turn and proceeded along the incline towards the property.

'You know it does, but I don't want to think about Llys Faen Hall,' replied Jemima.

'Me neither. I'm just hoping this isn't some sort of omen,' he said.

Llys Faen Hall had been a shockingly violent case with numerous victims. Getting inside the killer's mind had required extensive lateral thinking. Jemima had even doubted herself when she'd uncovered the truth behind those murders. The killer's motivation and modus operandi were so warped that no one apart from her had thought along those lines.

Off to the right, several sizeable outbuildings were visible in the distance. They were too far away to make out any definite features but appeared to be of wooden construction and were well-maintained as far as they could tell. It suggested they were either currently being used for something, or the owner had something specific in mind for them.

'I don't recall seeing those structures on the Ordnance Survey maps or Google Earth,' said Jemima.

'Me neither. I guess they must be fairly new.'

Further speculation ceased when, moments later, West Winds came into view. Jemima's jaw dropped in awe. It was the most architecturally stunning property she had ever seen. With a mixture of old and new, it combined a renovated farmhouse with a large, modern, steel-and-glass extension. The successful marrying of two eras ensured that what could have so easily been a design disaster was instead a breathtaking triumph. And the remoteness of its location added further to its appeal.

Broadbent laughed. 'Dream on.' He had clearly read her mind. 'Even if the whole squad clubbed together, we'd never be able to afford something like that.'

It was true. Should West Winds ever become available on the open market, the price tag would preclude anyone who was not a multi-millionaire. As it was, she was a single parent living in her sister's house. There was no chance.

They parked up in front of the property, and Jemima rang the doorbell. When the chime ceased, the only sound came from a few small birds chirping in a nearby tree. Jemima pressed the doorbell once more. They waited, but it seemed that no one was at home, which was unsurprising as the Johnson's had a business to run, and the children would be at school.

Broadbent walked to the side of the property as Jemima pressed the doorbell once more. He was just returning when a Land Rover appeared, heading towards the house.

A woman cut the engine and stepped out of the vehicle. 'Can I help you?' she asked. She was in her late thirties, tall, with shoulder-length auburn hair. Her eyes were obscured by a pair of oversized designer sunglasses. It was clear that her well-cut country casual clothes cost more than most people would spend on an entire wardrobe. Her voice lacked any hint of a local accent and oozed assertiveness. It suggested that she was not intimidated by the presence of two strangers.

Jemima held out her warrant card for inspection. 'Detective Inspector Huxley and Detective Sergeant Broadbent. And you are?'

The woman closed the gap between them and inspected the identification before answering. 'I'm Gabrielle Johnson, and this is my property.'

'We're making a routine call, Mrs Johnson. We're doing the rounds, speaking to every resident in the vicinity of Leighton Meadow. I take it that you've heard about the recent murder?'

'The young woman at the church? Yes, I have, but I can't see how I can possibly be of help. It's so remote here that we wouldn't see or hear anything that occurs down in the village.' There was no mistaking the iciness of her tone, though the woman stopped short of outright hostility. 'Now if you don't mind, I've things to get on with.' And with that, Gabrielle Johnson sidestepped them and headed towards the entrance to her property.

There was nothing more they could do. They had no grounds to force Gabrielle to engage in any further conversation. Though they both thought that her lack of interest in the murder was unusual. Most people displayed either morbid curiosity or were clearly worried about any potential threat to either themselves or family members. Yet this woman didn't appear to care.

Broadbent turned the key in the ignition. 'She's hiding something,' he said. 'But the question is what?'

'I agree. I also think we need to get a closer look at those outbuildings. Stop the car once we're out of sight of the house. I'll get the binoculars out of the glove compartment and take a closer look.'

'OK, but stay in the car. Remember, Charlie said it's important that we don't let on that we suspect that anything's wrong.'

Jemima adjusted the binoculars' focus in time to see the door to one of the wooden outbuildings open and a man wearing a hazmat suit step outside. She dropped the binoculars and grabbed her phone.

'What is it?' asked Broadbent.

'We've got a problem.' Jemima suddenly felt uncomfortably hot despite the pleasant air temperature.

CHAPTER 19

'What's your exact location?' demanded Charlie. His voice was rapid and overly officious as it boomed through the speakerphone. It was as though he was a sergeant major whipping new recruits into shape.

Jemima bristled yet somehow managed to sound calm as she explained they were on the long driveway that connected West Winds to the lane. 'As far as I can tell, it's the only way in or out of that property.'

'Turn your vehicle diagonally so that it blocks it completely,' ordered Charlie. 'We're on our way.'

Before Jemima had a chance to say anything further, the line went dead.

'What do you think is going on inside that structure?' asked Broadbent as he released the handbrake and repositioned the car as Charlie had instructed.

'Search me, but whatever it is, we're staying well back. You don't get dressed up in a hazmat suit for no good reason, and we're not equipped to deal with it. Charlie Morgan can handle that side of things. The NCA will either have the appropriate equipment or will contact specialists to enter the structure. I'm more than happy to leave that side of it to him and his team.'

At the sound of an approaching vehicle, Jemima stiffened. It would either be the NCA officers or someone likely to cause trouble. In next to no time, the vehicle skidded to a halt, and Charlie Morgan could be seen in the front passenger seat. He was animated and shouting into his phone.

An officer got out of the driver's seat and two more out of the back. The driver identified himself as Rick. His voice was as smooth as chocolate, and his face exceptionally attractive. A dark T-shirt strained across well-developed pecs, and his biceps looked as though they could easily crack nuts. Jemima felt a wave of heat work its way up her neck until her ears felt as though they were on fire.

It was the second time she had experienced such a feeling in as many days. She silently reprimanded herself for finding herself attracted to this stranger. It was an inappropriate thought, and the timing was lousy. After all, she was very heavily pregnant, and they were gathered there because of a potentially dangerous situation. Her hormones were all over the place, which meant that her judgement was compromised. She promised herself that as soon as this case ended, she would begin her maternity leave.

Thankfully, Rick was oblivious to Jemima's inappropriate thoughts. As soon as he had introduced himself, he turned away to use some binoculars to take a closer look at the outbuildings. 'At least two perps, both in hazmat gear,' he called over his shoulder.

'Reinforcements should be with us in twenty,' said Charlie. He'd ended his call and was out of the vehicle. 'They'll have protective equipment and can deal with whatever's inside. How certain are you that there's no one inside the house apart from Mrs Johnson?'

'As sure as we can be, without having gone in. We saw no evidence of anyone else there,' said Jemima.

'OK, well, here's where we are. I've a couple of officers in a van who have blocked the lane so no one else can get here.'

'Won't that look suspicious?' asked Broadbent.

'They're posing as workmen, so it should be fine. My team will keep our distance but surround the outbuildings. It's not ideal as there are only the four of us, but it'll have to do. I want you two to move your vehicle further up this driveway, but keep clear of the house for now. I don't want to risk Gabrielle Johnson making a run for it. Once reinforcements arrive, you get inside that house and arrest her.'

'On what grounds?' asked Jemima.

'Oh, I don't know, how about murder?' said Charlie. His words dripped with sarcasm as he shot a contemptuous look towards Jemima. 'The reason's not important. All that matters is that you two are up to the job. I appreciate that in your world, you're used to just plodding along. But this is a dynamic situation, and all the bases have to be covered. We can't allow her to tip anyone off because God only knows what we're dealing with here. I would have thought that even plods like you would appreciate that you don't need hazmat suits for people trafficking.'

Jemima felt her complexion redden even further, though this time, it was through anger, not lust. Every fibre in her body compelled her to retaliate with a put-down. But common sense told her that it was neither the time nor the place.

Sensing that Broadbent was about to say something they might later regret, she shot him a warning look. As her nails dug painfully into her palms in an attempt to ground herself, she lowered her voice. 'Don't worry about us. We're more than up to it.'

Jemima and Broadbent watched as Charlie Morgan and the other three NCA officers made their way towards the outbuildings. Not wanting to break cover and alert the perpetrators, they used the trees to hide their presence. Each of the officers was armed, though their weapons would only be used as a last resort. The perpetrators could leave at any time. If that were to happen before reinforcements arrived, it would be a whole different ball game, as the NCA squad had no intention of allowing these people to escape.

'Charlie Morgan's a prick,' said Broadbent.

'He sure is. I've no idea what's up with him, but he definitely has a problem with us. The sooner we find out who murdered that girl, the better. I won't be sorry to cut ties with that lot.'

Jemima kept glancing at her watch. The NCA reinforcements seemed to be taking a long time to arrive. Thirty-five minutes passed before a van appeared. It stopped about twenty yards further down the driveway, and six officers got out. One of the guys approached their vehicle. 'You'll need these earpieces,' he said. 'I take it that you're capable of using this?' It was a battering ram.

'More than capable,' said Broadbent. He suddenly wished that Ashton and Peters were with them, as he knew that in her current state, Jemima would be a liability if things kicked off up at the house. She was the one who usually looked out for him. He just hoped that he was up to the task. Especially if they discovered that Gabrielle Johnson wasn't alone.

'When you receive the order, head up to the house ASAP and use this contraption to gain entry,' said the officer. 'You mustn't allow the occupant time to communicate with anyone.'

Jemima and Broadbent exchanged glances. They both knew it was foolish for Jemima to be there, but as things stood, they had no alternative but to head up to West Winds and arrest Gabrielle. Watching the NCA officers put on their hazmat suits and seeing the weapons they had at their disposal made their own tasers and Kevlar jackets seem very inadequate. It was like turning up to work to find you were only dressed in your underwear.

CHAPTER 20

They swapped places in the car so that Broadbent could exit the vehicle as quickly as possible. Broadbent was well aware that Jemima wasn't quick on her feet at the moment, and there was no way she could be expected to use the battering ram. He fully appreciated that the success or failure of their allocated task would most likely be down to him.

The moment the order came through, Jemima slammed the car into gear. Her knuckles were white as she gripped the steering wheel and floored the accelerator. Broadbent held the battering ram ready to jump out and force entry to the property as soon as the car skidded to a halt. There was no time to wonder about what was going on back at the outbuildings.

As he raced out of the vehicle in readiness to break down the door, he wished once again that Ashton and Peters were there to back him up. Apart from deploying her taser, there was no way Jemima could be expected to have his back. She was about ten paces behind him. Broadbent changed his grip on the battering ram, adjusted his stance and swung his arms back. He took a deep breath and was about to drive the implement forward when the front door opened.

Gabrielle was listening to music through a set of headphones, clearly oblivious to the two officers' presence immediately outside the entrance to her property. She screamed and staggered backwards.

Luckily Broadbent managed to stop himself from following through on the motion, though he was forced to shuffle slightly to remain upright as the battering ram changed his centre of gravity.

'Police! Don't move! Keep your hands where we can see them!' yelled Jemima, immediately taking control of the situation. 'Gabrielle Johnson, I am arresting you on suspicion of the murder of Dominika Jelinková. Hold out your hands.' She secured handcuffs around the woman's wrists, and then removed the headphones.

'You've no right to do this!' growled Gabrielle. The initial shock had worn off quickly. With her hands firmly secured, it was clear that they meant business and Gabrielle's fear turned into belligerent fury. 'You have no right to come into my home and arrest me. This is ridiculous. I demand to speak to my lawyer.'

'And you will, but not yet, Mrs Johnson. There'll be plenty of time for you to call your lawyer once you're at the station. Now let's go and sit down. I don't know about you, but I could do with taking the weight off my feet.' Jemima had already spotted the sitting room through an open door and headed in that direction.

Broadbent placed a hand on Gabrielle's shoulder and told her that she should do as she was told. Gabrielle shrugged his hand away but followed compliantly and sat on one of the sofas. 'You'll both be lucky to direct traffic when I finish with you.' She glared defiantly at them.

'Your threats won't change anything, Mrs Johnson. So, I suggest you calm down,' said Jemima. 'Is there anyone else in the house?'

'No,' said Gabrielle.

'Will you be OK while I take a look around?' asked Broadbent.

'I'm fine. Take your time,' said Jemima. 'My sergeant's going to take a look around to make sure that there's no one else hiding inside this property. We have to satisfy ourselves that there is no one else here.'

Sensing that it was in her best interest, Gabrielle shrugged her shoulders, settled back on the sofa and stared at the ceiling. The two women sat in silence, neither inclined to speak until Broadbent re-entered the room.

'All clear.' He sat opposite them.

'What are you doing? Why aren't you taking me to the police station?' A hint of fear in Gabrielle's voice was noticeable to the trained ear. Many years of work in law enforcement had given both officers first-hand experience of listening to and watching people attempt to bluff and lie their way out of situations they were suddenly desperate to distance themselves from. There were nearly always telltale signs to watch out for — changes in eye movement, muscle tics, voice cadence and the sudden appearance of excessive perspiration. With practice and determination, much of it could be controlled. Still, if the pressure was maintained or even ramped up throughout the interview process, then usually something had to give.

'We're waiting,' said Jemima.

'Waiting for what? This isn't right. Are you even police officers?' The woman looked from one to the other, eyes narrowing as it crossed her mind that the warrant cards she'd seen earlier were possibly not genuine.

Jemima and Broadbent both ignored the woman.

'Waiting for what?' she repeated. This time her voice was more forceful.

'Just be quiet,' said Jemima.

'I'd like an answer,' said Gabrielle.

Broadbent glowered at the woman. Obviously, Gabrielle was used to calling the shots. They were both aware that she would be unsettled by her question going unanswered. Anyone would know that being arrested, cautioned and cuffed yet kept waiting inside their own home was highly unusual. But with the operation underway at the outbuildings, it was essential to keep her out of the loop. It would shake the woman's confidence, which could ultimately play into their hands. Until they got the all-clear from the NCA team, they had to stay put.

Jemima made the most of the current downtime and settled back into the chair. It was a strange situation, having to wait in a suspect's home until they could return to the station to question them. It was one she had not encountered before. She used the time to formulate a questioning strategy and also to study Gabrielle. She could tell that the woman's mind was in overdrive. After all, it would be unnerving to be arrested, only to be kept in one place and not immediately transferred to a police station.

Almost an hour had elapsed by the time a message was relayed to them through their earpieces. They were given the go-ahead to leave the property and transport Gabrielle Johnson to the police station. The message was brief, with no update on how the operation at the outbuildings had gone.

As they travelled along the driveway to join the lane, there was nothing to suggest that a major operation had just taken place. The NCA vehicles were long gone. Everything looked peaceful, and Jemima thought how deceptive appearances could be. But as things stood, there was no reason for Gabrielle Johnson to suspect that a covert police operation had just occurred on her land.

The three occupants of the car sat in silence. Broadbent was at the wheel, and Jemima kept a close eye on Gabrielle, watching her in both the vanity and side mirrors. The woman appeared to be lost in her own thoughts. If Gabrielle Johnson was aware of or at all concerned about whatever had gone on inside the outbuildings, then she was doing an excellent job of hiding it. She neither glanced in that direction nor looked nervous.

As soon as they arrived at the station, Jemima received a message that Ray Kennedy wanted to speak with her immediately. Broadbent booked Gabrielle in while Jemima headed upstairs to Kennedy's office.

'It's all kicked off,' said Kennedy. 'Charlie Morgan let me know that they arrested two as yet unidentified men and rescued—'

'The missing girls,' interjected Jemima. She was so relieved that she was unable to let the DCI complete his sentence.

'No, Huxley. That's not what I was about to say. Now, if you'll allow me to continue . . .' He raised his eyebrows in mild annoyance, though his voice remained calm and measured. 'The NCA team rescued a man. Details were sketchy — I don't think they had a name — but the victim was tied up, badly beaten and found in one of the other outbuildings. He's been taken to hospital, and they won't be able to speak to him until the medical staff allow it.'

'A man? There wasn't any suggestion that any men were trafficked.'

'I suppose they couldn't rule it out. Just because they were made aware of a group of women going missing doesn't mean that there wouldn't be other victims,' said Kennedy.

'Any update on whatever was going down in that outbuilding? There were men in hazmat suits.'

'Nothing so far. All I know is that Morgan's team have arrested them and taken them in for questioning. You know what they're like. We'll only be told the bare minimum when it suits their purposes. The only thing they knew for certain was that there was a metal drum containing hydrochloric acid. They weren't able to establish what was inside, but it's a very effective way of disposing of evidence. That stuff will eat through just about anything.'

Jemima couldn't help but shiver. These people were ruthless. At best, they could be disposing of inanimate evidence. But if they'd got wind that the police were on to them, they could have panicked and decided to dispose of the bodies in a way that was likely to leave little, if any, trace.

'Do you know if they managed to track down Gabrielle's husband, Chester Johnson? He wasn't at their home, so I presumed he must be at the haulage yard,' said Jemima.

'Charlie confirmed that a team raided the haulage yard, but there was no sign of Chester Johnson as far as I know. He's either unaware of today's turn of events, or else he's on the run,' said Kennedy. 'As long as you stay away from anything linked directly to the people-trafficking operation, its fair game for you to push the Johnson woman on her husband's whereabouts. Let's face it, he could have committed the murder and legged it afterwards.'

CHAPTER 21

It took a while for Gabrielle Johnson's lawyer to arrive. Usually, Jemima would have been itching to make a start. Still, she was feeling weary, uncomfortable and was glad of the respite.

The squad settled around the main table in the incident room and used the time to review where they were on the case. They were all aware that given the NCA's involvement, this was likely to be their one and only shot at Gabrielle Johnson. They had to throw everything at it and make the interview count.

As yet, there was no physical evidence directly linking Gabrielle to the murder. Indeed, it was possible that she had not committed it herself. It would be easy to think that a successful businesswoman and a mother of two young girls would not be involved in people trafficking, let alone venture out in the middle of the night, hunt down and kill a young woman with a crossbow. But that would be playing to stereotypes. And everyone on the squad knew that that was a dangerous thing to do. Plenty of women were more than capable of committing the most heinous of acts without feeling even the slightest bit of remorse.

It was agreed that Jemima and Broadbent would be the ones to interview Gabrielle. Having already spent time with her, they would have a greater familiarity with what pushed her buttons. Given her apparent wealth, it was highly likely that she would have a hotshot lawyer who would advise her not to answer any questions, but there was always the chance that Gabrielle would ignore the advice of her counsel and believe that she knew better. If that were the case, they had a chance of getting potentially valuable information out of her.

As Jemima and Broadbent entered the interview room, DCI Kennedy watched the proceedings on a monitor. Gabrielle's lawyer was unknown to them and introduced himself as Vernon Foley. He was dressed in a sharp suit, which both officers knew would cost more than they earned in six months. Beneath the cuffs of his jacket, diamond-encrusted cufflinks glittered. His full head of hair was pulled back tightly and fixed in a top knot. Compared with the uptight solicitors who usually frequented the premises, he appeared rather bohemian. He spoke with no discernible accent, flashing his dazzling veneered teeth as though auditioning for a toothpaste advert. There was no mistaking the fact that this man was expensive and showy. But he also had to be good at his job. No client would pay the fee he was likely to command without getting exceptional service in return.

With the preliminaries out of the way, the interview began in earnest.

'Where were you on Monday night and Tuesday morning between 9 p.m. and 8 a.m.?' asked Jemima.

Gabrielle glanced at her solicitor, who nodded to indicate that it was appropriate for her to answer. 'At home.'

'Can anyone verify that?'

'Not for the entire period, but my brother was also in the house. He lives there at the moment.'

'Your brother?'

'Yes, Perry Cook.'

This information was unexpected. They had not been aware of Gabrielle having a brother, let alone one who lived at West Winds.

'How long has your brother resided at the property?' pressed Jemima.

'Approximately three months.'

'Does anyone else live at the property?'

Gabrielle's breath caught in her throat. 'N-no.' The response was short and clearly emotional.

'Really? What about your husband, Chester, and your daughters, Blythe and Roslyn?' Gabrielle's chin dropped to her chest, but not before Jemima spotted a flash of fear in the woman's eyes. 'I asked you a question, Mrs Johnson. Were your husband and children at home with you on the night in question?'

Gabrielle was about to say something when her solicitor placed a hand on her arm. She glanced sideways and he shook his head, warning her not to answer. 'No.' The short statement was barely more than a whisper.

Sensing that she wasn't going to get more information on Chester Johnson at this point, Jemima changed tack. 'As we speak, officers are going over every inch of your house, garage and garden. Once they have finished there, they'll move on to examine your outbuildings and the remainder of your land. All of your electronic devices will be removed and forensically examined. We have experts more than capable of gaining access to every file stored on them, even if you've taken precautions to password protect or encrypt those files. We'll crawl over every aspect of your life. Neither you nor your husband will be able to hide anything.'

'That's enough, Inspector. It sounds to me that you're on a fishing expedition and have little, if any, evidence to hold my client. So, I suggest you stop the scare tactics, present your evidence and either question my client or release her,' said Foley.

As Jemima was about to respond, there was a knock at the door. Gareth Peters entered the room and passed his colleagues a handwritten note. It contained bad news for Gabrielle Johnson.

'How long have you owned a crossbow?' asked Jemima.

'I don't—' She stopped in her tracks as her solicitor once again placed a hand on her arm. 'No, I'm sorry, Vernon, I'm going to answer because I don't have anything to hide.' The solicitor's eyes narrowed as he silently attempted to bring his client into line. But Gabrielle was having none of it. 'I don't own a crossbow, and neither did my husband.'

'I find that hard to believe. You see, we've just been informed that a crossbow was found concealed in your attic during a search of your property. It's being tested as we speak.'

'Tested for what? I've already told you it's not mine.'

'The victim, Dominika Jelinková, was murdered with a bolt fired at close range from a crossbow. And you have to admit that it's a huge coincidence that such a weapon has been found hidden away in your attic,' said Broadbent.

'You're not going to be able to link it to me. I've already told you that I don't own a crossbow. This is ridiculous. I'm a respectable businesswoman. I'm not some psychopath who goes about killing people with a crossbow or any other weapon, for that matter. You can do all the tests you like. It's not going to change the fact that I haven't seen or touched that weapon. Whoever's put it there is obviously trying to set me up.'

'And who would that be?' asked Jemima.

Before Gabrielle had a chance to reply, Vernon Foley's hand shot towards his client's arm and forcefully grasped her wrist. 'I-I've no idea,' she muttered. Shaking herself free of his grip, she dropped her gaze and shifted as far away from her legal representative as she could without physically moving her seat.

The dynamic between the two of them was puzzling and concerning. The woman was evidently distraught and doing the best she could to keep a lid on her fear and emotions, while Vernon Foley was coercing his client. What his motive was remained, as yet, unclear.

'Mrs Johnson, are you happy to be represented by this man?' asked Jemima. For the sake of the case, she felt compelled to ask the question. The last thing they wanted was for the case to be compromised because the suspect had been coerced by someone who, without question, should have her best interests at heart.

'Really, Inspector! Your question is completely inappropriate, and I resent the implication,' said Foley.

'Mrs Johnson?' Jemima ignored him. She had no intention of being put off getting an answer.

'Mr Foley is and has been my chosen legal representative for many years. I have no doubt that he has my best interests at heart. Even though we might not see eye-to-eye at the moment.'

'What I don't understand is why you used a crossbow. There are other weapons you could have chosen. Weapons which would have been far easier to conceal,' said Broadbent.

'I don't hear a question there,' Foley countered.

'On the night in question, what time did you arrive at the church?' asked Jemima.

'I didn't go to the church. I've not set foot inside that or any other religious establishment. I abhor everything they stand for.'

'That's a very sweeping statement. You can be sure that we will check it, Mrs Johnson,' said Broadbent.

'What possible reason could I have for killing some unknown woman?' The exasperation in Gabrielle's voice was undisguised.

'What possible reason indeed?' Jemima decided to change tack once more. It was frustrating that they had to veer away from the people-trafficking link. 'Let's return to something you said a few moments ago. When I asked about the crossbow, you said, and I quote, "I don't own a crossbow, and neither did my husband." You referred to your husband in the past tense. I'd like you to clarify exactly what you meant by that.'

The colour blanched from Gabrielle's complexion, and her shoulders suddenly sagged as though weighed down with unbearable force. 'I didn't mean anything by it.' The denial sounded desperate.

'My client is here to ans—'

Jemima cut the lawyer off mid-sentence. 'That's enough, Mr Foley.' She held up her hand to emphasize her annoyance. But before she was able to continue, Gabrielle began to sob. This was no false show of emotion. She was genuinely distressed.

'Don't say another word,' hissed Foley. His face was inches from his client's ear.

'I've had enough. I can't take it anymore,' wailed Gabrielle.

'What can't you take?' pressed Jemima.

'Think about what you're about to say. There's too much at stake,' whispered Foley.

'What have I got to lose? They might even be able to help,' said Gabrielle.

Jemima swallowed hard as her heart rate increased. She had no idea what Gabrielle was about to reveal. But whatever it was, she was determined to hear it. 'Help you how?'

Gabrielle clenched her lips tightly together as she emitted a high-pitched squeal which threatened to shatter their eardrums. She shook her head furiously as she fought the urge to spill her innermost fear.

'Look at me, Gabrielle. I'm a mother, just like you. Now tell me what you're afraid of,' demanded Jemima.

'Chester's dead! My brother killed him. This whole rotten mess is Perry's fault. He's behind everything that's happened.'

'Why didn't you contact the police when he killed your husband?' asked Jemima. She was blindsided by Gabrielle's admission. It was so unexpected and made no sense.

'Because Perry's abducted my daughters, and I've no idea where they are. He's threatened to kill them unless I go along with everything he says. You've got to get them back. You have to save my girls. They're only six years old — they'll be terrified. God only knows what he's done to them.'

'When did this happen?'

'Fifteen weeks ago. I came back from the haulage yard and saw an unfamiliar van outside our place. I got out of my car and heard Chester yelling from inside the house. It was so unlike him, as he was always so laid back. He was arguing with someone, but I didn't know who. The next thing I knew, the front door opened, and Chester and my brother came tumbling out. Perry had turned up out of the blue.' For someone who had been so reluctant to speak, Gabrielle's words gushed from her lips in a raging torrent.

'Chester was gripping and pushing Perry. I'd never seen him that angry, and I had no idea why he was so upset. They were struggling and shouting at each other. Chester kept shoving him towards the rear of the van. I was trying to make sense of things, but everything happened so quickly.'

Barely allowing herself time to take a breath, she continued, 'I kept shouting at them, telling them to stop. But they didn't listen to me. I'm not sure they even realized I was there. The next thing I knew, Chester had Perry pinned against the van. He was yelling at him, demanding that he return the girls. It didn't make any sense. I tried to break them up, but there was no reasoning with Chester. He'd completely lost it. He was screaming that Perry had abducted the girls. But Perry's their uncle. I couldn't understand why he would have done it.' She stifled a moan, her agony laid bare for them to see.

'I eventually managed to separate them, but as soon as I did, Perry pulled a gun on us. It was surreal, as Perry was always such a sap. I backed off. I was more concerned about getting my daughters back, and I was sure I could talk Perry round. I quickly figured out it must be about money — he's always been hopeless with it. I tried to defuse the situation. I remember saying, "Look, we can work this out. You can have whatever you want. There's plenty of cash in the safe. Just let us have the girls back, and we'll say no more about it." But Chester had to go and play the hero. He launched himself at Perry. There was a struggle, and the gun went off. Ches didn't stand a chance. He took a bullet to the chest. It killed him outright.'

As tears streamed down Gabrielle's face, Jemima passed her a handful of tissues. In that moment they were no longer police officer and suspect. It was a genuine display of compassion from one woman to another. She allowed Gabrielle time to compose herself, to stop crying and get her thoughts together. But the questioning had to continue.

'What happened to your husband's body?' asked Jemima. A few minutes had elapsed since anyone had spoken.

'I helped Perry load him into the back of the van. Perry said that if I got the police involved, he'd kill the girls too. He told me to sit tight, keep my mouth shut and act as though everything was normal. I did as I was told. I had no choice.

'Afterwards, I spent weeks going out of my mind, jumping every time the phone rang. Perry turned up three weeks later. There was no sign of Blythe or Roslyn. He told me he was holding on to them as they were his insurance policy.'

'Did you happen to notice the van's registration mark? It's possible there could still be forensic evidence inside it.'

'No, it was the last thing on my mind!'

'What about a logo? Or anything that would help us trace it?'

'I don't remember. It was white. That's all I can recall.'

Jemima felt her heart sink. Without a registration mark or any other distinctive information, there was absolutely no hope of tracing the vehicle.

'Have you spoken to your daughters since their abduction?' asked Broadbent.

'No. I asked, but Perry wouldn't agree to it. He didn't want to allow me a way of tracing them.'

'So, forgive me, you've had no proof of life?' asked Jemima gently. She had a bad feeling about this.

Gabrielle swallowed hard and shook her head. The idea of her daughters being dead was far too painful for her to articulate.

'What has Perry been up to since he returned to West Winds?'

'I'm not entirely sure. He's uptight and cagey, but whatever's going on involves one of my trucks and the outbuildings on my land. I was told to stay away from them, or else I'd regret it. He made me hire a new driver, no questions asked, and said that a particular truck would operate through him from that point forward. The driver's name is Neil Henney. I'd have no say on where it went or what cargo it carried. I just had to sign off on the paperwork as and when required, without seeing what it said. If I didn't fall into line, my girls would b-be k-killed.'

The confession was the final straw for Gabrielle. Her final shred of composure dissipated. 'P-please save my g-girls,' she sobbed.

Jemima's heart lurched as she witnessed the woman's distress. 'We'll do everything we can. Do you have a recent photograph of your brother?'

'No.'

'What about his previous address? It could help us locate your daughters.'

'I'll write it down for you,' said Gabrielle.

'And when did you last see Perry?'

'Early yesterday evening. He was in a strange mood.'

'Angry?'

'No . . . at least, I don't think so, but there was something up with him. He was pacing about like a caged animal.'

'Did you ask him what was wrong?'

'Why would I? We barely speak. I do everything I can not to antagonize him in case it has repercussions for my girls. Just being in the same room as him makes me feel sick. I want to rip his head off, but I can't do anything until I find out where they are and know that they're safe.'

Jemima could see the torment in the other woman's eyes. Gabrielle had been living under enormous pressure. It was unthinkable that she had been forced to share her home with someone who had killed her husband and snatched her children as a form of insurance policy. 'What about recent photographs of your daughters?' she asked.

'There are some on my phone. The code to unlock it is—'

'I'd advise you not to—' began the solicitor.

'Shut up and stay out of it. This has nothing to do with you,' ordered Gabrielle. She gave them the passcode.

'We'll get it out of evidence and follow it up. It'll be treated as a priority,' said Jemima.

'Please be careful. I don't want any harm to come to my girls.'

'The address you've given us is a long way outside our area, so I'm afraid that officers from another police force will have to deal with it. I'll ensure they're fully briefed about what you've just told us, and I'll let you know as soon as we've heard back from them. But I'm afraid that for now, you'll have to return to the holding cell until we either verify what you've told us or have the forensic results rule you out of the murder.'

'But he'll kill my girls if he finds out I've been speaking to you!'

'He won't find out from us, but you still have to return to the cell. We'll release you as soon as we can, but you won't be allowed to return home as things stand. Realistically, it might be a few days before you're allowed back there.'

Jemima and Broadbent gathered their papers together.

CHAPTER 22

They had all known that Gabrielle Johnson's arrest was a desperate throw of the dice. With no forensic evidence linking her to the murder, they had been relying on the flimsiest of circumstantial evidence. Finding the crossbow hidden in the attic at West Winds had taken them closer to reaching the threshold for the burden of proof. However, it didn't necessarily link Gabrielle to the murder. Unless they found evidence directly linking her to the weapon, they couldn't prove that she had used it to kill Dominika. Especially since the woman claimed that she had not been aware of its existence.

The interview had revealed a whole new case. Gabrielle's allegations were a shocking turn of events that no one could have predicted. In a few hours, they had gone from investigating one murder to being informed of yet another, not to mention the abduction of two small children. If Gabrielle Johnson was telling the truth, these were all crimes outside the NCA purview and would fall to Jemima's team to investigate.

The squad assembled in the incident room.

'Didn't see that coming,' said Broadbent.

'None of us did, lad. But we're going to have to follow up on it pretty sharpish. If the Johnson woman's telling us the truth, then her daughters have been separated from her for fifteen weeks. That's a hell of a long time in a child's life, especially when they're that young. She's only got her brother's word that they're being taken care of. And since he's spent much of that time back at West Winds, who the hell's looking after them? He could have offloaded them to God knows who. Those kiddies could be dead or being used as playthings by a gang of paedophiles.'

'Don't even go there. It makes me sick to the stomach just thinking about it. Cook's beyond evil to do something like that. I wouldn't be responsible for my actions if someone abducted my Harry,' said Broadbent.

Kennedy ignored him and turned his attention to Jemima. 'Are you able to continue with the case?' He was aware that she would be going on maternity leave soon, and if Gabrielle Johnson was telling the truth, it added at least two other dimensions to the investigation.

Jemima bristled at Kennedy's question. She readily acknowledged that the closer it got to the birth, the less energy she had. Everything was such an effort at the moment, and exhaustion was making her snappy. Her immediate thought was that Kennedy was suggesting that she was not up to the task. And if the thought occurred to her, surely the rest of the squad would think so too. 'I'm more than capable of handling this,' she replied.

'That's fine, Huxley. It's just with your due date approaching and the scope of this investigation spreading, it could take a while before we're able to wrap things up. Your capabilities and commitment have never been in doubt. I just don't want to add to your workload if you feel that it's time for you to slow down.'

In the last few days, Ray Kennedy had started to feel as though he was walking on eggshells. He felt protective towards Jemima. She was one of the best officers he'd ever encountered and certainly rose to every challenge life threw at her. But he was also aware of the stress she was under following the rape. Despite having no children of his own, he knew that any pregnancy's last trimester was challenging and exhausting.

Jemima had left him in no doubt that she felt as though he had overstepped the mark with his question, which had not been his intention. He just wanted her to look after herself and not put herself or the unborn baby at risk. Or get to the stage where she felt compelled to cut herself again. But of course, he couldn't voice that final concern.

'This development calls for a rethink of our strategy.' Kennedy addressed this statement to everyone in the room, keen to take the focus away from Jemima. 'So I'm making a unilateral decision. As of now, all communications with Charlie Morgan and the NCA will go through me. I'll be assuming the role of designated liaison officer, leaving you lot free to follow up on everything else.

'Morgan's displayed overt animosity towards this squad,' Kennedy continued. 'Though God only knows what his problem is. With the latest developments, you'll all have your hands full without having to tiptoe around him. If he tries any of his nonsense with me, he won't get away with it. If he's anything but professional, I'll see to it that his superiors get to hear about it. I know the NCA sees itself as a cut above, but the very least we can expect is a bit of professional courtesy.'

The team nodded their appreciation.

'Does anyone have any further updates to share?' Kennedy asked.

'I've just run a PNC check on Perry Cook,' said Gareth. 'In 2006, he was arrested for, and subsequently found guilty of, affray. He was twenty years old at the time and received a community service order. Since then, he appears to have been clean, as there's nothing on the system for him.'

'Do you have a photograph of him?' asked Jemima.

'Yeah, I printed it off. Though, given how old it is, his appearance could have changed a hell of a lot in that time.'

'I know, but it'll have to do. Gabrielle Johnson doesn't have a photograph of her brother, so we haven't got anything else to go on.'

'Let's take a look at it.' Kennedy snatched the image from Gareth's outstretched hand and placed it on the table. He then proceeded to put another set of images next to it. 'These are photographs of the men the NCA have in custody.'

They all gathered around and stared intently at them, each trying to imagine how the face Gareth had pulled off the PNC would have changed over the years.

Jemima was the first to voice her opinion. 'They don't have Perry Cook in custody,' she said. 'There's no way he could be either of those men.'

'I agree, but since that lowlife's not one of them, it means that Perry Cook is still out there, which puts those Johnson kiddies in imminent danger. Even if he goes to ground because of recent events, it'll just take a phone call to whoever's watching over them to end those girls' lives.' Kennedy fixed his gaze on Jemima. 'Set the wheels in motion, Huxley. There's no time to waste. With the amount of time elapsed since their mother claims they were snatched, those little ones could already be dead. But until we've evidence to prove otherwise, we approach this as though they're still alive. Now get to it. Every second counts.'

Jemima was already furiously tapping away at the keys, her hands shaking as a sickening feeling of dread settled on her. She didn't need anyone to tell her how time-crucial this was. Even the most inexperienced of officers would know. Just the thought of two little girls being held against their will, terrified and not understanding why they had been taken from their parents, was almost too much to bear. But even that thought was preferable to one where they were already dead.

Jemima swallowed hard as she did her best to focus on the task at hand. It would be all too easy to allow her imag-ination to run away with itself, with thoughts of emaciated, dehydrated bodies, or little girls at the mercy of paedophile rings. The best thing she could do for Blythe and Roslyn Johnson was to act and not think. She needed to get the ball rolling and ensure that the relevant police force had all the necessary information to take things forward.

When Jemima eventually found what she was looking for, she picked up the telephone and dialled her counterpart at the appropriate police force. She sighed impatiently, drumming her fingers on the desk as the phone continued to ring out unanswered. She was about to hang up and try again when someone picked up.

'DI Jack Chalmers.'

'Hello, I'm DI Jemima Huxley from the South Wales police force. We've an urgent situation and need your help.'

It was almost twenty minutes later when Jemima ended the call. She allowed herself a moment to recover before heading to Kennedy's office. The door was closed, and she was getting ready to knock when he raised his head and spotted her through the window. Kennedy's head was cocked sideways, a telephone receiver nestled between his ear and shoulder. He beckoned her inside while continuing to listen to whoever was on the other end of the line. He gestured for Jemima to take a seat, then lowered his gaze to concentrate on what he was being told. Every so often, he scrawled some information on a pad of paper.

Jemima waited patiently, curious about what Kennedy was being told. His expression was dark. 'OK . . . Uh-huh . . . Yeah, keep me informed,' he said. When he replaced the handset, he sat back in his seat and rubbed his face with his palms. He sighed heavily, then turned his attention to Jemima. 'It appears that there's no end to people's depravity.' As he spoke, his voice cracked.

In all the years she had known him, Jemima had not seen Kennedy this emotional. He frequently said that he'd seen everything the job had to throw at police officers and doubted that anything could ever shock him again. Whatever he had just been told must be awful for the DCI to look and sound as he did.

'What's happened?' she asked, placing her hands protectively over her stomach in an attempt to shield her unborn child from the horror she was about to hear.

'They opened the barrel. It contained the remains of a human body. There's not much left of it. The acid had done a pretty thorough job.'

Jemima swallowed hard as she fought a sudden urge to vomit. She placed a hand over her mouth as she struggled to get out of the chair.

Kennedy quickly upended his wastepaper bin and rushed to the other side of the desk to hand it to her. He placed a supportive hand on her shoulder, all the while hoping that she wouldn't need to use the receptacle. When the feeling of nausea passed without incident, they were both relieved.

The use of acid to dissolve a body was something that until now they would have associated with drug cartels. Without such indisputable evidence, it would seem inconceivable that such an atrocity could occur in a sleepy rural setting. It hammered home the fact that the NCA hadn't captured members of an ordinary criminal gang. These people operated on another level — a level they had previously not encountered. These men were monsters, individuals for whom apparently nothing was off limits.

'The other thing you need to know is that they found an old BMW in the barn. It's registered to Perry Cook. So if Cook doesn't turn out to be the one in the barrel, there only seem to be three possibilities,' said Kennedy.

Jemima supplied them. 'Either he's hiding out close to his sister's property, or he escaped by using another vehicle. Other than that, he's got to be on foot.'

'My thoughts exactly. What did you want to tell me?' asked Kennedy.

'Only that I contacted my opposite number, a DI Jack Chalmers who covers the area where Perry Cook's address is located. I filled him in on what we've been told, and he's organizing a team of officers to raid the property. He's aware that it's potentially a life-or-death situation. They'll have medics and child protection officers standing by, and he assured me that as soon as everything's in place, they'll be good to go.'

'Excellent. Time is of the essence, Huxley. We need to know one way or the other and get those kiddies to safety.'

'For now, we'll search for Perry Cook,' said Jemima. 'I'll get Ashton to return to the village and obtain any footage from home-security cameras for the last few days. I can't say I've ever noticed any, but if there are, it'll be easy enough to establish which are local vehicles. We might just get lucky and get a make, model and registration mark of any other vehicles.'

'I suppose it's too much to hope that your sister has security cameras?'

'She does, but they cover the driveway and the log cabin. The property's set well back from the road. So it's not going to be of help to us.' As she said this, Jemima's thoughts briefly returned to the night of the murder. It suddenly occurred to her that even if she had looked out of the window at the exact moment when Dominika had run past, it would have been impossible to see her. She had been beating herself up for no good reason. There was nothing to feel guilty about.

Kennedy spoke again, shaking Jemima out of her reverie.

'Until we know otherwise, we have to assume that Cook's out there somewhere. Of course, there's always a chance it could be the remains of his body in that barrel. Then again, it could be Chester Johnson's or any of those other trafficked young women. The bottom line is we're not going to know for a while — if ever. The acid could have destroyed all DNA traces, in which case we'll be none the wiser.' He rummaged in his pocket, extracted a handkerchief, and used it to wipe beads of sweat from his brow. He was feeling the pressure. This case was intense and appeared to have a life of its own. Every time he thought they were getting a handle on events, something else was revealed. It was like peeling away layers of a rotting onion, where each one turned out to be more revolting than its predecessor.

'If Cook's still at large, it'll be down to us to find him. The NCA have their hands full. They're currently undertaking a thorough search of the outbuildings. They're aware that apart from Gabrielle Johnson, there was no one else present at the house, but Morgan has arranged for it to be gone over with a fine-tooth comb,' said Kennedy.

'I know it's not part of our remit, and it'll be a long shot, but I'm going to have a word with the Vice squad and ask them to visit local brothels,' said Jemima. 'Find out if any new Czech girls have arrived. They're better placed to do that as they know the local trade inside out. And who knows, even if they haven't been farmed out locally, someone might have heard something. Chances are they'd be more likely to talk to Vice officers than to any of us.'

'Good idea,' Kennedy agreed. 'Cook could have tried to sell the girls on quickly. The longer they keep them, the greater the risk that one or more of them will try to escape. I'd put money on it that they'll want rid as quickly as possible. It's a whole different ball game now that one of those girls was murdered.'

Jemima nodded. 'Yes, and at least by offloading that task to Vice, it'll free us up to concentrate on finding Cook.'

'Put the idea out there, but tell DI Wansley at Vice to hold off until I've spoken with Morgan,' said Kennedy. 'I don't need to tell you that the NCA are very territorial. It would be better to have their agreement. The last thing we need is to tread on their toes and have something come back to bite us.'

CHAPTER 23

Gabrielle Johnson agreed to sit with a police artist to enable her brother's photofit picture to be created. Meanwhile, Gareth Peters was still doing his best to find an up-to-date photograph of the man. But as time was of the essence and Gareth's efforts were getting him nowhere, there was a strong possibility that an artist's impression was the best they would get.

Sometime later, Kennedy marched into the room with an expression that bordered on smug satisfaction. He announced that after a great deal of wrangling, the NCA had given the green light for a search of the local brothels. As he uttered the words, Jemima reached for the phone and wasted no time updating Vice officers. Armed with photographs of the missing Czech girls, the officers set out across Cardiff and nearby towns to see what they could find.

It was good to get things moving again. Still, as they had no part in any of the active investigation areas, everyone in the team felt sidelined. It was frustrating given the seriousness and complexity of this multifaceted case. Then again, there was no point in taking action when the team hadn't yet come up with a decent plan.

Jemima and Broadbent were finalizing their strategy for locating Perry Cook when the telephone rang. When she realized it was DI Jack Chalmers, Jemima put the call on speakerphone. Everyone was keen to know whether or not Gabrielle Johnson's daughters had been found.

'Thought I'd let you know that we're on the move. We're a couple of minutes out from the property. Given that there are children involved, I thought you might want to stay on the line. I'll patch you through to our network, and you can listen in as the operation goes down.'

'That'd be great.' Jemima did her best to hide her surprise. DI Chalmers' offer was an unexpected bonus. It would not have occurred to Jemima to extend such a courtesy to another police force.

Word spread quickly, and despite having tasks to get on with, everyone stopped what they were doing. There wasn't one among them who didn't want those little girls to be found alive and unharmed. And as each of them had participated in similar exercises, it was easy to picture the scene. Tension in the room was palpable as they silently and collectively willed Jack Chalmers and his team on.

A female voice was the next sound they heard. 'Bravo Team in position at the rear of the property.'

'Go! Go! Go!' Chalmers' voice was loud but calm.

There were crashing sounds as the front and rear entrances were forced open with battering rams. Everything had to be perfectly timed so the occupants had no chance to attempt an escape or harm the children if they were inside.

Hurried footsteps and heavy breathing could be heard as the police officers systematically searched the building. With no visual link to the proceedings, the wait for information was almost unbearable. Eventually, a voice called out, 'Downstairs clear!'

'I'm heading upstairs now,' said Chalmers. They could hear the creak of the treads as his weight systematically transferred to each step. 'Something's not right up here.' His voice was now more whisper than anything else.

Jemima was eager to find out what was wrong but knew better than to say anything. Chalmers and his colleagues had more than enough on their plate. The last thing she wanted to do was distract them at a vital moment, especially when the stakes were so high.

'Do you hear that?' he asked. Even over the phone line, there was no mistaking a hum, which became louder with each passing second. 'I have a bad feeling about this. It can only mean one thing. I'm gonna open the door.'

Jemima was aware that her heart rate had increased to an unhealthy level. Being so far away and blind to the action made her feel impotent. There was nothing she could do. Her imagination was running haywire as she was caught up in an operation occurring more than a hundred miles away. The tension was excruciating. She winced as her teeth broke the skin on her bottom lip. She hadn't even realized that she had been biting it. She forced herself to take a deep breath. She needed to stay calm for the baby's sake, if not her own.

'Shit! It's bad,' said Chalmers. He was clearly shouting, but his voice was almost drowned out by the sound of buzzing. 'Get some windows open in here!'

Broadbent placed a protective hand on Jemima's shoulder as they waited to be told what now seemed inevitable. Experience told them that the sound was coming from blowflies, which meant that whoever was inside that room was dead.

'I can't see any children. We've got two bodies, both adults,' said Chalmers. 'Looks like a drug overdose.'

'All clear in the remainder of the property,' called another officer.

'Is there anything to suggest that the girls have been there?' pressed Jemima.

'Give us a minute,' said Chalmers. The silence seemed interminable before he spoke again. 'You can rest easy. There's no evidence that young kids have been at the property.'

Jemima gave a sigh of relief. 'Any chance you'll send us a photograph of the victims? We'll need to establish if one of them is Perry Cook.'

'Sure thing, but it's not going to help you,' said Chalmers. 'These people have been dead for a while. Their faces don't look anything like they would have when they were alive.'

'You say they've been dead for a while. How long are you talking about?'

'I'm not an expert in that sort of thing, but as there's no heat in the house and the weather hasn't been particularly warm, I'd say we're talking weeks. But that's just a guess. We'll need a pathologist to narrow it down.'

Jemima and the rest of the squad knew from what Chalmers had told them that Perry Cook wasn't one of the dead junkies. His sister had insisted that he had been at West Winds on the previous evening. There was a chance that his body could be the one discovered in the acid barrel. But for now, they had to proceed as though he was very much alive.

'I hate to ask you this,' said Jemima, 'but there's every chance that Cook still has the girls. Cook and his sister were born and brought up in that area. Their parents still live there, and there's a chance Perry could have friends in the area. There's every possibility he could be holding those children somewhere in the vicinity. Can you dig around and see if you can find another lead?'

'Will do.' Chalmers' voice was more level now that the uncertainty of the operation was over. 'Email me everything you have. At least with names and addresses, we'll have something to go on. I s'pose there's a chance that Perry's parents will know who his friends are and perhaps have a more up-to-date address for him. Even though we've drawn a blank here, I'll still treat it as a priority. You have my word that I'll follow it up today.'

CHAPTER 24

The live auditory feed that Jack Chalmers set up for them had proved to be one of the hardest things Jemima had ever listened to. She appreciated the inspector's generous gesture and had eagerly sat there as her imagination had conjured up a scene to make sense of what she was hearing. It had been helpful to have a real-time update on what Chalmers and his team had discovered at the property. But unfortunately, the end result was that they were nowhere closer to finding the Johnson twins.

'Why is nothing simple? I so wanted them to find those little girls safe and well,' said Broadbent.

'Let's not lose focus,' said Jemima. She was just as disappointed that the children had not been found. Still, given what Chalmers' team had witnessed, she was relieved that there was no evidence to suggest that the children had ever been at the property. 'It was always going to be a long shot. So put it out of your mind. We've lost nothing apart from fifteen minutes or so. At least we found out that it was a false lead at the earliest opportunity, and Jack Chalmers will follow up with Gabrielle's parents.'

Jemima frowned. 'Of course, as things stand, we're blindly accepting Gabrielle's assertion that her daughters are missing. Whereas perhaps we should consider whether her claim is actually true. It could all be bollocks, a deflection tactic. We've no proof that she isn't up to her neck in it with the people-smuggling operation and the murder. She's an astute woman.'

'I suppose she must be,' Broadbent agreed.

'Exactly, she runs a successful haulage company and seemingly has the respect of other business leaders. Neither of those things would come easily.'

'What are you implying?'

'Considering everything Gabrielle's achieved, I'd say she's a shrewd operator. So put yourself in her shoes. The evidence is piling up against her. Now, if I was her, I'd do my best to deflect the attention away from me. We've only got her word that her brother has kidnapped her daughters. She could have taken one look at me and thought that because I'm pregnant, I'd automatically believe that her kids are in danger. And I have to admit that it worked.'

'But why would she do that?'

'There's any number of possible reasons. Right up there is the fact that it buys her time.'

'For what?' asked Broadbent. He didn't seem to be buying Jemima's theory.

'For starters, for her accomplices to sell on or dispose of the rest of the Czech girls. While we're wasting time looking for her kids, we're taking resources away from the trafficked girls.'

'But we're not. The NCA are all over that.'

'You forget that Gabrielle doesn't know that. We haven't told her that we know about the people trafficking. As far as she knows, we're only investigating her potential involvement in a murder. And she certainly has no idea that the NCA were at her property. She obviously knows that there's something we're not telling her. But she doesn't know what it is,' said Jemima.

Broadbent considered this. 'There was definitely something off about her brief.'

'I agree. It was a strange dynamic. Foley was supposedly representing her interests, yet he seemed to be doing everything in his power to stop her from telling us about her daughters' supposed abduction. The more I think about it, the more convinced I am that something's not right.'

'So should we forget about the Johnson kids?'

'No, we can't do that. We have to follow up on Gabrielle's claims, as there's a chance she's telling us the truth. And if she is, then we have to find her daughters. I'm going to make some inquiries to establish when those girls were last seen. In the meantime, I'd like you to look at how Perry Cook could have got away from West Winds. Ashton's already checking out local CCTV, which should allow us to identify the possible use of a vehicle. So you should concentrate on how he could have made it out of there on foot. The area is popular with walkers. There are likely to be several established routes he could have taken that would allow him to stay off the roads.'

'You're surely not suggesting we send out search teams or the police helicopter?'

'Not at the moment. But if Cook did follow one of those trails, he'd have to find food and shelter sooner or later. Use the OS maps to establish villages or towns along the various routes. Then we can show shopkeepers and publicans the artist's impression in those targeted locations. Someone might have spotted him.' She sighed. 'Let's face it, with no real leads, we need to cast the net wide. But we have to find him quickly. The longer he's out there, the more chance he has of evading capture.'

Jemima picked up the telephone and dialled her sister's number.

Lucy picked up on the third ring. 'Everything OK, Jem?' There was a noticeable level of concern in her voice.

'Everything's fine, Luce. I just have a quick question. Do you know which school the Johnson twins attended?'

'It's the local primary — the one James transferred to.'

Jemima was surprised that the Johnsons with all their apparent affluence hadn't arranged for their children to attend a private school. The fact she had so readily presumed it would be the case made her acknowledge the possibility that she could quite easily have read the woman wrong.

It was usually easy for Jemima to be objective about a stranger. It was a necessity for doing her job. Yet despite not knowing Gabrielle personally, Jemima realized that her impartiality had been compromised by Lucy's evident admiration of the woman. It was silly, really, as despite being academically intelligent and an extremely capable person, Lucy was not worldly-wise. She was fortunate that bad things rarely happened to her, which resulted in her always seeing the good in people. There had been occasions when she'd even suggested that perhaps Jemima was too cynical for her own good.

Jemima realized that in recent weeks she had been losing her edge. Being pregnant wasn't just compromising her physical abilities. As the baby's birth approached, her thought processes were becoming woolly. Ideas would begin to form in her consciousness only to be obliterated by the slightest distraction. It was frustrating for her and dangerous for everyone who relied on her. It seemed as though it was nature's way of telling her to slow down, and she acknowledged that perhaps she should listen to what her body was telling her.

If it had been any other case, Jemima might have decided to start maternity leave there and then. But as the murder had taken place only a matter of yards from where she lived, she felt compelled to push on with the investigation. Deep down, she recognized that the rest of the squad were more than capable of continuing without her. But knowing that there was a killer still out there, someone who might pose a threat to her family, was not conducive to taking things easy and putting your feet up. And then there was the alleged abduction of the Johnson girls . . .

Jemima's attention returned to the six-year-old twins. She already knew the headmaster at the local primary school, having met Ken Wong only a few months earlier when James had transferred there. She hoped he would be amenable to answering her questions about someone else's children.

Having rung the school and with the formalities out of the way, Jemima began the conversation. 'Mr Wong, my call today has nothing to do with James. Instead, I'm speaking to you in an official capacity, and I'm hoping you'll answer a few questions I have about two of your pupils.'

'This is highly unorthodox, Inspector. I'm immediately uneasy on two accounts. Firstly, I can't begin to imagine what a couple of primary school pupils could have possibly done to warrant investigation by a senior police officer. After all, I can assure you that we've not had any hint of trouble at this school. Secondly, the most appropriate course of action would be for you to approach their respective parents, to gain whatever information it is that you feel you need.'

The conversation hadn't started as well as Jemima had hoped. 'Let me explain myself, Mr Wong. In the last few hours, I have been made aware of an allegation that the welfare of two of your pupils is at stake. The allegation has been made by one of the parents.'

'I see . . .' The headmaster's tone immediately softened, and Jemima could clearly hear the concern in his voice.

'The pupils in question are Blythe and Roslyn Johnson.'

'The Johnson twins?'

'That's right.'

'They were pupils at this school, but they haven't attended for the last few months.'

'Did either parent provide any explanation for the girls' absence?'

'Not at first. It took everyone by surprise. Until that point, neither of the girls had missed a day of school. Their first day of absence coincided with a class assembly. The children worked very hard on a special presentation that all the parents and other close family members were invited to. And I know for a fact that Blythe, in particular, was looking forward to it. She had one of the main roles. There hadn't been any suggestion that they wouldn't attend. It was highly irregular and upsetting for some of the other children as they had all worked so hard to make it a special occasion.'

'Did either of the parents contact you later?' Jemima was busy scribbling notes so she would have an accurate record of everything the headmaster said. 'No, but I attempted to contact them. It was so out of character. I had no reason to think that either girl was in danger. They were happy, outgoing children. At first, I felt that there must have been some family emergency, so I gave it an hour or two. When I dialled Mr Johnson's number, I immediately got a message to say that the number was no longer available. Mrs Johnson's number was just ringing out, but she didn't pick up. I left numerous messages, asking if everything was all right with the girls, and told her to contact me if there was anything I could do to help.'

Jemima heard him swallow as he took a drink before continuing. 'Mrs Johnson finally got back to me about a week later. But I got the impression she did so because I'd told her I'd have to contact the relevant authorities, as I was gravely concerned about Blythe and Roslyn's welfare. It's not unusual for some parents to take their children out of school during term time for things such as a holiday or a family emergency. The former is frowned upon, and the latter is unavoidable. We have a duty of care to our pupils, and as such, we expect parents to inform us of any absences. When it comes to family emergencies there can be a delay, as keeping us informed is not a top priority in such circumstances.'

'What explanation did Gabrielle Johnson give you?' Jemima was eager to know.

'Very little, I'm afraid. She said that there had been an emergency on her husband's side of the family, and he had taken the girls with him. I did my best to press her on where they had gone and how long they were likely to be away, but she was vague and non-committal. It was quite unsatisfactory.' The headmaster's frustration was apparent in the tone of his voice.

'I see. And did you follow up on things?'

'Yes, I flagged it up by submitting a report to the appropriate authority, but that was all I could do.' He sighed.

'It's been about four months since the girls last attended the school. If you want to know more, I'm afraid you'll have to contact the bureaucrats yourself, and I wish you luck. Perhaps they'll be more forthcoming with you.'

It took the better part of an hour of being passed from one telephone extension to another before Jemima finally got to speak to someone at the appropriate department within the local authority. Her patience was wearing thin. And if that wasn't bad enough, she had to force herself to remain polite when it was finally revealed that Mr Wong's email had not been acted upon. The faceless apology was both perfunctory and insincere.

Jemima knew better than to make her feelings known. If people had done their jobs correctly, the missing girls' plight might have come to light sooner. But as it was, she had established that they had not attended school for the same period that Gabrielle Johnson claimed her daughters had been missing.

CHAPTER 25

Broadbent entered the room to the sight of Jemima slamming the phone's handset back into its cradle. 'Everything all right?' he asked, his eyes wide with concern.

'Uh-huh,' she muttered. From his expression, Jemima realized that she hadn't kept her rising sense of frustration under wraps. 'How's it going with you? Any progress?' It was a deflection technique to take the focus of attention away from herself.

'I've established that there are five possible routes Cook could have taken. Two of them would have required him to head through the village. He'd have needed to walk down the lane at least until the church before he had access to off-road paths.'

'I think we should discount those for now. It's usually a quiet lane, but it's crawling with police at the moment. He'd be crazy to risk heading down that way.'

'I agree,' said Broadbent. 'That's why I thought we should concentrate our efforts on the other three routes. With that in mind, I've just come back from having a quick word with Gabrielle. She confirmed that Perry isn't an outdoorsy sort of person. Apparently, he'd get in the car to go a hundred yards. He doesn't own a pair of walking boots and certainly isn't familiar with the local terrain. He knows how to get from the village to the main road, though only from a driver's perspective. He's reliant on satnav to make his journeys.'

'In other words, he's not equipped for life outdoors and could easily get into trouble if he took to the hills,' said Jemima.

'I'd say it's a safe bet.'

'Well, if he's opted for one of those tracks, it would have been a random choice. And I'd guess that since he doesn't have walking boots, he'd be forced to stick to a well-trodden route. Otherwise, he'd risk injury. Which ones have you identified?'

Jemima studied the map as Broadbent traced the routes with his finger. 'They all look like reasonable possibilities.'

At that moment Ashton entered the room. 'Well, that was a complete waste of time. A few residents had installed security cameras, and they were all happy for me to take a look to see if they'd recorded anything we'd find useful. But there was nothing. They're a friendly bunch of people. I've turned down so many offers of tea and biscuits this afternoon. But I did succumb to a piece of homemade carrot cake, which was absolutely delicious.'

'Oh, you lucky git. I love carrot cake,' moaned Broadbent.

Despite the overriding feeling of frustration that had blighted the mood of the last few hours, Jemima couldn't help but laugh. This was so typical of Dan. Ever since she'd known him, she'd thought that his stomach was a bottomless pit. He was forever complaining that he was hungry, and he had a particularly sweet tooth.

Broadbent turned his attention back to Jemima. 'So what's the plan?'

'It's too late in the day to start now — it'll be going dark soon. And there are too many unknown variables. Cook could have taken any or none of those routes with any number of the other abductors. He could be travelling alone or with the missing Czech girls. It's even possible that there was a vehicle waiting somewhere to meet up with Perry. If that's the case, he'd be long gone, and we'd be none the wiser. We just don't have a clue. Even if we weren't running out of daylight, there's no way we could get an agreement for a search helicopter to be sent up as they wouldn't know what they were looking for.'

She furrowed her brow as she tried to hold on to the incisive ideas among her scrambled thoughts. 'We'll head back to Leighton Meadow armed with Perry's photofit and the Europol photographs of the Czechs. We'll search out-buildings and show the images to everyone. Someone might have spotted him or the young women. After all, when we spoke to people yesterday, we hadn't even heard of Perry Cook and didn't know what those girls looked like.'

'And what if they haven't seen them?' Broadbent asked, clearly sceptical of how useful the villagers would be.

'If we have no luck in the village, we set out early tomor-row and expand the search. We can't spare the manpower to follow the routes. Cook's had more than enough time to cover a reasonable distance if that's his intention. So the best course of action is to have teams of officers target villages and towns along these two routes.' Jemima pointed them out. 'They can visit pubs and shops and knock on doors to show everyone the artist's impression of Perry and the photographs of the trafficked women. Someone might have seen them. After all, if they're sleeping rough, they're going to have to find food. And on that note, the search teams will also need to check out any empty properties, barns or even garden sheds. If Perry's sister's to be believed, he's no Bear Grylls. He'll look for shelter. Of course, he could have enough money for a B & B or a room at a pub, so they need to keep that in mind. If he's trying to save his own skin, it's odds on he'll have gone off alone.'

'Why only two teams?' asked Broadbent.

'Because the four of us are going to be the other team, and we'll be following the other route. It could turn out to be a complete waste of time, but right now, it's the only

169

course of action open to us. I'll update Kennedy, and he can arrange the manpower for tomorrow morning. In the meantime, round up ten flashlights and tasers.'

Broadbent nodded.

'Gareth, get six more officers to join us today. With ten of us, a search should be manageable within a reasonable amount of time. We'll head back to the village in thirty minutes.'

'Great,' muttered Ashton. 'I've only just driven back from there.'

* * *

The search team arrived at Leighton Meadow. Jemima had brought along a list of names and addresses, together with maps showing the location of the more remote properties that it would be necessary to visit. She split the group into five and allocated areas. As usual, Jemima and Broadbent teamed up together. They were to search the cattery, the vicarage and two other houses.

'We'll begin at the cattery as it has several outbuildings. Its remoteness makes it an ideal hiding place,' said Jemima.

Unlike their previous visit to the cattery, they arrived when the business was open to collect and drop off pets. Broadbent navigated the car slowly up the long driveway. The surface was uneven and speeding into a pothole would do the vehicle's suspension no good at all. They approached the parking area, where three other cars were parked and another was reversing out of a space.

'Seems to be a popular time.' Broadbent switched off the engine.

'Let's get this done. We need to make the best of little daylight,' said Jemima. She felt that searching the village and the surrounding properties would be a necessary yet fruitless exercise. They needed to cover all the bases with so many lives hanging in the balance. This case's scope was spreading like an oil slick, and they had to get a grip on things before anyone else ended up dead.

Violence of any kind sickened and saddened Jemima. She was well aware of the evil people were capable of. There were many occasions when it seemed to her that there was very little goodness left in the world. But at those moments, she recognized that it was a cynical and skewed viewpoint and would redouble her efforts as she strived to maintain a professional distance.

Over the years, she had nevertheless felt acutely for each victim she encountered, whether they were alive or dead. Dealing with the aftermath required her to root into people's lives and get to know things about them that sometimes those closest to them had failed to appreciate. By getting up close and personal, her job went far beyond the salacious media headlines and personally intrusive news reports that the public was exposed to.

Jemima's experience of real-life tragedy was beyond most people's comprehension. People enjoyed reading headlines or watching news reports giving a passing flavour of someone else's misfortune. Yet like goldfish, they often let it drift straight out of their minds. Some people existed inside tiny social bubbles. It was as though they believed that it somehow protected them. Of course, it was a fallacy, but it was a way of life that they clung to. This introspective approach inadvertently nurtured the ability to ignore, or at the very least, airbrush away any heinous acts committed around them. The recent murder was all the more shocking, given its location. Yet the world kept on turning, and people continued to go about their lives as usual.

As they made their way towards the office, they passed a young woman escorting a couple to the fancy cage that would confine their pet for the next week. 'Going anywhere nice?' she asked.

'Minorca,' the man replied.

They approached the office door. Winston Mundell stepped outside carrying a cash box and a ledger. He was whistling a tune, oblivious to their presence. He stopped abruptly the moment they caught his eye. 'What's happened?'

His eyes darted about as though he expected the murderer to jump out at him.

'It's nothing to worry about, Mr Mundell,' reassured Jemima. 'We're looking for someone and were hoping to search your outbuildings.'

'Is this linked to the business up at the church?'

'At this stage in the investigation, the man in question is a person of interest along with several others. There's currently no evidence to link him to the crime. It's a belt and braces approach, not meant to alarm you. As far as we know, there's no immediate danger.'

'But you think he could be here?'

'It's a possibility, but no more than that,' said Jemima. 'The cattery's fairly isolated. You've got several outbuildings. If I was looking for somewhere close to the village to hide out, this place would be fairly high up on my list. But don't think you've been singled out. We're searching the entire village this evening.'

'If the murderer's a local, surely they'd carry on as normal so as not to draw attention to themselves?' suggested Winston.

'I would have thought so.'

'So, you don't think he's local?' Winston was fishing for information.

'As I've already said, at this point in the investigation, we're just covering all of the bases. Take a look at these photographs and tell me if you've seen any of these young women in the last twenty-four hours.' Jemima handed him the pictures of the missing Czech girls.

Winston stared at the images, his brow furrowed. 'No, no, I haven't. Are they suspects? Or are they other victims you haven't told us about?' he asked.

'That's really not your concern, Mr Mundell. What about this man? I'm afraid we only have an artist's impression.'

'No, he doesn't look familiar.'

'Thank you. Are you happy for us to undertake a search of your outbuildings?' Jemima wanted to close down the conversation as soon as possible and get on with the search. They had a busy few hours ahead of them, and she was determined not to drag things out longer than necessary.

'Be my guest. We've got CCTV covering the office and the animal pens. If anyone suspicious has been hanging around those areas, we'd know about it. But the outbuildings are a different matter. We use the first two every day, but the furthest is where we keep the ride-on mower and other equipment used infrequently. To be honest, there are parts of the year when no one ventures inside. I walk around every day and check that it's locked, though.' He raised his hand holding the cash box. 'Once I've secured this, I'll update Christina and the others so they don't get spooked if they spot the two of you wandering around. The outbuildings should all be locked. You'll need these.' Winston removed a selection of keys from his key ring. 'Drop them off at the office when you've finished.'

Jemima and Broadbent set off towards the nearest of the outbuildings, glad to part company from the man. 'It seems doubtful that we'll find anything here,' said Broadbent. 'Especially if they routinely keep those buildings locked.'

'I agree, but we still need to check them out. Hopefully, it won't take up too much of our time, and then we can move on to the next location.'

The nearest of the outbuildings had recently been constructed on a substantial concrete base. It was a large, metal, garage-type construction with roller-door access. Broadbent quickly walked around the structure and established that there was only one point of entry. There was no sign of damage to the outer walls, and it appeared to be large enough to house more than one vehicle.

The roller door was firmly secured with a hefty padlock fixing it to a substantial security device bolted into the concrete. There was no way it could be compromised by a casual passer-by. It would require a significant amount of effort and specialist equipment to bypass the security measures in place.

'My gut says this is a waste of time, but give us the keys anyway,' said Broadbent. As the padlock was at ground level, there was no way Jemima could comfortably reach it.

Broadbent raised the door to reveal the internal space, and Jemima used her flashlight to illuminate the area. Because of its outward appearance, she had fully expected to find that it was being used to house vehicles. Instead, they were confronted with four rows of neatly stacked and labelled shelving. It was where the food and other essential supplies were stored for the cattery. For an outbuilding, the space appeared scrupulously clean. There was no evidence that anyone had ever used this building as a hideout. Given the limited free space, it seemed impossible that the Mundells would not have spotted an intruder immediately.

'At least we haven't wasted much time on this. Lock up and move on,' said Jemima. Moments later, she stood outside the second of the structures, as Broadbent set about unlocking the door. It was just as organized and clean as the previous outbuilding. But when they arrived at the entrance of the final outbuilding, there was no sign of a padlock. The hasp had been forced from its fixings.

Broadbent gently placed a warning hand on Jemima's shoulder. 'Stay back. You can't risk the baby,' he whispered.

Having both sustained serious injuries in an incident in the Brecon Beacons, they had subsequently trained to carry a firearm. As had Ashton and Peters. None of them relished the idea of shooting a suspect, but given the nature of the cases they investigated, they had reluctantly agreed it was a necessary precaution. They didn't routinely carry a gun. But as Gabrielle had already told them that Perry had a firearm, they had to be prepared for any eventuality.

Jemima appreciated his concern and stepped sideways, out of the direct path any intruder would be likely to take. She reached for her weapon, noticing that Broadbent already had his in his hand. After switching on her torch, she nodded that she was ready.

Dan took a deep breath and resolutely stepped forward, using his free hand to fling open the door. The flashlight lit the internal space.

Two sets of eyes looked up at them.

'Don't hurt us!' pleaded a teenage girl. 'We've nowhere else to go.' She sounded fearful, and there was no mistaking a strong Valleys accent. This wasn't one of the Czech girls.

'Who's that with you?' asked Jemima.

'He's my brother. He doesn't speak.'

'C'mon, get up. You can't stay here,' said Broadbent. It was the line he knew he had to take, but he despised the harshness of his own words.

As the pair rose to their feet, it was clear that they were no more than children. The boy was the youngest by some years. He clung to his sister as though his life depended on it.

'D-don't s-send us home,' implored the girl.

'First things first, what are your names, and why is hiding inside this building better than being at home?' Jemima's voice was gentle. 'We're police officers. If you're in danger, we'll do everything we can to help you. You can trust us.'

The girl held Jemima's gaze, looking her up and down as she assessed whether or not this was an adult she could believe. She held her brother close. His arms were tightly wrapped around her, and his face was buried in the grubby material of her jacket, which had clearly seen better days.

'I'm Summer and my brother's Harley. You can't send us home. He'll hurt us again.'

'Who'll hurt you?' asked Jemima.

'Our mum's boyfriend. He hates us. It wasn't so bad when it was just me he had a go at. But he's started on Harley now, and he's too small to take it. He's covered in bruises and fag burns.'

Jemima swallowed hard as an incandescent rage ignited inside her. It was intolerable to think that these children had been abused by their mother's boyfriend. It was also inconceivable that any parent could allow someone to share their home if that person abused their children. 'You don't need to worry, Summer. We'll arrange for an officer to take both of you to the station. They're a good bunch. They'll sort you out with something to eat, and I wouldn't be surprised if you both get a mug of hot chocolate too.' Harley turned his face to look at Jemima and took half a step back from his sister. 'We'll need to inform Social Services and get a doctor to check you both over. We'll see to it that you're both kept safe. Your mum's boyfriend won't hurt you again, but later on this evening, you'll need to tell the officers where you live and give us the names of your mum and her boyfriend.' Jemima guided them towards the door.

'Aren't you going to stay with us?' The pitiful plea in her voice conveyed the girl's vulnerability, and she suddenly appeared so much younger than her years.

'We can't, sweetheart. We're in the middle of an investigation, but I promise you that I'll get one of our best officers to take care of you and Harley. The worst is now over, Summer. You've done the hard part, and it's time to trust us. We take things like this very seriously. You're safe now.'

Although Jemima hadn't asked him to, Broadbent had known to set the wheels in motion. 'I've contacted the station and asked them to send Stacey Frewin to accompany the kids.'

'Stacey's the best. I'm sure you'll like her,' said Jemima, addressing the children in what she hoped was a reassuring voice.

'I've also informed Finlay and Gareth that we'll be delayed. I've asked them to undertake the search of the two houses but said that we'll go to the vicarage ourselves.'

'Excellent,' said Jemima. 'How about we get you two back to the cattery's office? You never know, they may be able to find you both something to drink.'

'Won't they be cross with us?' asked Summer.

'I'm sure that when I've explained why you were there, they won't be cross with you. The Mundells seem like nice people, and we're going to stay with you until Stacey arrives.'

CHAPTER 26

Jemima fully appreciated the importance of keeping the mood light with the children. She had no reason to doubt that they had already suffered so much and desperately wanted them to feel that their ordeal had finally come to an end. They needed to believe that better times were ahead of them.

With James being of a similar age to Harley, she found it easy to talk about things that had become favoured topics of conversation at home. It wasn't long before Harley began to relax. The boy made no attempt to speak but did at last peel himself away from his sister and sat beside her. He sipped greedily from a carton of orange juice and helped himself to handfuls of biscuits.

It took the best part of an hour for PC Stacey Frewin to arrive. Throughout that time, Jemima's focus appeared to be entirely on the children. However, she was secretly counting down the minutes until they could safely hand over their young charges and get back to what they should have been doing in the first place.

At first, Summer and Harley were both reluctant to go with Stacey. However, the officer had plenty of experience of dealing with youngsters in such distressing situations and was one of a select band trained to deal with vulnerable children.

Although Stacey's role didn't require her to be at the so-called sharp end of policing, Jemima was in awe of the work that those officers did on a daily basis. Even before her pregnancy, Jemima could not have imagined having to spend her shifts dealing with such troubled children. She knew that it would leave her feeling emotionally drained and wanting to beat the monsters who had abused them. She wouldn't have sufficient self-control as there was no way she would be able to remain detached.

'How're you holding up?' asked Broadbent, as they headed back to the car.

'Much the same as you, I guess — tired, angry and hungry. At least we've only got the vicarage, and then we can call it a day.'

'That's something, I s'pose.' Broadbent's stomach growled loudly as they pulled into the driveway.

Jemima reached down to disengage her seatbelt and stifled a yawn. The vicarage was a large old building. The sort of place that had been constructed many decades before fuel efficiency had become a concern. As far as she was aware, Father Mason Roy lived there alone. The residence came with the job and was far too large for a single person, though light was blazing from various rooms throughout the property's ground floor.

'Well, at least the vicar's home,' said Dan.

'C'mon, let's get this over with.' Jemima opened the passenger door and carefully manoeuvred her body out of the car seat.

Even before they reached the front door, the sound of raised voices could clearly be heard. One was indisputably female, and although it was impossible to make out what was being said, she sounded upset.

'We'd better get in there. Don't bother ringing the bell. Just try the door,' ordered Jemima. Since their arrival at the cattery, things had not gone to plan. What should have been a straightforward search of local premises had thrown up an unforeseen scenario. It was slowing down their search for

Perry Cook, the Johnson twins and the missing Czech students. Jemima hoped that the other search teams were having better luck and making some progress.

Broadbent pressed the handle and pushed the door inwards. As he did so, the voices became louder. They both stepped into the hallway.

'They're at the back of the house,' said Jemima.

As the voice of the unknown female became clearer, it became apparent that she was scared. 'You idiot! We trusted you. What the hell did you think you were doing?' she screeched.

'Just . . . leave . . . it,' instructed a male voice. The words were spoken in a local accent. The speech was laboured, implying that whoever uttered the words was either exasperated or possibly in pain.

'I can't just leave it. You've been unbelievably stupid. I can't begin to imagine what you were thinking. Your brother's still out there somewhere. God only knows the danger he's in. Sorry, Father, I meant no offence.'

'None taken, Rosie. You've far more important things to worry about at the moment. Now, I suggest you take a deep breath and think carefully about your next move.' Father Roy's voice was immediately recognizable. The Canadian accent was unmistakable in this part of the world. Despite the short amount of time she had spent in his company, Jemima detected the strain in the priest's voice.

The only Rosie who came to mind was Rosie Forbes, who ran the pub with her husband, Wayne. Jemima recalled that the couple had twin boys. Whatever was being discussed wasn't a run-of-the-mill issue, though it didn't necessarily follow that it was a police matter.

Broadbent turned to Jemima for guidance. There was still time to turn around, step outside and close the door. They had entered the vicarage without just cause, but Jemima was determined to find out what was going on. She shuffled past Broadbent and strode defiantly into the kitchen.

'Curtis can take care of—' Nathaniel Forbes stopped mid-sentence as Jemima entered the room, closely followed by Broadbent. 'You promised you wouldn't call the police!' he shouted.

He struggled to his feet. The teenager was clearly in a great deal of discomfort, wincing at the sudden movement. He moaned loudly, grasping his ribs with one hand while using the other to force his body off the chair. He'd evidently taken quite a beating. His face was bruised and bloodied, the skin surrounding his left eye dark and swollen. His lip was split, which partly explained why his speech was slow.

'No one called the police, Nathaniel,' reassured Father Roy. 'But as they're here, perhaps it's time you told them what's going on.'

'No way!' The defiance in the teenager's tone was noticeable. Yet, instead of being a command, it rendered him more childlike.

'If you don't, then I will.' His mother looked directly at Jemima. 'You'll understand the need to protect your child. Well, that's what I'm doing here. My boys have been first-class idiots. If I'd had any idea of what they've been up to, I would have done something about it sooner.'

'Mum, you can't say anything.' The way Nathaniel spoke emphasized the fact that he was a recalcitrant teenager. There was a note of fear in his voice too. 'You've no idea what these people are capable of. They don't mess about. You might as well put targets on our backs. It's not just me and Curtis that'll be in the firing line. It'll be the end for all of us. They'll torch the pub.' He turned his attention to Jemima and Broadbent. 'Please, I'm begging you, just walk away and pretend you haven't heard anything.'

Jemima pulled out a chair and sat down heavily. Having barely spent a minute in the vicar's company, his voice made her go weak at the knees. The man was attractive. So much so that she dared not glance in his direction in case she made a fool of herself. She needed to put these inopportune thoughts out of her mind and establish what was going on with Nathaniel and Curtis Forbes. 'I'm afraid we can't do that,' she said. 'It appears that you and your brother have got yourselves mixed up with some very dangerous people. And if they are that dangerous, I guarantee they're not going to just let you walk away. So, if you want to protect yourself and your family, I suggest you tell us what happened.'

'No w—'

'It's drugs! They've got themselves involved in drugs!' wailed Rosie.

'Using or dealing?' asked Jemima.

'Dealing. As far as I'm aware, they're not dumb enough to take anything,' said Rosie.

Jemima exchanged a worried glance with Broadbent. Drug dealers were two a penny in urban areas. But somehow, it seemed far more disturbing and threatening to realize that the village was not immune from such an activity. From a health perspective, it was good that the Forbes boys had not acquired a drug addiction. However, the dealing of drugs was a criminal act that she could not ignore.

'You'd better tell us what's going on.' Jemima's voice was flat with weariness.

Just to keep going day-to-day, juggling the pressures of work and trying to be everything for James, had been an enormous amount of pressure on Jemima's shoulders. When Nick walked out, she had been well aware that she couldn't allow negative thoughts to get her down. There wasn't just herself to consider. It was imperative that she put James's needs first and ensured that she gave him the sort of life he deserved.

The pressure was intense, and keeping the urge to self-harm at bay had proved incredibly challenging for Jemima. At times of extreme stress, the allure of the razor blade was every bit as compelling as any powerful drug. It was destructive enough to deal with by oneself. It was not something she wanted to inflict on James.

Jemima had first-hand experience of how a parent could mess up a child's life. Through her counselling sessions, she had learned that her mother's abhorrent treatment of her was at the root of her mental-health issues. She had been damaged from an early age, accepting the continued emotional abuse heaped on her as being normal behaviour. Eventually she had been brainwashed into believing that she must be a bad person and less deserving than others of being treated well. This early belief had become deeply entrenched. Even though she outwardly acknowledged that it was a lie, she had so far been unable to free herself from her mother's warped doctrine.

Those who knew Jemima said that she was doing a great job bringing up James. She could not be there for him as much as she would have liked. Her career choice made it all but impossible. Giving up work had never been an option as they needed her wage to live. Moving in with her sister had given Jemima the peace of mind of knowing that there would always be someone there for James, and ultimately the baby. As Lucy had pointed out, it had been the only practical solution to enable Jemima to continue with her career.

It had taken a great deal of persuasion to convince Jemima that it was the best thing for everyone. Still, once the move had taken place, she had soon realized that it was for the best. She had been keen to believe that village life was far removed from the problems she encountered in the city. But in the last few days, she had begun to realize that Leighton Meadow was just as rotten as anywhere else. The closer she looked, the more she saw that the villagers had hidden their problems behind the idyllic facade they presented to the rest of the world.

'Do I look stupid? I'm not a grass,' said Nathaniel.

'Don't test my patience, sunshine,' growled Broadbent. 'You look like a pathetic little boy who's trying to play the hard man. But it's not working. You're in over your head. They've doled out a punishment beating to warn you off. The one thing you can count on is that this won't be the last time. You step out of line with them again, and you might not walk away. Kids like you are expendable. You're not special. You're ten a penny, and your poor mother could soon be identifying your body in the local mortuary. So if you've got any working brain cells inside that thick skull of yours, you'll spill your guts to us right now.' It was unusual for Broadbent to take up the mantle of bad cop, but he was doing an excellent job of it.

'You don't fright—'

'Cut the attitude, lad. If you've got any sense, you'll park your backside in that chair and think very hard about the next words that come out of your mouth. Unless you cooperate, you're looking at time behind bars.' It was an empty threat, but Broadbent was banking on the fact that the teenager wouldn't know better.

Jemima's attention was focused on Nathaniel until she sensed a movement in her peripheral vision and realized that Rosie Forbes was about to interject. She shot the woman a warning look, which startled her into remaining silent. The last thing they needed at this moment was for Nathaniel to think that his mother was on his side. They needed the teenager to be scared so that he would tell them everything he knew.

Father Roy moved towards Rosie, placing his hand gently on her elbow as he guided her out of the room. 'Best leave them to it, Rosie. Think of Curtis.'

'Don't leave me, Mum,' begged Nathaniel. The teenager attempted to stand.

Broadbent was having none of it. 'You move your bony backside out of that seat, and I'll haul you off to the station right now! This is your one and only chance to get out of this mess without spending a significant amount of time in a prison cell.'

'He's right, Nathaniel,' said Jemima. 'Prison's no place for a lad like you. You might think you're tough, but you're not. You practically wet yourself when your mother walked out of the room. You wouldn't survive five minutes with the big boys. Young offender units are not the sort of cushy number some people would have you believe. There'd be no PlayStation or Xbox. You wouldn't get your own room, and there'd be very little privacy. You'd soon be transferred to prison, and that's something you really wouldn't want to experience. You'd be at the mercy of any number of head-cases who wouldn't think twice about treating you like a piece of meat. You'd serve your time and come out with more physical and mental scars that you can ever begin to imagine.'

Jemima and Broadbent were sufficiently experienced to spot any weakness and chip away at it. They acted like a tag team as they ramped up the pressure. It was an effective routine they'd honed over the years. The first sign that their tactics were working was when the teenager's shoulders slumped. Shortly after that, his chin wobbled momentarily, though he inhaled sharply and somehow managed to regain his composure.

Both officers knew they still had a way to go, but it didn't matter. Neither doubted that they would break the lad down.

Broadbent continued seamlessly from where Jemima had left off. 'Put it this way, you'd never sleep easy again. And here's something else for you to think about. If you don't tell us everything now, how do you think your parents will feel if things go wrong for your brother? Those thugs gave you a beating, but you've been fortunate enough to walk away. What if Curtis isn't so lucky? What if they beat him senseless and put him in a coma? Or even kill him? How do you think your parents will react? Knowing that you could have said something to us right now which could have saved your brother's life, but you chose not to.'

As Broadbent spoke, Jemima quickly weighed up her options and decided the best approach was to lay it on thick. Nathaniel needed a reality check. He needed to hear the worst-case scenario and understand that it could easily become a reality for someone in his situation.

The lad was at a crossroads. Despite the advantages of coming from a supportive family, he had made some terrible choices, but there was still a chance for him to veer away from the path of self-destruction. It would be difficult, but he could turn his life around. Make his parents proud. But to do that he needed to fully appreciate how quickly and easily he could lose everything he took for granted if he continued to associate with dangerous people.

Any lingering doubt about what she was about to say was dispelled when an image of James flashed before her. She knew without a shadow of a doubt that if he ever found himself in Nathaniel's shoes, she'd want someone like her to do everything they could to force him to change his ways.

'Your life wouldn't be worth living,' said Jemima. 'You'd be begging on the streets because your parents would want you gone. They wouldn't be able to look at you. You'd have flushed away your future and most likely be shooting up to make life more bearable. Once you're out on the streets, people would step over you rather than acknowledge your existence. As winter comes, you'd be so cold that your bones would ache. You'd lose your pretty-boy looks. You'd have permanent stomach cramps, either from hunger or from craving your next fix. You'd spend every moment being terrified, and that feeling would never go away.'

'She's not kidding,' Broadbent interjected, determined to keep piling on the pressure. 'We've lost count of the number of times we've seen it happen to kids who mistakenly think they'll always live a charmed life. What the inspector's just told you is the best-case scenario. You see, I think you're soft, Nathaniel. You don't have what it takes. I'd give you a week tops before you became someone's bitch or you tried to off yourself. But I'd put money on you messing that up. I don't think you'd be capable of doing it right.'

'I'm guessing, Nathaniel, that even if you don't care about your brother, you care enough about yourself. So stop wasting our time and start talking,' said Jemima.

Their pressurized approach worked. They knew they'd broken him down the moment Nathaniel's shoulders began to shake. Seconds later, he was sobbing like a baby until he was sufficiently composed to tell them everything he knew.

CHAPTER 27

Jemima's frustration ratcheted up with every passing moment. She knew that if she allowed the feeling to escalate any further, there was the distinct possibility that it would compromise her ability to do her job. She needed a clear head, now more than ever, yet the focus she usually so effortlessly applied to tasks eluded her.

She was determined to do everything she could to ensure the best possible outcome for the Czech students and the Johnson twins. More than anything, Jemima wanted to go out on a high, with the satisfaction of knowing that she had saved lives. But it was looking increasingly likely that there would be no successful resolution before she was forced to take leave. She had become so ineffectual. It wasn't long ago that she had successfully led a team of detectives, that she would have been the first one into the fray, leading by example. Now those days were behind her. There was the baby to consider, and everyone on the team knew it.

Jemima felt she was being buffeted about like a leaf on the wind. It seemed as though she had no control over the case. Whenever she tried to forge ahead in one direction, events forced her along a different path.

A gut feeling told her that the key to getting things back on track was to find Perry Cook. Once they had that scumbag in custody, they would stand a far better chance of locating the missing Johnson twins and the Czech students. Plus, there was every chance that they would be able to solve the murder, which had initially been their only objective.

Even so, with all available officers deployed to search for Cook, they had still been hampered by discovering the runaway children at the cattery and by walking in on the unexpected events at the vicarage. There was no denying that these were both good outcomes. They had ensured the safety of the runaway siblings and had also stumbled across evidence of a drugs gang operating in the area, which, if Nathaniel Forbes was to be believed, was part of a well-established operation. Before searching the vicarage and its grounds, Jemima had passed on the drug gang's information to Narcotics. They were sending someone out to speak to Nathaniel and would set about trying to locate the whereabouts of Curtis Forbes.

Everywhere she turned, it seemed that there were parents with missing children. One minute their offspring was there, but in the blink of an eye, they were gone. It was a scenario Jemima hoped never to find herself in. She wanted the best for her unborn child and for James too. Yet, even as the thought occurred to her, she realized that those parents must feel exactly the same way too. No one wanted someone they loved to suddenly be gone.

The truth of the matter was that events like these were often outside a parent's control. You could only try to do your best. Sometimes life didn't work out the way you wanted it to. After all, this unborn child of hers was a prime example. She'd spent so many years desperately wanting a child of her own, only to become pregnant as a result of being raped.

It was almost eleven o'clock by the time Jemima tumbled into bed that night. She was exhausted. It had taken a monumental effort for her to keep raising her legs as she had made her way up the stairs. If it hadn't been for the handrail, she wouldn't have made it. She had reached the stage where she knew that she couldn't continue like this for much longer. Her body was telling her that she needed to rest, but her professionalism compelled her to see this case through to the end.

Perry Cook had so much to answer for. He'd abducted the Johnson twins, and those poor girls would both be terrified. But as Perry had returned to West Winds, who if anyone was looking after the children? For all they knew, the twins could be locked up, unable to fend for themselves and totally reliant on a man who was no longer there. It wasn't beyond the realms of possibility that they had been imprisoned inside a dark, dank space, where they were running out of air, food and water. And if that were the case, then every second counted. Their very survival depended on being found. The thought of finding them too late was too much to bear.

The best thing she could do now was to get some sleep. After all, she needed to be sharp and fully functioning when she went back on shift in the morning. It wasn't as if the search for Cook would grind to a halt overnight. Officers on the nightshift would continue with the task. Jemima couldn't shake the idea, however, that they would be less effective than her own team. Whether it was fact, hubris, or pure dread of what these children were going through, she couldn't put the thought out of her mind.

It seemed wrong that no matter what was happening to the twins, Jemima and the others were continuing with their everyday lives. They were each spending time with their loved ones and resting in comfortable beds — even if they were struggling to get to sleep. Try as she might, she couldn't switch off from the awful images that haunted her imagination. They became incredibly vivid, and continued until exhaustion eventually won out.

The next thing she knew, Jemima was waking up to the sound of the alarm. It was time to haul her body out of bed and start all over again. Her first cogent thought was that she hoped that the day's ensuing efforts would successfully resolve the various cases. As things stood, everything was such a mess. Their murder investigation had tendrils that had spilled out into other areas over which she had no control. It was like watching an oil slick spread across the surface of the sea, knowing the damage it would cause but being powerless to do anything about it.

Within their own investigation, things impacted on the work of other police forces and law enforcement agencies. It was a complex situation that required coordination between the various bodies. It had rapidly become a logistical and bureaucratic nightmare. They were all too aware that if you trod on someone else's toes, it could ultimately backfire and have a negative effect on your own investigation.

Jemima placed a call to Kennedy, dialling his number as she bit into a slice of buttered toast. Kennedy answered almost immediately and gave her an update. He told her that as the crossbow had been found at West Winds, they had been granted extra time to hold Gabrielle in custody. So far, they only had her word that her brother was behind everything that had happened. They had no choice but to investigate her allegations, but until they had some actual evidence to place Perry Cook in the frame, there was a chance that Gabrielle could have fed them a pack of lies.

No progress had been made overnight. There had been no reports of stolen vehicles in the surrounding area in the last few days, so they should continue to presume that Perry Cook was still on foot. Of course, it wasn't beyond the realms of possibility that someone with a vehicle had met him at a pre-arranged rendezvous point. If that were the case, they would be long gone. But until they had evidence suggesting that this was the case, they would have to continue to search the area as thoroughly as possible.

Perry Cook was the key to everything. He could easily have killed Dominika Jelinková and was responsible for the abduction of the Johnson twins. According to Gabrielle, he had already killed Chester. There was no doubt in Jemima's mind that this man was a dangerous, ruthless individual, and the lives of the young women and two little girls hung in the balance.

As the nightshift had had no success in finding and apprehending Cook, Jemima called the others on her team and told them to meet her at Lucy's house. It would be a waste of time to assemble at the police station only to have to travel back out from the city centre to conduct the search.

Broadbent was the first to arrive and found Jemima studying an OS map of the area. It was littered with breadcrumbs.

'Help yourself to a slice of toast,' she said distractedly.

Dan didn't need to be asked twice. He'd already had a large breakfast but invariably displayed a seemingly infinite capacity for food of any kind.

'What's the plan?' he asked with his mouth full.

'I thought we'd set off in this direction.' Jemima traced her finger along a route. 'There are three villages along the way, and we can keep an eye out for anyone travelling on foot across the fields. As far as we know, Perry doesn't have any transport. Also, we've no way of knowing if he's on his own or with the Czech students. But whichever it is, he's been out there long enough to need food and shelter.'

'We don't know that they're travelling as a group,' said Broadbent. 'Cook knows we'd be looking for him. So perhaps he's got rid of the Czechs.'

'You mean killed them? I don't think so,' interjected Jemima.

'Why not? They'd slow him down, and it'd be easier for him to go unnoticed if he travelled alone. The more I think about it, the more convinced I am that that's what he's done. Let's face it, there are four of them and only one of him. How would he control them? It'd be virtually impossible.'

'And you don't think he'd have thought of that before he set off? You're misreading the situation, Dan. He wants those women alive. It's the only reason he took them and at considerable risk to himself. They're cold hard cash to him. He's going to sell them on. He'll have made arrangements.'

She frowned at the map. 'I just hope that we get to them before the buyer collects his cargo. If we don't, they'll disappear for ever along with Perry Cook.'

Broadbent marvelled at how emphatic Jemima could be when speculating on the motives of someone they knew so little about. He knew from experience that there would be no point in continuing to suggest that she might have misread the situation. When she got something into her head, it was best to run with it. 'So how are we going to approach this?'

'We split into two teams and go door-to-door. Ashton and Peters can take the nearest village. It's about five miles away. We'll head for the next one, three miles further on. I've spoken to Kennedy, and he's arranging for teams to cover the other directions.' She fixed her gaze on his. 'Today is a final throw of the dice, and the stakes couldn't be higher. There are lives riding on it.'

CHAPTER 28

The village was less than ten miles from Lucy's house, but it was a community that Jemima knew nothing about. For one reason or another, she had never ventured over that way. The routes to Cardiff and to James's school were the ones she regularly travelled, and they were in other directions.

Despite her police officer's inbuilt radar for detecting trouble, Jemima had somehow failed to be alert to the possibility that these areas could also be hotbeds for crime. There was something about the rural landscape and its inherently slower pace of life that had idealized her perception of the way things were. With the extensive catalogue of awful events she had endured, Jemima had readily bought in to her sister's assertion of guaranteed security. Lucy had assured her that apart from the occasional break-in, the village was a safe haven.

She had desperately wanted a secure and happy life for James and the baby. Now, after the events of the last few days, Jemima acknowledged her own naivety. She had always known that there was the potential for danger wherever you went. The truth was, bad things happen. You just needed to open your eyes and keep your wits about you.

'How many properties d'ya reckon there'll be?' asked Broadbent.

'Your guess is as good as mine,' said Jemima. 'I'd suggest driving along the main street until we get to the end. Perhaps that way, we'll get a feel for the place. Once we've done that, we can park and work our way along.'

'This already feels like another big waste of time.'

'Yeah?' Jemima felt her hackles begin to rise. She was as disillusioned as the rest of them. Perhaps even more so, as these days, all she wanted to do was to sit down, put her feet up and conserve what little energy she still had. 'Do you have a better suggestion, Dan?'

'No. I was just saying.'

They were both on edge. Frustrated with the enforced impotence, a multi-organization investigation imposed on them. But they were on the same team, and it was essential to commit to a course of action, no matter how futile it seemed. There were numerous lives at stake, and no matter how ineffective they felt they were being, they had to give it their all. No one on the squad wanted to look back and think they could have saved lives if only they'd knocked on a few more doors. Better to do the groundwork than live with a lifetime of regret.

Jemima and Broadbent trudged door-to-door, each armed with a set of photographs of Perry Cook and the Czech students. The question they asked was always the same — 'Have you seen any of these people?' The answer was always, 'No.'

When she reached a small local shop, Jemima went inside to find a middle-aged woman serving an elderly couple. She identified herself as a police officer and placed the photographs on the counter. 'Have you seen any of these people?' She was anticipating a negative response when the shopworker spoke.

'Yes. The man and three of the women.'

Jemima did a double take and steadied herself against the counter. The lethargy of recent days melted away as it dawned on her that this could be the break they'd been hoping for. 'When and where?' she demanded, her heart thumping.

'My sister's place, yesterday. I pop up there most evenings. Cassie's got a smallholding off the beaten track with a holiday cottage on-site. Out of season, it's not unusual to go for days without seeing anyone apart from the postman, so it was quite a shock when they turned up.'

'And you're certain it was only three of the women?' Despite the initial relief of hearing that Cook and most of the women had been seen, Jemima was concerned that not all the students had been with him.

'I'm positive.'

'Which one wasn't there?'

'Her.' The shopkeeper pointed at a photograph of the woman they knew to be Pavla Coufalová.

Jemima swallowed hard, forcing herself to concentrate on the recent sighting of the others. This was the first viable lead they'd had. If these people were still in the area, they could still rescue the women and apprehend Cook before anyone else got hurt. It was an opportunity they couldn't afford to miss. Yet it was far from ideal. If one of those women had already been sold on, they'd have to deal with that later. When they had Cook in custody, Jemima would force him to tell her what had happened to Pavla, and efforts would be made to find her. But for now, she couldn't allow herself to become distracted by it.

'Were they in a vehicle?' Jemima pressed on.

'No, they were on foot. They trudged up to us while we were out feeding the chickens. There was no sign of a vehicle, and the young women all looked the worse for wear. They weren't dressed for the outdoors. If anything, I'd have put money on them having been out on the town. At least, that's the sort of clothes they were wearing, but they were dirty and ripped in places. It was very unusual.' She frowned. 'My first thought was that it must be some kind of prank. It even crossed my mind that they were homeless. But the man paid in cash. He had a wad of notes.'

'So no credit card?' asked Jemima. With a card payment, it would have been easy to check his identity. Without it, there was always the chance that these were not the people they were looking for, unlikely as it seemed.

'I guess not.'

'What else did you notice?'

'He sounded English, but the women were foreign. They spoke English too, but I don't think it was their first language. They had strong accents.'

'How did the women seem?' asked Jemima.

'Scared, dirty, exhausted and hungry. We didn't ask them any personal questions, but it was obvious that something awful had happened to them. Cass had just made a huge pot of chilli. We were going to have some for supper, and she was planning on freezing the rest. Anyway, she told them they were welcome to share the food with us. When she dished it up, they cleared their plates pretty quickly. It was as though they hadn't eaten for weeks.'

'Were they scared of this man?'

'They were scared of something or someone. But I don't think it was of him. Should they have been?'

'You tell me.'

'No . . . No, there's no doubt in my mind that they trusted him, and he appeared to care about them too.'

The statement took Jemima by surprise. It made no sense. 'Are they still at your sister's place?'

'As far as I know. We made up beds for them in the holiday cottage, gave them fresh towels, bread, eggs, bacon and sausages. That way, they could make themselves breakfast.'

'Tell me about the layout of the place,' said Jemima.

'What do you mean?'

'Well, when you approach the smallholding, do you reach the holiday cottage first or is your sister's house closest?'

'You can't see the holiday cottage when you drive up there,' the woman replied. 'When you park, Cassie's place is straight in front of you. There are barns on either side. The only way to reach the cottage is on foot. You'll need to take the path to the left of the house. So you have the house on your right and the barn on your left.'

'From inside the cottage do you have a clear line of sight of anyone approaching?' pressed Jemima. It was essential to clearly understand the place's layout, as they didn't want to have any nasty surprises sprung on them.

'No. The holiday cottage is side-on. There are no windows facing in that direction. In fact, there are only doors and windows to the front and back of the place. The rear door gives access to a walled garden, which in turn goes on to the fields. The wall's well-maintained and about five feet high. I'd struggle to get over it.'

'Thanks. That's useful to know.' Jemima's voice softened and she smiled to show her gratitude.

'You've got me scared now. It's worrying that you're asking all of these questions. Is my sister in danger?'

'I wouldn't have thought so. We just need to speak with these people. But to be on the safe side, call your sister and tell her to lock herself inside. However, before you do that, I need you to tell me exactly where the property is, as I'll be heading up there with a team of officers.'

Jemima noted down the exact location and gave the woman a final warning. 'When you speak to Cassie, make sure she understands that it's important for her not to alert these people about us going there. It's essential that they don't realize that we're on our way.'

Jemima exited the shop, her mind whirring. She dialled Ashton's number and glanced up to see Broadbent walking towards her.

Ashton picked up on the third ring. 'What's up, guv?'

Jemima quickly filled him in as Broadbent listened to her side of the conversation. They walked as she talked. When they reached the car, they set off for the smallholding, hoping Perry Cook and the young Czech women would still be there.

CHAPTER 29

Jemima was on the phone to Kennedy as Broadbent negotiated the lanes. Every so often, the annoying satnav voice
called out the directions he should take. Although useful for
Dan, the interruptions set her on edge. The voice was pierc-
ing and particularly disruptive as she tried to impart important information to her superior officer.

She gave the DCI the address of the property along
with a précis of her conversation with Cassie's sister. He
promised to send some vehicles to transport the women and
Perry Cook in case they were still at the location. Due to the
potential risk posed to the young Czech women's lives, they
agreed that once Jemima and the other three were in place,
they were to apprehend Cook and rescue the women. As they
had set out to find and apprehend Perry, and there was the
possibility that he could be armed, each officer was carrying
a firearm.

When Jemima ended the call and glanced across at
Broadbent, it was clear from his expression that there was
something on his mind.

'Wassup?' she asked.

'OK,' he sighed. 'Don't go off on one. I appreciate that
you're the senior officer, but—'

'But what?' she interjected. 'Spit it out, Dan. We don't have much time. We're almost there.'

'I want you to promise that when we get there, you'll stand back and let the three of us deal with this situation. You'll be giving birth in a few weeks, and the last thing we need is to be worried about your safety.' Dan looked across at her, momentarily taking his eyes off the road. 'Cook's ruthless. To have murdered his brother-in-law, kidnapped his nieces and also be involved with people trafficking shows he's got no scruples. He'll not think twice about hurting you and the baby if it gives him some sort of advantage. That's not a risk I'm prepared to take, and it's not something you should expect from any of our team. I don't want that on my conscience, and I know that Fin and Gareth will feel the same way.'

'I've no intention of putting anyone in danger,' said Jemima. 'In normal circumstances, I'd tell you where to go, but I agree with you. I'm not up to it. I can't move quickly, and I certainly don't want to put my baby at risk.'

'Glad we're on the same page.' Broadbent had been reluctant to voice his concerns, but now that his thoughts were out in the open and Jemima had responded positively, he felt relieved. It took the pressure off, knowing that he and the others could focus on apprehending Cook. Which was precisely how an operation such as this should be executed.

Vehicle headlights flashed behind them. Broadbent glanced in his rear-view mirror and smiled. 'Fin and Gareth have caught up with us.' It was good to know that they'd all arrive at the property together. Having the three other officers there from the get-go meant that there was no need for Jemima to feel obliged to get stuck in. She could stand back, let things play out and focus her attention on the trafficked women.

As there was never much traffic on these out-of-the-way roads, they arrived in good time, and without the need to deploy the lights and sirens for the entire journey. Both vehicles were unmarked police cars, and the last thing they wanted to do was draw attention to their arrival. This way, they stood a chance of being mistaken for ordinary tourists should Perry Cook happen to see them coming.

There was no denying that the smallholding was in an isolated location. It was a perfect place to lie low and rest up. From what Cassie's sister had said, it seemed that Cook hadn't planned to make this journey. The women had been inappropriately dressed for a trek across country terrain, and apart from having a large amount of cash, he hadn't packed any practical provisions or a change of clothes. It suggested that Cook had somehow got wind of the NCA raid on his sister's property and had got out of there while he was able to. The fact that he had taken the young women with him suggested that he was somehow hoping to meet up with the buyer and offload his charges as soon as it was safe for him to do so.

Jemima just hoped that they would arrive in time. After a frustrating few days of floundering about and getting nowhere, they were now so close to finding the majority of these women and arresting Perry Cook. She didn't think she could bear it if they arrived there only to discover that they'd already moved on and they had missed them by a few hours.

Broadbent slowed the vehicle. A large wooden sign announced that they had arrived at Vale View Holiday Cottage. Jemima shivered as goosebumps erupted along her arms.

'Stay put,' ordered Broadbent.

Jemima got out of the car with him. She had no intention of staying inside as it was cramped and uncomfortable. She leaned against the side of the vehicle, watching Dan and the others briefly gather together for as long as it took to agree on the strategy they would use to approach the holiday cottage and apprehend Perry Cook.

She watched them, feeling a sense of loss. In a few days, she'd be at home getting ready for the birth of her child. There would be months when she would no longer be a part of this team. She had reluctantly let go of the reins, knowing that they needed to operate effectively without her input. This was the first time she had been relegated to the sidelines, being a spectator instead of the one calling the shots. It crossed her mind that this was how she might feel a few years down the line when James inevitably became independent, and she would be forced to stand back and let him make his own decisions. Without warning, the breath caught in her throat and her eyes filled with tears. This emotional response felt both irrational and inappropriate. Still, she could do nothing about it other than quickly wipe the tears from her eyes.

As the rest of the team made their way up the path, a movement at one of the main house's upper windows caught Jemima's eye. A middle-aged woman was standing there. Both women raised a hand to acknowledge the other. Cassie pointed towards the holiday cottage and gave her the thumbs up. It suggested that to the best of her knowledge, Perry Cook and the women were still there.

Jemima's heart beat a little faster. In a few minutes, it would all kick off, and if Cook somehow managed to make it past the rest of the team, he would have to head in her direction if he was to stand any chance of making an escape. She should still be prepared should things not play out the way Dan and the others hoped. With that in mind, she took out her firearm and slowly made her way towards the path at the side of the house. If Perry Cook was about to make a run for it, she'd be the one to bring him down. The scumbag wouldn't know what had hit him.

Standing there waiting, her anxiety levels began to rise. It was doubly hard for someone used to being in control, not knowing how events were playing out. She had no idea how long she had been in position, but her hand was beginning to cramp as she clutched the taser. It was such a strange feeling not to be in the thick of it, making snap decisions as things took unexpected turns.

A breeze tickled Jemima's skin, and she became aware of the sound of birdsong. As she glanced around, she fully appreciated why the area would attract holidaymakers, especially those who spent their lives in urban areas. These surroundings were peaceful, idyllic and wholesome. The place provided a short respite from a more hectic pace of life, allowing visitors a chance to step out of the rat race, breathe clean air and commune with nature. It was cathartic, special.

Of course, it was easy to see these things as positives when the sun was shining. It was equally conceivable that it could lose its appeal during prolonged periods of bad weather.

The silence was shattered by a series of shrieks and the sound of raised voices. The team had breached the property and was attempting to bring about a resolution. This was the time when the officers would be at their most vulnerable. Jemima hoped that there would be no injuries.

The minutes passed, and the urge to get closer to the action reached an unbearable level. Common sense told her to stay put, but the shouting had stopped. She was worried that something was wrong.

She decided to take a look. Just as she was about to head off up the path, she heard the familiar voices of the team. As far as she could tell, there was no sense of urgency in any of their voices. Jemima lowered the weapon.

Broadbent was the first to appear, leading a tall, slight man, whose hands were cuffed behind his back. 'We've got them. They're safe,' he said.

As if on cue, there was the sound of approaching vehicles. Two police vans pulled up, and Broadbent marched Perry Cook towards the nearest one. Jemima noticed how tired the man appeared to be. For someone facing many years in prison, he was unusually compliant. In fact, he seemed almost relieved to have been captured.

Ashton and Peters accompanied the young women towards the other vehicle, where a female officer was waiting. It was a heartbreaking sight to witness the students clinging to each other for support. Their body language and wide-eyed expressions demonstrated the stress of their recent suffering and their mistrust of strangers. Jemima could only begin to imagine how their ordeal would affect their mental and physical health. The one thing she knew for sure was that it would take a long time for these young women to fully recover, if indeed they ever would.

The plan was to transport the women back to the police station. Once there, a doctor would assess them, and any medical needs would be seen to before they gave their written statements. They would also be allowed to contact their families, which would undoubtedly lift their spirits and reassure all concerned. Perry Cook had already been arrested and would be placed in a holding cell until they were ready to question him.

Jemima headed back towards the car, and Broadbent strode to meet her. Hot on his heels were Ashton and Peters.

'Well done, guys! Great result.' Jemima already felt as though a heavy weight had been lifted from her shoulders. This was the best possible outcome, at least for the Czech students. Although, there was still one missing. And once they got back to the station, she could interrogate Cook, break him down and force him to tell them where he was holding his nieces, and what had happened to Pavla. As her mind raced ahead, she was surprised to see the sombre expressions on the rest of the team's faces.

'Wha . . . What's the matter?' she asked, suddenly fearing the worst. 'Please tell me he hasn't killed the children.' Her knees went weak at the thought of it. She lurched precariously towards the side of the car, and Dan rushed forward to prevent her from sinking to the ground.

'No! God, no, nothing like that. It's just if Cook is to be believed, then we've got this all wrong,' said Broadbent.

'What do you mean?' she said, her legs still trembling.

'Get in the car. I'll explain on the way.'

CHAPTER 30

Jemima barely uttered a word throughout the entire journey back to the police station. She sat motionless and open-mouthed as Broadbent recounted what had happened when they entered Cassie's holiday cottage. What he told her was the last thing she expected to hear, and by the time he had finished, she felt as though her brain was mashed.

They agreed that Broadbent, Ashton and Peters would fully brief DCI Kennedy on the events at the holiday cottage. It was impossible to know at this stage whether or not they had finally arrived at the truth or whether this was all an elaborate lie. First, Jemima needed to interview Perry Cook and speak with the Czech women.

Back at the station, DCI Kennedy was pacing back and forth like a caged bear. 'Excellent teamwork rescuing those young women. You've done us proud. But what's this about us being fed a pack of lies?' He looked from one to the other of the four officers, demanding answers.

'I'll let the others fill you in. I wasn't there when Cook dropped the bombshell. To be honest, I'm still trying to get my head around it.' Jemima sank into her seat.

'Right, lads, there's no time to lose. Take me through it step by step. This case is a bloody nightmare, and we need to get to grips with things. I want a blow-by-blow account. Someone's not telling the truth, and I want to know who that is.' He handed Peters a marker pen. 'Write this up on the whiteboard as we go. I want it up there in black and white to help us make sense of things.' Kennedy rubbed both hands over his face as he perched on the edge of the nearest desk. There were dark shadows beneath his eyes, and his brow was more furrowed than usual. He was clearly as perplexed and frazzled as the rest of them.

Broadbent stepped forward and cleared his throat. 'I'll kick things off.' As Jemima was about to go on maternity leave, he was keen to demonstrate his leadership qualities, to show the DCI that he was more than capable of stepping up and taking on additional responsibility.

DS Ashton muttered something, so low as to be virtually imperceptible. He was perching on the edge of one of the other desks, his legs stretched out with only his heels resting on the floor. His arms were folded across his chest, and he was scowling.

Jemima immediately recognized the beginnings of a power struggle. It was inevitable, really. Both men were sergeants. Ashton was the one with an impressive range of qualifications to his name, while Broadbent had been in the post longer and had far more operational experience.

There was no denying the fact that Ashton had more potential. He was a graduate in computer forensics. His skills were highly sought after throughout the police service and in the outside world. They all knew that it was only a matter of time before he moved up the ranks, possibly even right to the top. Either that, or he'd leave the force altogether to take up a far more lucrative offer somewhere in a corporate setting.

Jemima felt an unexpected pang of sorrow. This team was like a family to her. With the exception of the DCI, she'd nurtured each of these men. It hadn't been an easy task, gaining respect and toning down testosterone-fuelled, alpha-male behaviour to ensure that they gelled effectively as a team. She had taken on a dual role. Firstly, leading this group of men, and secondly, being the glue that held them together. Each of them had worked hard and demonstrated exceptional commitment. As a result, they had become a highly effective unit.

Both of these men were capable and competent. But given the dangers they regularly faced, they needed to have each other's backs. They had demonstrated that willingness today when they and Peters raided the holiday cottage to take down Perry Cook and rescue the Czech women. Broadbent, Ashton and Peters had been prepared to put Jemima's welfare first. Of course, there had been numerous occasions when she had protected each of them. But it had been a heart-warming moment when they had chosen to protect her.

But now the jostling for position between the two sergeants was about to get underway. Jemima realized that with everything going on in her personal life, she'd taken her eye off the ball. She silently scolded herself for allowing this to happen. Even before her temporary departure, the fracture lines were already opening up. The competition between the two men would ensure that these gaps would inevitably widen. It made Jemima question whether or not she would have a team to come back to. It was a sad thought, a scenario that would not have crossed her mind a few hours earlier.

She made a mental note to ask Kennedy to keep an eye on the dynamic between Ashton and Broadbent while she was away. She also decided to call the team together at the earliest opportunity. They needed a pep talk, and she'd take the opportunity to ram home the need for them to put egos aside and support one another while she was away.

'I suggested that the inspector should not put herself or the baby in danger by taking an active role in entering the holiday cottage,' Broadbent began. 'As far as I was concerned, the risk was too great as we didn't know what we were going to face. I briefly discussed this with the others, and they agreed.'

'Sensible call, lad,' said Kennedy.

Broadbent did his best not to smirk, but Jemima noticed the slight twitch at the corner of his mouth. Buoyed on by the DCI's apparent approval, Dan continued with his narrative.

'I suggested that as we had limited numbers, we split our resources. Fin and I would focus on capturing Perry Cook. Given what we've been led to believe about him, it was a reasonable presumption that he posed a significant threat to us as well as to the trafficked women. In my opinion, it was essential we neutralized any potential threat as efficiently as possible.'

'You're making it sound like a SAS operation. It's nothing we haven't done before,' said Ashton.

'You'll get your turn to speak later.' Kennedy shot Ashton a warning look. 'Continue, Broadbent.'

'Thank you, sir. I was about to say that it freed up Gareth to reassure the Czech women that we were there to rescue them.'

'A sensible approach to take,' said Kennedy.

'I understood the need to advance towards the building cautiously. I didn't want Cook to get wind of us being there. We had tasers ready to be deployed at a moment's notice,' Broadbent went on. 'As we approached the cottage, I noticed the curtains were closed. This was a double-edged sword. It made it easier for us to reach the property without being seen. On the other hand, we had no way of knowing where the targets were or what they were doing.'

Kennedy was hanging off Broadbent's every word.

'There was no easy entry point, so we forced the front door and caught a lucky break. Given that it was late morning, we'd expected everyone to be up and about, but the occupants were still asleep.'

'On reflection, perhaps that wasn't so surprising,' said Jemima. 'They'd spent a couple of days roughing it on foot. They didn't know the area and were terrified of being caught. I'd have thought they wouldn't have got much rest during that time. They'd have been exhausted.'

'My thoughts exactly,' interjected Kennedy. 'And let's not forget that those young women had been subjected to a terrifying ordeal. In the last week, they would have suffered immeasurably. Quite frankly, it's down to luck that they're still alive.'

'Absol—' began Broadbent.

But he wasn't quick enough. Ashton proceeded to take up the narrative, and this time, he wasn't going to be silenced. 'We were lucky that the place was small. Cook was spark out on the sofa when we burst in. He barely had time to sit up before I restrained him. He was cuffed in no time. It was a pretty slick rescue operation.'

The self-congratulatory tone of Ashton's voice surprised Jemima. It revealed a side of him she hadn't seen before, and it was something she found a little distasteful. It was as though he had regressed, reverting to teenage one-upmanship.

Kennedy turned his attention to Peters. 'What about the young women?'

'They proved to be more problematic than I anticipated. It didn't help that they were terrified. They were asleep upstairs when they heard us break the door down. In all fairness to them, they didn't know that I was a police officer and was there to rescue them.'

'I take it they gave you a hard time, Gareth? I'd noticed the scratch to your cheek,' said Kennedy.

'Yeah. They were on me like a pack of wild animals. I haven't had a chance to take a look, but I think I've got a fair few bruises.' He tentatively patted his midriff. 'I was lucky that Dan raced to the rescue.'

'You'd have done the same for me,' said Broadbent. 'They were difficult to control, but it helped when Perry Cook shouted up to them and confirmed that we were the police and that they were safe. That's when I began to wonder about things. Fin had already cautioned him. So, when I came downstairs, I asked Cook why the women trusted him. That was the moment everything we thought we knew was turned on its head.'

'Of course, we don't know if Cook's told them the truth. It could easily be another pack of lies. But we need to check it out,' said Jemima.

'I've a feeling he's telling the truth. You weren't there to see how those women reacted. They trusted him,' said Gareth.

'This is wasting time. Someone tell me what happened. No speculation. Just tell me what was said!' Kennedy's patience was wearing thin. His voice had a dangerous edge to it, and a red flush spread across his face. He was annoyed that everyone else appeared to know more than him.

'We searched the place top to bottom. Cook didn't have a weapon. He claims that he was an unwilling participant in the people trafficking. At the earliest opportunity, he risked his own life to get the survivors away from the others. He reckons that he was saving them,' said Broadbent.

Kennedy resumed his pacing. 'Huxley, I want you and Broadbent to interview him now. You need to get to the bottom of this. I also want you to push him on who murdered Dominika Jelinková. He might have been responsible. If not, he might have witnessed it. There's every chance he knows something that could lead us to the killer. And why is one of those students missing? We need to know what's happened to her. I also want you to question him about the murder of his brother-in-law and the abduction of his nieces. You've got to get him to tell you where those kiddies are. I just hope it's not too late for them.'

'We're on it.' Jemima and Broadbent headed for the door.

'Do we need a translator to enable us to interview the Czechs?' Kennedy asked Peters.

'There's no need. They're fluent in English.'

'In that case, I want you to take their statements. Get one of the PCs that escorted them to the station to sit in with you. I don't want to stress them out. Take it easy but remain focused. They've been through so much. We have to be sensitive. They might not feel comfortable with two male officers in the room. And find out what's happened to the other girl, because as far as I'm aware there should have been four of them.'

'Yes, sir.'

'The bottom line is that we've got a murder to solve, and we need to ascertain what happened,' Kennedy continued. 'There's no suggestion that any of those women were at the church when it took place. But the murder victim was trafficked along with them, so they would have witnessed the events leading up to her escape. They might be able to identify whoever went after her when she made a run for it.'

'What about me?' asked Ashton. It was apparent that he felt slighted.

'Liaise with DI Jack Chalmers, and establish if they're any closer to finding those kiddies. Once you've done that, you can start writing up your report. The quicker we get on top of things, the better. We're juggling so many balls, and I don't want us dropping any. Meanwhile, I'll get on the blower to Charlie Morgan, update him on these recent developments.' Kennedy frowned. 'I'm damned sure that as soon as he knows that Cook's in custody and that most of the trafficking victims are safe, the NCA will attempt to pull rank.'

CHAPTER 31

Jemima strode into the interview room closely followed by Broadbent. A bored-looking uniformed officer was already in there leaning casually against one of the walls. He had been tasked with keeping an eye on the suspect. Acknowledging their arrival, he abruptly straightened his stance and dropped his hands to his sides, hoping that they hadn't picked up on the fact that he had been biting his nails. Jemima ignored him and made a beeline for the nearest chair on the opposite side of the desk from where Perry Cook was already seated.

She had brought several files with her. It was only the top file that contained case notes. The others were stuffed full of blank pieces of paper. It was a tactic to create the illusion that their investigation had progressed to a greater extent than it had. She wanted Perry Cook to believe that they were well briefed and already had a significant amount of evidence against him. It was a mind game, but a method that had proved successful over the years.

Cook's body tensed slightly. It was a good start. She'd already put him on the back foot without saying a word.

With the recording device switched on, they identified themselves. Although it was given at the time of his arrest, Jemima repeated the caution, just to be on the safe side.

'You don't have a solicitor?' She was surprised, given the seriousness of the charges against him.

'I can't afford one, and I don't need one. I've done nothing wrong. I'm a victim just as much as those girls.'

'Give me a break.' Broadbent shook his head.

Jemima knew the importance of doing everything by the book. 'You do know that you are entitled to legal representation? If you can't afford a solicitor's services, we can arrange for a duty solicitor to represent you. Considering the gravity of the charges, I would suggest you have one.' Given everything he had done, Jemima would quite happily see him go down for a long stretch. What she didn't want was for him to claim at a later stage that he was denied legal representation. It would unnecessarily muddy the waters and could ultimately harm the case against him.

'I'm aware of my rights. I just choose not to be represented at this point in time.'

Jemima longed to question Cook about the abduction of his nieces. But she chose not to lead with that line of questioning. Kennedy had made it clear that he was keen to make headway on the murder investigation. And in light of Charlie Morgan's almost hostile takeover of the human-trafficking investigation, she needed to try to find out what had happened when Dominika was killed. If they failed to extract information from him now, then they might never get to know.

Jemima was sure that she had Charlie Morgan all figured out. He was NCA through and through. His loyalties lay with his own organization, which he clearly saw as being a cut above ordinary police forces. His focus was on shutting down the people-trafficking operation and convicting those responsible. The right result would undoubtedly bolster his career prospects. If that came at the expense of South Wales Police's investigation, then so be it. He was more interested in the so-called bigger picture. The fact that one of the young women had been murdered at a village church was a side issue as far as he was concerned.

'We've got you bang to rights with those trafficked women, Perry. Yet you seem to be labouring under the misapprehension that you haven't done anything wrong,' she said.

'I was trying to help them. I risked my life to get them away from those maniacs. If it wasn't for me, they'd most likely be dead.'

'But you were involved in the trafficking.'

'No . . . Well, sort of, but not in the way you think. And I didn't do anything willingly. I meant what I said. I'm a victim, a total fuck-up. I know it's my fault. I've made so many bad choices. One thing led to another, and before I knew it, I was way out of my depth. I'm not a bad person. I've just been forced to do bad things to survive.' Cook sighed heavily and covered his face with his hands.

'I don't buy that, Perry. You are a bad person. Good people don't abduct innocent young women,' said Broadbent.

'I didn't do that. It wasn't down to me. All I did was let those bastards use one of my sister's trucks.'

'And that makes it all right? You're in it up to your neck.' Jemima's words dripped with incredulity. The man was deluded if he thought that because he played no direct role in the abduction, it absolved him of any responsibility.

'I know I enabled it to happen. But they forced me into it.'

'What do you mean, they forced you into it? You're a grown man. You had a choice.'

'No, I didn't. They've controlled me for months. Let me explain.' Perry's speech quickened as he became more agitated. His eyes were wide and he was sweating. The man was clearly scared. 'I'm a gambler. I'm not talking about the occasional flutter. I'm an addict. It's out of control and it's destroyed my life.'

'What's that got to do with anything?' snapped Broadbent. He was clearly annoyed that Cook was trying to make them feel sorry for him.

Jemima shot her sergeant a warning look. 'Tell us more,' she said to Perry, in what she hoped was a more neutral tone.

She wanted to dial down the tension in the room. With so much at stake, the last thing they needed was for Cook to clam up altogether.

'I-I u-used to have my own business. In fact, I had it all. Fancy car. Big house. Even had a stunning wife. But look at me now. I'm the lowest of the low. I've lost everything I valued, and I've only myself to blame. It started off with a flutter on the Grand National. A five-hundred-quid stake — the amount was nothing to me at the time. The horse I backed came in two hundred to one. I couldn't believe my luck. It was the easiest money I'd ever made. I started placing regular bets, and for a while, I won big. Pretty soon, I was hooked. I'd bet on anything. If there were a couple of cockroaches on this table, I'd bet on which would make it to the other side first. That's how bad I am. It's a compulsion, and I can't stop myself. It's pathetic, but it's the way it is.' He sniffed. 'In less than a year, I'd lost more than three hundred grand, but I still kept telling myself I could win it back. Of course, I didn't. I just kept going until I'd lost everything. With the debts mounting up, I was forced to borrow money. When I'd reached my overdraft limits and my cards were maxed out, the only option was for me to borrow money from the sort of people you don't want to get involved with. You know how the saying goes — "If you lie down with dogs, you get up with fleas." Well, that's where I'm at.'

'So this person started to lean on you?' asked Jemima.

'If only it was that simple. You've no idea! My debt got sold on three times, and the interest rates increased astronomically. There was no hope of me ever being able to pay back what I owed. This latest lot are the sort of people you don't cross. If you're stupid enough to try, you don't live to tell the tale.'

'Are you telling me that they're loan sharks?' asked Jemima. She knew the answer before Cook had a chance to reply. And she also appreciated that his response would strengthen the case for the NCA investigation.

'That's part of their operation, but they're into so much more. There's an organized-crime gang behind this outfit.

They've got fingers in so many pies. People trafficking is just one of them. These people don't mess about. They threatened to kill me and feed my body to the pigs unless I paid off my debt or proved myself useful in another way. I didn't want to die. Giving them use of my sister's haulage firm was my last throw of the dice.'

Jemima shook her head in despair. If Cook was telling them the truth, she had some sympathy for his predicament. Yet, even now, the hold that gambling had over the man was there in his choice of words. She doubted that he'd ever find the strength to beat his addiction. 'We'll come back to the haulage firm in a moment, Perry. First, I want the names of all the traffickers.'

'They'll kill me if I talk.'

'It's not that simple. If you're not completely honest with us, you could go down for this. So far, we only have your word that you were coerced. We'll need definitive proof. If an organized-crime gang is behind this, then you're not going to be safe in prison. They know you're weak, and they'll let you take the fall. But once you're inside, you'll become a liability. There's a significant chance you could talk at any time, and they're not going to risk that.' She placed her hands on the table in front of him. 'Gangs like that have people on their payroll in every nick up and down the country. It could be a prisoner who stabs you in the shower. Maybe someone will put broken glass in your food or rat poison in your tea. They'll have guards on the payroll too, happy to take a bung to look the other way. You'll be lucky to make it through your first week inside.'

Jemima had conducted enough interviews to know when she was getting through to a suspect. She sensed that Perry wasn't a hard man. In the last few minutes, his complexion had paled, and he was sweating profusely, despite the room temperature being quite pleasant.

'If I g-give you their n-names, will you p-promise to p-protect me?' he asked.

'I can't make you any promises. The only thing I can say is that, dependent on the information you give us, it's a possibility.'

He groaned. 'You're not making this easy for me.'

'How about we start with something a bit easier? What happened with the woman who was killed at the church?' pressed Jemima.

'You can't pin that on me. I had nothing to do with it.'

'So tell us what you know.'

'I was just the gofer. I knew there might be problems, as they'd been delayed, something to do with extra checks at the port. They had a customs officer on the payroll. But they still had to wait in line when they came off the ferry.' He fidgeted as he talked, his anxiety keeping him from being still. 'Shortly after two in the morning, I got a call to say that they were thirty minutes away. So I left my sister's place and headed down to the barns, as we'd agreed. The only thing I had to do was open up, wait for them to arrive and then leave them to it. I was to have nothing to do with the cargo—'

'You're talking about a group of young women, for fuck's sake. Not some flat-pack furniture!' yelled Broadbent. He thumped the table as his anger boiled over.

Perry Cook jumped and leaned back in his seat to distance himself from the detectives.

'Interview suspended,' said Jemima. 'Sergeant Broadbent, a word outside.' Her voice was low and controlled as she stared him down. She stood up, picked up the files and headed for the door. Broadbent followed in her wake and dutifully closed the door behind him.

Once outside the room, he went to plead his case, but Jemima was having none of it. 'Not here,' she snapped. 'Office, now!'

They walked in silence, their usual camaraderie no longer present. Jemima was glad that Broadbent didn't attempt to speak again. She didn't trust herself to be civil with him.

She understood that emotions were running high. After all, she'd had months where her body was awash with hormones that caused extremes of emotion. These days, she frequently felt like a boat lurching precariously in a stormy sea. But she had taken charge of the interview and had managed to keep it together. Whereas Broadbent had the far easier task of backing her up to ensure Cook gave them the information. Disappointingly, he had allowed his personal feelings to rise to the surface and had reacted badly over a poor choice of words.

Jemima agreed that it was particularly distasteful to refer to the trafficked women as 'cargo'. But in the end, it wasn't important. What mattered was that they got the information they needed as quickly as possible. Broadbent's unprofessional behaviour could have ultimately jeopardized that. As things stood, they required Cook's cooperation. The last thing they needed was for him to stop talking.

As they turned into another corridor, DCI Kennedy came storming out of the viewing room. His face was like thunder, and it was clear that he'd been watching the proceedings as they unfolded in the interview room. Broadbent opened his mouth to speak, but Kennedy was in no mood to listen to anything he had to say. 'Shut it, lad. Get yourself back to the office and find something useful to do. I'll speak to you later.'

Broadbent skulked off, hanging his head in shame. In a matter of seconds, his aspiration to fill Jemima's shoes while she was on maternity leave had evaporated into the ether. He had blown his chance, big time.

'You all right to continue?' asked Kennedy.

'Yeah,' said Jemima.

'Good. I'll take Soft Lad's place. Let's get to the bottom of things once and for all.'

'Did you update Charlie Morgan?' asked Jemima.

'Not exactly. I called his number, but he didn't answer. Ended up leaving him a vague message telling him that it was a courtesy call and asked him to call me back.' He huffed. 'I'm banking on the fact that he'll ignore my request. After all, that's what he's done so far. Hopefully, it'll buy us enough time to complete our enquiries. After all, it's not my fault that the guy doesn't think our input is important enough to warrant immediate attention.'

'Nice one, sir,' said Jemima.

CHAPTER 32

Perry Cook's arms were folded on the table, his head resting listlessly on them. He glanced up without raising himself as they entered the interview room. His brow furrowed with consternation when he noticed that Jemima was accompanied by a man he had not encountered before. Sensing an imminent shift in the dynamic, he lifted his head, shuffled backwards and adopted a more appropriate seated position. His eyes darted from one to the other of them, giving him the appearance of a cornered animal. 'Where's the other bloke?' he asked, his voice shaky.

Kennedy ignored the man, pulled out a chair and proceeded to get comfortable. He eventually nodded at Jemima, who reached across to switch on the recording device. When Ray Kennedy identified himself for the tape, he explained that he had replaced Daniel Broadbent.

'I've been speaking to Inspector Huxley, and I'm disappointed at your lack of cooperation,' Kennedy said. 'I'm a busy man, Mr Cook. I don't have time to waste, so let's hear your version of events. And you should know that playing the self-pity card is not going to wash with m—'

'I was coerced,' interjected Cook.

'Don't interrupt when I'm speaking!' Kennedy pounded the table with his fist and leaned forward, closing the gap between them.

Perry flinched and backed away.

'You're a small fish, Perry,' Kennedy said, inches from the man's face. 'In fact, I'd go as far as to say that you're a minnow swimming in a sea of sharks. When they smell blood, there'll be nowhere for you to hide. You say you're a betting man?'

Cook nodded.

'Well, you'll understand this analogy. At this moment in time, your fate is a fifty–fifty gamble. Not unlike the toss of a coin. Only this time, you're placing the ultimate bet. Heads, you live, tails, you die. The only certainty in all of this is that whichever criminal outfit you've got yourself involved with will see to it that you're killed.'

Cook blinked under Kennedy's cold stare.

'Don't make the mistake of sticking to misguided loyalty,' Kennedy continued. 'Now that you've been brought in and interviewed, they'll never be able to trust you again. Even if you keep your mouth shut and are lucky enough to walk away from this a free man, they won't know for sure that we haven't flipped you. And if you go down for it, the inspector here was right when she told you that you won't last a week inside. So stop messing around. Make the smart choice and save your life.'

Jemima had to give it to Kennedy. The man was impressive. If she was in Cook's shoes, she'd have been ready to cave in and tell them everything.

Kennedy leaned back in his seat and crossed his arms. It was an unspoken signal for Jemima to take up the reins. She opened the top file, extracted a crime-scene photograph of Dominika's dead body, and pushed it across the table. 'Take a look at this,' she commanded.

Cook's skin visibly paled. He pushed the photograph away. 'I don't want to.' His voice was hoarse, barely more than a whisper.

'Look at the damned photograph.' Jemima shoved it back across the table.

'I don't want to.' His voice was small, almost childlike. He reached out to return the photograph once more.

'Don't you touch that!' Spittle flew from Jemima's mouth, and there was a moment when she appeared almost feral. 'Open your eyes and take a good look at her. That's the corpse of Dominika Jelinková, a nineteen-year-old student from Prague. She had her whole life ahead of her, until she was bundled into the back of one of your sister's trucks. She had hopes and dreams and was desperate to live. When she managed to escape, she was hunted down like an animal and slaughtered as she lay on a church pew. Shot in the chest with a bolt from a crossbow. Did you do that to her, Perry? Did you murder Dominika?'

'No! I swear it wasn't me.'

'You might not have fired that weapon, but you certainly played a part in her death. So take a long look at what you did!' Jemima could feel the blood pounding in her ears.

'It wasn't me. I couldn't kill anyone.' Tears streamed down Cook's face. He wiped at them with his hands.

'Well, who did it, Perry? We need a name, and we need it now,' Kennedy demanded.

'It was Eamon. Eamon McClennen.'

Jemima extracted mugshots of the men currently being interrogated by the NCA. 'Which one is he?'

Perry jabbed a finger at the unflattering image of a youngish man who appeared to be dead behind the eyes. 'That's him,' he replied. 'You don't mess with Eamon. He's a psycho. I've seen him take a bolt-cutter to someone's fingers, and I swear he got off on the man's screams. He's one of the enforcers. He'll stop at nothing to get the job done.'

'One of whose enforcers?'

'The Waverleys. They're based up north, but they're looking at expanding their territory. Leonard Waverley heads it up. He runs a cut-throat operation. If anyone dares to take him on, they've signed their own death warrant. There are stories about people that have gone missing, never to be seen again. I've heard rumours they're planning a turf war, looking at taking over someone else's patch. And from what I know about them, they'll stop at nothing to get what they want.

'Joseph's scared of his father. That's why he gave Eamon a beating. Jo and Eamon are friends, so it's the last thing either of them wanted. Eamon knew he'd messed up, and that when Leonard got to hear about him killing that girl, he'd have him killed to keep everyone else on his payroll in line. Eamon's only chance was to allow Joseph to dole out a punishment beating. It suited them both. Joseph knew his father would see the gesture as a show of strength, and if Eamon was seen to suffer enough he might get to live.'

'Who are these other men?' Kennedy gestured at the remaining mugshots. This information was interesting but way outside their remit. However, it would do no harm to present the NCA with their findings later that day. He'd be sure to ring the officer in charge, someone far more senior that Charlie bloody Morgan.

It would give Kennedy a great deal of personal satisfaction if he discovered that Morgan had failed to get any useful information from the suspects they had arrested. After all, they were hardened criminals, and there was every chance that the gang members would refuse to talk. It would also go down well with the chief constable if Kennedy's squad was instrumental in bringing down an organized-crime gang, especially if the NCA had failed to get anywhere. It would be a nice boost to his pension if he could end his career as Superintendent Kennedy.

'That's Neil Henney,' Cook said. 'He drove the truck. And that's Joseph Waverley.'

Kennedy's lips twitched with excitement. They were finally starting to get somewhere.

'Joseph Waverley . . . As in one of Leonard's blood relatives?' As he asked the question, Kennedy was careful to keep his voice calm. He tried to push thoughts of career progression to the back of his mind.

'He's Leonard's youngest son and has recently taken over the people-trafficking operation. He's ambitious. Wants to prove himself and is out to impress his old man. Joe runs a string of brothels throughout the north-east. I've even heard him boasting about a speciality gentlemen's club where his girls cater for every sort of proclivity you can think of. He hasn't named names, but he's boasted about having some seriously influential clients. He reckons that he keeps them sweet as they're the sort of people who can open doors for him. Whatever that means.'

Jemima shivered in disgust. These men were the lowest of the low. They'd doubtless destroyed countless women's lives and would continue to do so until they were stopped. The only consolation at the moment was that by rescuing the Czech women, her team had saved them from a life of sexual slavery. Although, it was likely that Pavla hadn't been so lucky. It was a small victory in the grand scheme of things. Still, it would reunite some families and give them some sort of happy ending — if they could ever truly be happy again.

'What makes you so certain that Eamon McClennen was responsible for Dominika's death?' asked Jemima.

'I watched her escape as the others were getting out of the lorry. They were terrified, following orders like sheep. She must've thought it was her one and only chance of getting away. She was towards the back of the line. She leaped out of the vehicle and made a run for it.' Perry's words spilled out quickly as he recounted the story. Now that he'd started, it appeared that he was eager to tell them everything. 'They hadn't counted on anyone trying to make a run for it, and it gave her a slight advantage. I'm not part of their operation, so I was never going to be asked to go after her. Or look after the other women, for that matter. Only three gang members were present at the time, and suddenly someone had to go after the runner, leaving only two to deal with the others. It was a risk, whatever they did. The women were still out in the open at that moment. They needed to get them inside the barn and tie them up. Otherwise, more of them could do a runner.'

'I can imagine that Dominika's escape didn't go down well,' Jemima said.

Cook shook his head. 'Joe did his nut. He'd gone from being in control to having to think on the hoof. He knew that if she managed to get away and raise the alarm, it'd blow the whole operation. And if that happened, Leonard wouldn't trust him again. Joe ordered McClennen to go after her and bring her back. McClennen was into hunting. He had a crossbow stashed in the nearest shed, so he grabbed it along with a couple of bolts. His motorbike was there too. It seemed like a good option as he could go off-road with it if he needed to. There was no way she'd be able to outpace him. He was confident of catching her before she got too far.'

Despite his earlier aversion to the photographs, Jemima thought Cook was rather enjoying telling the tale, now he was getting into it.

'He knew he wasn't supposed to hurt her, as she was going to be a good little earner for the Waverleys,' he went on. 'We all thought he'd only taken the crossbow to scare her into returning with him. But I think he was thrilled by the hunt, and when he cornered her, he forgot about Joe's orders and killed her. He was gone for hours and when he eventually returned, he'd blooded himself.'

'What do you mean by that?' asked Kennedy.

'You know, like in hunting when someone's made their first kill. It's like a rite of passage. They get smeared with the blood of the animal. It was a hell of a shock when we realized what he'd done. But McClennen was buzzing. Said he couldn't find her at first. Looked everywhere. I think he even abandoned his bike at one stage as he realized that he stood a better chance of tracking her down if he went on foot. He told us that when he eventually found her inside the church, it was like a switch flicked inside his head. He knew it was his job to bring her back alive but murdering someone in a setting like that was something he'd fantasized about for ages. So, when the opportunity arose, he didn't have the willpower not to see it through.'

Kennedy made a noise of disgust somewhere in the back of his throat.

'Joe asked him where he'd hidden the body,' Cook continued, 'and when McClennen told him that he'd just left her inside a church, Joe went wild. He'd always known that McClennen was a sandwich short of a picnic, but for some reason, he'd trusted him to do as he was told.'

'What happened after that?' asked Jemima.

'Joe ordered me to get rid of the crossbow. I knew the body would be found in the next few hours, and I wasn't stupid enough to risk getting caught with the murder weapon. So I hid it at my sister's place. I was pretty freaked out by what they'd done. It didn't help that one of the women had already died inside the truck. So now there were two dead women.'

'What do you mean one of them had already died inside the truck?' asked Jemima.

'One of the Czech girls. I think her name was Pavla. The other girls told me she had asthma. It's Joe's fault. He didn't think about making sure that the air could circulate properly. With her medical condition, it would have affected her more than the others.' He swallowed. 'I'd only got involved to clear my debts. I didn't want anything to do with what happened. I'm not a violent man. It's just not me.' The tremble in his voice had returned. 'I was trapped. I wanted out, but knew I had to play the long game. I've always known that I'm expendable, and I did what I did to survive. But as I keep telling you, I'm no killer.'

'That's not what we've heard,' said Jemima.

'What d'you mean? I swear, I'm telling you the truth.'

'You killed your brother-in-law, Chester.'

'No, no, no, no, no!' The denial was spat out as rapidly as gunfire. 'You've got it wrong.' Perry's body language changed instantly. His muscles tensed, and his voice sounded far more assertive.

'Your sister told—'

'I don't care what she told you. It isn't true. Chester's alive. He's my friend. I wouldn't do anything to hurt him.'

'So where is he? And more to the point, where are Blythe and Roslyn?'

'If I tell you, you've got to swear not to say anything,' demanded Perry.

'This isn't some teenage prank we're talking about here,' Jemima scoffed. 'This is three people's lives. Three people who are part of your family.'

'Look, it's not what you think. I promise you, they're safe.'

'Your promises don't count for anything, Perry. We only deal in cold, hard facts. As things stand, your sister has alleged that she witnessed you kill Chester. She also claims that you kidnapped her daughters and that she didn't report these crimes at the time because she was scared that you'd kill the girls if she didn't keep quiet,' said Jemima.

'Look, I admit I threatened her with that. But I was never going to do it. Those girls are safe with their father. It was all a ruse. A bit of theatre to convince Gabby that Chester was dead. Chester came up with the idea in the first place.'

'And why would he do that?'

'You've no idea what my sister's like.'

'Well, you'd better start talking, lad, because we're not letting this go,' Kennedy said. 'We need proof that those kiddies are safe.'

'I've got a contact number for Chester. But it was only ever to be used in emergencies.'

'Let's have it then,' said Kennedy.

'It's not a direct number for him. It's a burner phone that goes to his cousin. I'm the only one that has the number, and she'll only pick up if a call comes from my phone.'

Kennedy raised an eyebrow. 'That's a bit extreme.'

'It's necessary. You don't realize what's at stake.'

'So why don't you tell us? What's Chester so scared of that he had to fake his own death? And why would he take his kids away from their mother?' asked Jemima.

'Because my sister's the one he's scared of. He wanted out of their marriage, and he knew she wouldn't let him go. He loves those girls so much, and he didn't want them around Gabby. That's why he couldn't risk leaving them with her.'

Jemima frowned. 'What has Gabrielle done that's so bad?' Perry's vague accusations made no sense. Gabrielle Johnson was a pillar of the community, lauded by numerous influential people. She'd been named Welsh Woman of the Year for three consecutive years and was tipped to become Wales' first business tsar. The woman was up there on a pedestal.

'I'm not getting into that. Gabby's my sister, for God's sake. Let me make a call, and hopefully, within the next hour or so, I'll get Chester to speak to you. But I'm telling you now, he won't come to the station. It's too risky.'

'Well, that's no good. How could we be sure that it's him we'd be speaking to?' asked Kennedy.

'Perhaps I could get him to agree to do a video call. It's the best I can offer. Once he's spoken to you, I'm sure you'll understand why we did what we did. But you have to promise that what I've told you stays within this room.'

'That could be problematic,' said Jemima.

'What do you mean?' There was no mistaking the look of panic on Perry's face.

'We record the interviews, and there's a viewing room. It's standard procedure.'

'Well, that's it then, you've probably signed my death warrant and put Chester's life in danger too.'

Jemima shivered as she felt ice flow through her veins. As yet, she had no idea what they had stumbled across. But for some inexplicable reason, she believed that Perry Cook wasn't exaggerating.

'So how does this work?' asked Kennedy.

'What do you mean?'

'How do you contact Chester?'

'I'll tell you once I can be sure that no one's listening in.'

'This is ridiculous!' snapped Kennedy.

'You have my terms. I'm not putting lives at risk.' At that point, Perry folded his arms and refused to utter another word.

CHAPTER 33

Jemima and Kennedy headed back to the squad room. Perry Cook had been returned to a cell, where he could get some rest and refreshment. It was approaching midday, with hours to go until the end of the shift. Everyone knew that they would be required to work on into the evening because of the recent developments.

'This case is a bloody nightmare. It's like trying to hold on to a greased pig. Just when you think you're getting to grips with it, it slips through your hands and heads off in another direction.' The chief inspector looked and sounded jaded.

'It's just as well you applied for the extension to keep hold of Gabrielle. I believed her brother when he said he's scared of her,' said Jemima.

'Yeah, I believed him too. I think I made the right call. Better to have her in custody for now. At least until we've a clearer idea of what's going on.'

'Do you want me to ask Broadbent to retrieve Cook's phone from the evidence locker?' asked Jemima.

'Yes. Let him do something useful. It won't do any harm to bring him back down to earth. Let him know that he's not above doing menial tasks. Soft Lad and Ashton are starting to get on my nerves. They must think I'm stupid, the way they've started carrying on like a couple of teenagers, trying to impress me. In my opinion, neither of them is up to filling your shoes. They've both still got a hell of a lot to learn, and they need to realize that there's no room for egos on this or any other squad.'

'Quite right, sir. I'd noticed it myself and was meaning to talk to you about it.' At least that was one conversation she could cross off her to-do list.

Kennedy's voice softened. 'Once you've sent Daniel off to the evidence locker, go and take five. Get yourself some lunch. You need to look after yourself, Jemima. I don't want you passing out on me, and I certainly don't want to be called upon to deliver that baby of yours. That would definitely be a step too far.'

* * *

Thirty minutes later, the squad was assembled, ready to pool the latest round of information gathered.

'Ashton, you kick off,' ordered Kennedy.

'There's not much change. I spoke to DI Chalmers, who confirmed they've exhausted every lead and come up with nothing. There's no sign of the Johnson twins anywhere, and he said that his superintendent has pulled the plug on them continuing with the search. Apparently, they've got more pressing priorities. So much for the kids' lives.'

'Perhaps things are not as bleak as they once appeared to be, but we'll get on to that in a moment,' said Kennedy. 'Peters, how did it go with those young women?'

'It was hard going, very emotional. There were a lot of tears.'

'And that was just you.' Ashton laughed at his own joke but stopped when he saw Kennedy glower at him. 'Sorry. Inappropriate,' he muttered and dropped his gaze to the floor. As he'd uttered the words, he'd known that it wasn't a time for levity. Yet, for some reason, he had been unable to stop himself.

'Right, well, as I was saying,' Peters continued, 'they were upset but obviously relieved that they were finally safe. I didn't get much out of them about their ordeal, apart from what happened to Pavla. They were all pretty traumatized about it.'

'Pavla? The missing student?' asked Broadbent.

'Yeah. Unfortunately, she died while they were still in the truck. Suffocated. She had asthma.

'But they were keen to know what had happened to Dominika. One of them seemed to think that she must've raised the alarm, and it was somehow down to her that we found them.'

'Did you tell them she was dead?' asked Jemima.

'No. They've been through so much already. I couldn't do that to them. It'd push them over the edge, especially since they're trying to come to terms with Pavla's death.

'Anyway, I purposely steered the conversation away from Dominika, and I don't think they noticed.'

'That's good.' Jemima smiled supportively at Gareth, encouraging him to continue.

'Every one of them was concerned about Perry Cook. They were adamant that he'd saved them.'

'Classic Stockholm syndrome,' said Ashton.

'You what?' said Broadbent.

'It's when victims bond with their captors.' Ashton puffed out his chest as he demonstrated his knowledge.

'I'm pretty sure it wasn't that,' said Peters.

Ashton scowled and harrumphed loudly. Peters ignored him and continued to speak. 'Apparently they'd been tied up in one of the sheds. They were treated pretty harshly, by all accounts. Given basic rations, the occasional drink of water, and beaten if they dared complain. Perry smuggled food to them on a few occasions, and when he realized that they spoke English, he told them that he'd do his best to get them out of there. They all claimed that's what happened. That he saved their lives.'

'That's exactly what Cook told us, so perhaps it's the truth,' said Jemima.

'I think we should believe them,' said Kennedy. 'Just before this briefing, I was handed a copy of Cassandra Evans's statement. Cassie, as she likes to be known, has stated that there is no doubt in her mind that Cook was acting in the best interests of those young women. They all shared a meal with Cassie and her sister shortly after their arrival. Although the entire group were reluctant to enter into conversation, she sensed genuine concern and a bond between them. She also thought that every one of them, including Cook, was scared of something, and that whatever it was, they were dealing with their predicament collectively.'

'That's a turn-up for the books,' said Broadbent. 'But why show concern for the wellbeing of strangers when he killed his brother-in-law and abducted his nieces?'

'He may not have,' said Jemima.

Suddenly, all eyes were on her. For once, Ashton didn't attempt to say anything. Broadbent's jaw dropped.

'He claims that he colluded with Chester Johnson to fake Chester's death,' Jemima explained. 'He also says that the twins are alive and well. Apparently, they're living with their father.'

'What the hell?' Broadbent shook his head in disbelief.

'That's why we wanted Cook's phone. It seems that Chester and Perry are both terrified of Gabrielle. At the moment, we've no idea why that should be the case. Perry told us that it's imperative that we don't let on to Gabrielle that her husband's alive. Without knowing the facts, it all seems rather dramatic, but we're hoping that once we give Perry the phone and allow him to make contact with Chester, we'll get visual proof of life of both him and the girls.'

'Hopefully we'll be able to convince Chester Johnson to tell us why he's so terrified of his wife,' added Kennedy. 'But everything that you've just been told must remain between us. No one talks. If anyone does, I'll have their head on a platter.' As he issued this warning, he made eye contact with each of the three male detectives. His expression left them in no doubt that he was deadly serious.

'Has there been any further contact from Charlie Morgan or the powers that be at the NCA?' Kennedy asked. Everyone shook their heads. 'I left a message for Morgan to ring me. Should he or anyone else do that, I want you to tell them that I am unavailable at the moment. Under no circumstances let them know that we have Cook in custody or that the trafficked women are at the station.'

'Yes, sir,' came the reply.

'Whatever comeback there is, it'll all be on me,' said Kennedy. 'But if we update the NCA now, you can guarantee they'll see to it that Cook is taken from us. I don't need to tell you that were that to happen we'd no longer be able to make progress on our cases. So keep schtum. It sounds as though they've got at least one big player in an organized-crime gang. That should be more than enough for them to deal with at the moment.'

Kennedy held out his hand. 'Right, lad, let's have Cook's phone.'

Broadbent passed it to him.

'Get this morning's notes sorted if you haven't already done so,' he ordered. 'Huxley, get a key for one of the pool cars. I'll see you down at the cells.'

The others exchanged glances, clearly wondering what was going on, though they all knew better than to ask the DCI what he was planning to do.

Jemima headed off to pick up the keys for the unmarked police car, knowing exactly what they were about to do. She walked into the custody suite to find Kennedy already there with Cook, who had been handcuffed, and fully briefed on their plans. They left the police station in silence, and Cook got into the back of the car without complaint.

Kennedy drove towards the playing fields at Heath Park. It was an expansive area that would be relatively quiet at this time of day. Avoiding the car park, he stopped the vehicle on a quiet stretch of road overlooking the greenery. 'Get in the back, Huxley,' he said. 'I'd do it myself, but as we've no idea what we're dealing with, I think it's better that I remain behind the wheel and keep the engine running in case we need to move quickly. It's purely precautionary, but you never know.'

Jemima did as she was told and took a seat next to Perry Cook.

'This is the safest place I can think of to make the call,' said Kennedy. He turned to Cook. 'Here's your phone, so make contact. As I told you before, we need proof of life. You'll have to insist that he sets up a video call so that we can see him and speak with him too. We need to be satisfied that he and his daughters aren't being held somewhere against their will.'

'I understand, but it might not be quick. I've got no control over anything he does,' said Cook. 'My initial contact is always by text. It's a coded message we agreed on. Kathryn — that's Chester's cousin — will call me back to check that everything's OK. She'll ask me a pre-arranged question and will expect a specific answer. Once she's satisfied, she'll hand the phone over to Chester.'

'All very cloak-and-dagger,' said Jemima.

Perry sighed. 'You've no idea how necessary it is.' He scrolled through his contact list. Selecting 'Inglenook Bistro', he typed out a short message.

I'd like to book a table for one.

Perry pressed send, and they waited.

CHAPTER 34

If anyone had happened to walk past the unmarked police car and glanced inside, they would have undoubtedly thought that something was up. The two men and a pregnant woman just sat there, staring aimlessly out of the windows, waiting for Perry Cook's phone to spring into life. As the minutes ticked by and nothing happened, the tension became palpable.

It was Cook who finally broke the silence. 'What sort of sentence am I looking at?' His voice was flat and emotionless. He had clearly realized that his part in the people-trafficking operation had sealed his fate.

'Can't say,' said Kennedy. 'If what you've told us about Chester and his daughters is true, then there'll be no charges brought on that. You might very well have faked his death, but you haven't broken any laws. Also, if it turns out to be the case that your brother-in-law has taken his children with him, then that's nothing to do with you either.'

'What about my involvement with the Waverleys?'

'That's a different matter. Even if you were coerced into helping them, people trafficking is as serious as it gets. Plus, two women have died as a result of it. You told us that you weren't responsible for firing the crossbow, but you handled the weapon.'

'I wore gloves, so my fingerprints won't be on it, and I never even touched the bolts. McClennen's a meathead. He didn't bother covering his tracks. Your scientists should be able to link him to the weapon and the bolt.'

'If that's the case, you won't be looking at a murder charge in respect of Dominika. But one of those young women died in the back of your sister's truck. Whichever way you look at it, you played a part in that, as you gave the Waverleys access to the vehicle.'

'I'm going down,' said Perry.

'That part of the case is out of our hands,' said Jemima. 'Because it's an organized-crime gang, the NCA are in charge. But we've got the statements of the women you saved, so that should go in your fav—'

At that moment, Perry's phone vibrated. 'It's a text from Kathryn. She's given me a number to call. Oh, thank God. Hopefully, this'll all be sorted out soon.' The relief in his voice was evident.

'Go on then, don't keep us waiting,' Kennedy snapped. 'Make sure you put it on speakerphone. And tell Chester that he needs to speak to us on a video call.'

As Perry dialled the number, Jemima realized that she was holding her breath. She forced herself to exhale slowly as the ringtone sounded.

The call was eventually answered by a female. Her voice was gentle, with no discernible accent.

'Inglenook Bistro, how may I help?'

'I'd like to book a table for one,' said Perry. It was the exact same words he had texted less than half an hour earlier.

'What time and date were you thinking of?' asked the woman.

'Immediately, please, and I'd like a window seat.'

Jemima thought the conversation was the most bizarre she'd ever heard. It was like something out of a spy novel. But those thoughts soon disappeared when the woman next spoke. 'How are you doing, Perry? It's good to hear from you.'

'Hi, Kathryn. There've been some developments. I need to speak to Chester.'

'I'll put him on now.'

'What's up?' said a male voice.

'Nothing for you to worry about, Ches, Gabby's still none the wiser. The thing is, I've got myself arrested. It's a long story, but I need your help.'

'I'd love to, mate, but I can't take the risk of Gabby knowing that I'm still alive.'

'She doesn't have to, Ches. But she reported me to the police. They're under the impression that I killed you and abducted the twins. I'm in it up to my neck now, and I need you to get me out of it. I'm with the police now. They're listening to the c—'

'I thought you agreed that we couldn't trust the police? You've put us in danger, Perry!'

'Mr Johnson, this is Chief Inspector Kennedy speaking. I'm here with Detective Inspector Huxley. Your brother-in-law is correct. We don't know what's going on, but I can assure you that we pose no threat. Our sole concern is to verify the fact that you and your children are alive, unharmed and free to make your own choices.'

'Well, we're having a conversation, Chief Inspector, so I guess that proves I'm alive.'

'It's not that simple, Mr Johnson. Until we see your face, we have no proof of who you are.'

'And how do you suggest we do that? I'm not prepared to risk my life or that of my children by coming to see you. And I certainly have no intention of telling you where we are.' His voice went up a tone as his speech quickened. Despite not being able to see him, it was clear that Chester was becoming increasingly agitated.

'Think about this logically, Chester,' began Jemima. She sensed that the man was on the verge of ending the call. If he did that, there would be no easy way of clearing Perry of this set of allegations. 'We have no way of knowing where you are, and your location is not something we care about. From what Perry has told us, he helped you and your children get away from your wife. Whatever your reasons for doing that, I'm sure you didn't make that decision lightly. It sounds to me as if you were backed into a corner and feared for your lives.'

'That's exactly how it was, and we're still living in fear.'

'I'm sorry to hear that, Mr Johnson. Perhaps it's something that we could help you with, if you feel that you can trust us. But for now, our only concern is to investigate the allegations your wife made against her brother.'

'She's telling you the truth, Ches,' Perry said. 'You know I'd never put you and the girls in danger. I risked everything to help you. I just need you to return the favour and come through for me now. Please, mate. I'm desperate.'

Jemima glanced across at Perry and noticed that he was perspiring. 'A simple video call would suffice,' she said. 'I've seen a photograph of you, so I know what you look like. It's merely for us to confirm that you are who you say you are. We also need to see your daughters.'

'Can't you leave them out of this?' pleaded Chester.

'I'm afraid not, Mr Johnson. Following the allegations made by your wife, we've had officers out in various parts of the country trying to find your daughters. Missing children are treated as a high priority. We've allocated a lot of resources to try to find them as we were led to believe they'd been kidnapped. So you can imagine how concerned we were and still are. I assure you that we'll leave you to get on with your lives as soon as we're satisfied that the three of you are well and free to make your own choices.'

'Perry, do I have your word that Gabby isn't behind this?'

'She's not, Ches. Gabby's clueless. As far as she's concerned, you're dead. Look, I know it's a big ask, but unless you cooperate, I could go down for murder and kidnapping. Please, mate, I'm begging you. I've stuck my neck out for you, and now you're my only hope.' His eyes had filled with tears.

'When you put it like that, it seems I have no choice. OK, give me five. The girls are having a snack at the moment.

I'll set things up and call you straight back. But once the police have confirmed that we're alive, then that's it. Agreed?'

'That's absolutely your choice to make, Mr Johnson,' said Jemima.

When the call disconnected, Kennedy spoke again. 'So what is it with your sister? Why are you both so scared of her?'

'If I tell you, will it help my case?'

'It depends on what you have to say.'

'The bottom line is that once we've established that you didn't kill Chester or kidnap the twins, you'll be handed over to the NCA to face the people-trafficking charges,' said Jemima. 'But I'd have thought you'd be small fry to them. They're interested in serious and organized crime, not someone who's got themselves into debt and been forced into helping the big players to save their own life.'

'As I see it, you're in danger of ending up as collateral damage,' Kennedy added. 'The NCA will want to shut down the Waverleys' entire network, and by the sound of it, their reach goes way beyond people trafficking. It'll be a lucrative business with numerous profitable streams of income. So, if they can get to the bigger players by hanging you out to dry, then I wouldn't put it past them to do just that.'

'So I'm fucked?' Perry slumped back in his seat as the truth dawned on him.

'Not necessarily. You've suggested that your sister's a dangerous woman. So far, we've no idea what you mean by that. Both you and your brother-in-law have alluded to the fact that she poses a threat to your lives. If she's that dangerous, I'd guess that she's either a hardened criminal or she has violent tendencies. If it's the former, it could be something you could use as leverage.'

'What you need to ask yourself is whether Gabrielle would be of interest to either us or the NCA, but the clock's ticking, Perry,' said Jemima. 'To improve your chances of getting a lesser sentence or even being able to walk free, you're going to have to talk to us within the next hour. If

I was in your shoes, I'd think about it, because one way or another, you're soon going to be cut adrift. And once you're on your own, you'll have to fend for yourself.'

'Like I'd be able to do that.'

'I'm getting a sense that you're not a bad person, Perry. I think you're a victim of circumstances and not the hardened criminal we originally thought you were. I believe that you put yourself at risk to save those students, and it seems as though you were telling the truth about your brother-in-law. We'll know for sure if he calls back and lets us see him with the twins,' said Jemima. 'But if you're really not a hard man, then you're out of your depth. And if we're going to help you, you need to give us something to work with.'

CHAPTER 35

Perry Cook's sigh was pitifully loud and protracted. It shattered the silence as they waited for the phone to ring. The man was clearly in the depths of despair. Though he had no one else to blame but himself. Many bad choices had led him to where he now found himself, caught between a rock and a hard place.

He had a huge decision to make. His self-confidence had taken a battering, and he no longer trusted himself not to make things worse. It was all becoming too much for him. His brow was creased with deep furrows, ageing him considerably. He knew that if he ratted his sister out, it would open up a whole new raft of problems.

Before he said anything, he needed to weigh up the implications of what he was about to do. So, to get some clarity, he closed his eyes and leaned his head against the car window. The warmth of the glass provided no respite. It just made him feel trapped.

Jemima was in no doubt that the man was facing an all-but-impossible choice. It wasn't as if they were offering him an easy way out. When it came down to it, most people went with the option that caused them the least possible pain. But here, there was no standout alternative. They had already told Perry that there were no guarantees. He would be taking a hell of a risk, whatever he ended up doing.

Minutes passed. The only sounds inside the vehicle were of the occupants' breathing and Kennedy drumming his fingers on the wheel. The air was thick with tension. Even Jemima was starting to feel stressed. She restlessly shifted her position. Her abdomen and back ached, but no matter what she did, she couldn't seem to get comfortable. She hoped that it wouldn't be much longer before they returned to the station. The baby was pressing on her bladder. It was a discomfort she could do without.

When Perry eventually spoke, she almost jumped.

'She heads up a drugs ring.' It was a statement of fact, articulated with a noticeable lack of emotion. Cook could just as easily have been commenting on the weather.

Jemima's jaw dropped as she slowly turned to face him. 'What did you just say?' She was convinced that she must have misheard. Surely to reach the level of public seniority that Gabrielle Johnson had, thorough background checks would have been required? The politicians would need to ensure that there was nothing in her background that could cause the government potential embarrassment — and Perry's assertion went way beyond embarrassment. This wasn't some tacky affair or a string of one-night stands. This was an accusation that the woman was the head of an organized-crime gang.

Kennedy had been taken by surprise too. He hastily turned in his seat to face them both, clumsily hitting his elbow against the steering wheel and sounding the horn. He recoiled and cursed, but before he had a chance to say anything else, Perry's phone rang. The 'Inglenook Bistro' was requesting a video call.

'Uh . . . It's Chester. What shall I do?' asked Perry.

'Answer it,' demanded Kennedy.

The call lasted no more than ten minutes, which was more than enough time for Jemima and Kennedy to establish that Perry Cook had told them the truth. Chester confirmed that he had taken the twins to meet up with Kathryn on the morning of his supposed death. Kathryn in turn had driven them to a holiday let, where she had remained with the girls.

Shortly afterwards, Chester had met up with Perry again, to put the final part of the plan into action. The two men had carefully choreographed the death scene, both aware of the necessity to make it appear realistic. Gabrielle was no push-over and would have retaliated with force if she'd suspected that it was a ruse. The gun had fired a blank, while Chester had burst a sachet of fake blood on his chest. Perry had hired a van in which he would supposedly dispose of Chester's body. It had been the perfect way to allow his brother-in-law to make his escape.

The plan had worked. For once in her life, Gabrielle had been on the back foot. She was so distraught that she had done as she was told. Perry had loaded Chester's body into the back of the van and driven away.

The remarkable thing was that Gabrielle had no idea that her husband and children were alive and happy.

'I've told them about Gabby and the drugs,' said Perry.

'What the fuck! You're mad. You shouldn't have said any-thing!' Chester made no attempt to hide his anger and fear.

'I had no choice, Ches. I've got myself in some deep shit this time. I borrowed off the wrong people, and they sold my debt on. You know how it goes. I couldn't keep up with the repayments, and things got way out of hand.' His hands were shaking as he spoke. 'I've done some bad things, Ches. I'm looking at a prison sentence, and if I go inside, the people I'm involved with will have me killed. I'm on my uppers. The only chance I've got is to grass on Gabby. I don't want to, but there's no way around it. I have to.'

'Perry, you're an idiot. You promised that you'd stay away from gambling. We had an arrangement. That hundred grand I gave you should have enabled you to wipe your debts. You could have started over.'

'It did clear the debt, Ches. But you've no idea what it's like for me. Everywhere you go, there are adverts for gambling sites. They target you all day, every day. It gets inside your head and brainwashes you. It's like a junkie trying to get clean but being offered a fix forty or fifty times a day. It's impossible. I stayed strong for a couple of weeks, but I got to the stage where it was all I could think about. It was driving me mad. Then one day, I got a tip I couldn't ignore. It was way too good to p-pass up . . .' Perry's voice cracked as he began to cry. He sounded small, pathetic and weak.

'So you're back to square one? You're useless, Perry! Absolutely! Fucking! Useless!'

'I know,' he wailed. 'I wish I hadn't given in, but I am where I am.'

'You do realize that Gabby's not going to let this go? You're as good as putting another target on your back if you do this.'

'Yeah, but I don't have a choice. I was hoping you'd make a st—'

'No way! She mustn't find out that I'm alive. That was the deal when I gave you the money, and as far as I'm concerned, nothing's changed. Your sister's got a long reach, Perry. You need to think hard about what you're doing. There'll be no going back.'

'Chester, I realize you're scared, but this could be your one and only chance of getting your life back,' said Jemima.

'Oh, I'm way beyond scared. I'm bloody terrified. Why else do you think I got Perry to help me fake my own death? You've no idea what Gabby's capable of.'

'So tell us and let us help you. You and your daughters deserve to live a normal life,' said Jemima.

'It's impossible.'

Jemima appreciated that Chester believed this. He must have feared for his life to take such a drastic step, and he was worried about his daughters' lives too. 'It's easy for me to say this,' she said, 'but I believe you should reconsider. In a few years, your daughters are going to get curious about things. They're already at an age where they will remember their mother. They're going to start asking questions, and we all know that technology makes it so much easier to find things out. There's every chance that one or both of them will try to make contact with Gabrielle further down the line. If that happens, your cover is blown. If your wife really is as dangerous as you claim she is, then it's in your best interests to cooperate with us and help us bring her down.'

'I suppose you have a point . . .'

Jemima sensed that this hadn't occurred to Chester until now. She remained silent, reluctant to apply pressure, waiting for him to come to a decision. Her eyes didn't waver from the screen. She watched the man's thought processes play out across his face. It was clear that this was not an easy decision for him to make. When he next spoke, she had to force herself to suppress a smile.

'And if I played ball, how would you guarantee our safety?' asked Chester.

'If Gabrielle is the head of a large-scale narcotics operation and we've a strong enough case against her, there's every possibility that you could all be enrolled on the witness protection scheme. You'd be given new identities in exchange for your testimony,' Kennedy explained. 'You'd be able to start over again, much like you're trying to do now. The difference is that once we've taken Gabrielle down and dismantled her network, you wouldn't have to keep looking over your shoulder.'

'It wouldn't be easy for any of you,' said Jemima. 'But you'd all stand a decent chance of living a normal life. As your daughters grow up, you'd be able to tell them why things had to be this way. You'd have the evidence to show them how dangerous their mother is. There'd be press reports and other easily accessible documentation to back up your version of events. Otherwise, if you continue doing what you're doing, they'll only have your word for it, and that will make it more likely that they'll want to reach out to her one day.'

'I hear what you're saying, but it's a hell of a decision to make,' said Chester. His facial expression and tone of voice both suggested that he was giving it serious consideration.

'You can control your own actions, Chester. But once they reach their teens, your kids will start to think for themselves. Continue down the route you've taken, and you'll be forever looking over your shoulder, waiting for Gabrielle to come after you. Believe me, it's only a matter of time. So take the initiative. There's a good offer on the table,' said Jemima.

'But for the record, it's now or never, Chester,' Kennedy added. 'We can't ignore what Perry's told us. If you want in on it, this is a one-time offer.'

'Do it, Ches,' pleaded Perry. 'Between us, we can get Gabby sent down. You owe it to Blythe and Roslyn. When they're old enough to understand, they'll look back on this and realize what you've done for them. They'll be proud of you.'

'I suppose it makes sense,' Chester said.

It was the first time they had seen Perry smile. The knowledge that he was no longer on his own in all of this was clearly a relief.

'So how do we proceed?' Chester asked.

'We need proof,' Jemima said. 'If we're to take this forward, we need hard evidence of Gabrielle's involvement with the drugs network. We can't just arrest her on hearsay.'

'I'll give you all the proof you need. But you have to understand that until recently, I knew nothing about what Gabby was up to. She was always business-minded. She was destined to be an entrepreneur and has a phenomenal capacity to make things happen.

'When we set up Chesrielle Haulage, I decided to take a back seat and left the management of it to her. She's great at dealing with people and has an exceptional ability to multitask. I've never seen anyone with so much drive and determination. She's a human dynamo.' Chester smiled sadly. 'I'm nothing like that, just happier plodding away in the background. I'm a whiz with spreadsheets and have a background in accountancy. So it was only natural that that's where I concentrated my efforts. Gabby would have hated it if I'd interfered in the running of the business. And the figures showed that we were doing exceptionally well, so there was no need for me to have a more hands-on role.'

'When did you realize what she was up to?' asked Jemima.

'About a year ago. I stumbled on it quite by chance. I realized straight away that something wasn't right and somehow sensed that it was best not to ask Gabby about it. So I did a bit of digging around. I even followed her on a couple of occasions, and as things fell into place, I began to understand what she was doing.'

'That must've been a shock,' said Jemima.

'You've no idea. I was head over heels in love with Gabby and so proud of her. I couldn't believe my luck when she agreed to marry me. But I started to realize that I knew nothing about her. The woman I'd married wasn't the real Gabby. I discovered that she was someone with no conscience, happy to prey on the weak and vulnerable as long as it lined her pocket. I couldn't live with that, and I certainly wasn't prepared to let my daughters grow up with someone like her as their role model.'

'And what proof do you have of what she was doing?' Jemima prompted.

'You'll find everything you need at West Winds,' said Chester.

'We've already searched the property.'

'There's a hidden room. If you go into the kitchen, there's a walk-in larder cupboard. At the far end, fixed to the underside of the fifth shelf down, there's a button. You'd never see it as it's at waist height and far enough back so as not to be noticeable. When you press that button, the entire panel swings open. It takes you down to the basement. There's no record of it on any plans, and it's where Gabby keeps anything of importance.'

Jemima and Kennedy exchanged glances. 'And what should we find in that room?' Jemima asked.

'You're specifically looking for documents relating to a client named Rosewall Coffee Enterprises. The company operates on two levels. There's a legitimate coffee business, importing beans from South America. They're transported in sealed containers, graded by strength. Most of them are level four or five. A handful in each consignment is level six. As I understand it, the drug consignments are hidden among the beans inside those level six containers. The manager and foreman of the level-six factory unit are in on the drugs racket. It's their job to secure the packages and move them on to a residential property in Rumney, where the drugs are cut, packaged and distributed to a network of dealers. It's a slick operation.'

'What's the address of the property in Rumney?' asked Jemima.

'I've no idea. I was afraid it would have aroused too much suspicion if I had paid too much attention to what Gabby was up to.'

There was a pause as they took in everything Chester had told them.

'Well, there's no going back for me now,' the man said. 'I've just given you all the information you need to bring my wife down and dismantle her drugs empire. I've kept my side of the bargain, and I hope you'll be true to your word and arrange for us to enter the witness protection scheme.'

'We'll see how your information pans out, Mr Johnson. I'll be in touch via this number.' Kennedy ended the call, and the screen went blank.

Jemima shared a knowing look with him. This case had been like no other, with events continuing to snowball and expose other crimes. The murder investigation had revealed a people-trafficking operation, another apparent murder and child kidnapping. They had subsequently discovered that the crimes against Chester and his daughters had been a ruse. A supposed upstanding and influential member of society was actually the head of a criminal organization importing and supplying drugs to Cardiff and the surrounding areas. And the only reason she was linked to the murder was that she had been deceived into believing that her daughters' lives depended on her cooperation.

'And to think, I've been living in my sister's place for months, and I didn't have a clue about that hidden room. I've walked into that larder countless times and never saw what was right in front of my face. You've got to give it to her, Gabby's got brains and balls.'

Perry shook his head in admiration, closed his eyes and settled back into the seat.

CHAPTER 36

Kennedy drove them back to the station. Jemima was silent, lost in her own thoughts. Her mind raced as she tried to make sense of everything she had been told in the last hour. This entire investigation seemed to have a life of its own. From the onset, a series of unexpected revelations had thrown them in so many different directions. It was frustrating, unsettling and unwelcome so late in the pregnancy.

Jemima winced as the baby kicked her diaphragm. Over the last few weeks, the slightest movement had become noticeable and was often uncomfortable. She gently rubbed her abdomen, hoping to soothe the unborn child. She wished that this case would come to an end so that she could concentrate on making the final preparations for the baby's arrival.

Back at the station, Perry Cook was placed in one of the holding cells. While she was nearby, Jemima checked with the custody sergeant and was informed that Gabrielle was also still in one of the cells. Earlier that afternoon she had received a visit from her solicitor who had lodged a complaint about his client's unwarranted incarceration. Though, as they had been granted an extension, the police were within their rights to keep her in custody for the time being.

Having established that Charlie Morgan still hadn't returned his call, Kennedy left instructions that no one was to update the NCA should any of their officers make contact. Things had moved quickly in the last few hours, and it was important to sequester whatever potential evidence was hidden at West Winds. If the NCA discovered what they were about to do, they would undoubtedly pull rank and take over the case.

Until they saw the evidence to verify Chester's and Perry's claims, there was a chance that they had both been untruthful, though it seemed unlikely that they would have lied about what Gabrielle was up to. Any false information would be easily provable and would not benefit either man.

West Winds was still part of the crime scene, so they would be able to undertake a further search of the property without applying for another search warrant. And as Chester Johnson had told them exactly where to look, they would soon establish the validity of the men's statements.

If Gabrielle Johnson was heading up a large-scale drugs operation, she had managed to pull it off in the full view of everyone. It would have been natural to presume that having such a prominent public profile would have hindered her in this activity, but cultivating her attractive image could conversely have made it easier to pull the wool over people's eyes. People generally see what they want to see. Even her own husband had apparently been taken in by her.

Jemima knew to her own cost just how easy it was to fall so hard for someone that you became blind to their faults. The giddiness of being in love and the elation of shared happy experiences led you to see the world through rose-tinted glasses. By investing so much of yourself in a relationship, you sometimes failed to see — or perhaps chose to ignore — what any outsider would say was patently obvious.

It was completely understandable that if Chester Johnson had trusted his wife, it might have been years before he realized what she was up to. There had been so many things in Gabrielle's favour. She had put herself out there in the business community, readily offering advice and support to any would-be entrepreneurs. The face of a highly successful business, she had won over influential people, which had raised her profile even further.

Politicians and other important members of the community had readily embraced the squeaky-clean image Gabrielle had worked tirelessly to project. There were so many people who had been hoping to gain something from her success. It helped that she ticked so many boxes. Being a successful entrepreneur heading up a company with an annual turnover into the millions was impressive. But when you considered that she had started the company from scratch in a predominantly male-centric sector, the achievement became all the greater. Add to that the fact that she was a mother of two young children, the head of the local chamber of commerce and tirelessly raised funds for many local charities, Gabrielle seemed nothing but exceptional.

The more Jemima thought about things, the more credible Chester's claims appeared to be. If he had been oblivious to his wife's criminal activities, then when he found out what she was up to, it would have been too late for him just to walk away.

Criminal networks were notoriously ruthless and unforgiving. They thrived on money, power and fear. There would have been far too much at stake for Gabrielle to allow her husband to walk away and leave her to it. Chester had also had their twin daughters to think of, and he had known that his wife wouldn't be prepared to give them up without a fight.

As for Perry Cook, it seemed as though the man had a good heart. Jemima had initially been sceptical of his claims, coming from years of refusing to take people at face value. Yet it appeared that he had been truthful, as so far everything he had told them had been backed up by his brother-in-law. It was entirely plausible that he had found himself in the clutches of a criminal gang due to the substantial debts racked up as a result of a gambling addiction. He had admitted to being aware of his sister's drug empire, though he claimed that he had been oblivious to it until Chester presented him with the evidence. Perry had disapproved of what Gabrielle was up to but had been too weak to stand up to her. He and Chester were close. And when Chester had asked for his help to escape his marriage and leave with his twin daughters, Perry hadn't hesitated.

Kennedy interrupted Jemima's meandering thoughts. 'Huxley, I want you, Broadbent and Ashton to head over to West Winds. Gather up those documents Chester reckons his wife keeps there and whatever else you find. We'll go over everything once they're back here. Gabrielle Johnson's still in custody, but for some reason, Superintendent Deavers is sticking his oar in and demanding she be released. I'll have a word with him, but I don't know how much good it'll do. I believe he's been getting it in the neck from that solicitor of hers. Though why Deavers would give in to pressure, I don't know.'

'People like Gabrielle have friends in high places,' said Jemima. Her expression was grim as she shook her head.

'If the super ends up getting his way, I'll make sure that she's told that her home is still off limits. She's not to go back there until we give her the all-clear.'

'Surely the latest allegations against her should be more than enough to stop Deavers releasing her,' said Jemima.

'I'd like to think so. But who knows? It's hard enough battling the criminals, without the higher-ups on the force making life difficult for us,' Kennedy sighed. 'Peters, you can sit this one out. It won't take four of you to deal with the document retrieval, and there are a few things I need you to do.'

Gareth looked surprised but said nothing. The DCI had never asked for his assistance before. Although he had no idea what tasks Kennedy had in mind, he was pleased that the man had selected him.

Little did he know that Kennedy had decided that he should be the one to remain at the station as both Ashton and Broadbent had annoyed him earlier in the day. The DCI was tired and irritable, and didn't want to risk snapping at anyone, which would be a distinct possibility the way both of the sergeants had been carrying on. It was bad enough that he was going to have to plead his case with Superintendent Deavers.

* * *

Ashton collected the keys for one of the police vans. They had no idea how many documents they would need to transport, but it seemed the best option to take a large vehicle. The last thing any of them wanted was to have to leave a potentially important piece of information behind.

The three officers sat in silence for much of the journey until Jemima spoke. 'Are you both clear on our objective?'

'Totally,' said Broadbent.

'It should be a reasonably quick in and out,' said Ashton.

'Possibly — after all, the property should be empty.'

'You should allow the two of us to do the heavy lifting when we get there. After all, you should be taking it easy,' said Ashton.

'Thanks for your concern, Finlay, but I know my own limits. I agree that you two should do the lifting, but I still intend to look at things myself. I'm going to be right there with you when we set foot inside that treasure trove.' There was no way she was missing out on the action when they were this close to getting the crucial evidence to put Gabrielle away for a very long time.

'Gabrielle's no reason to think that we know about the hidden entrance in the larder,' she continued. 'After all, it was only her and Chester that knew about it. And as far as she's concerned, her husband's dead. She's no idea that Chester rumbled her involvement with the drugs. There's no way she'd realize that he's hung her out to dry.

'I'd have thought she'd be reluctant to risk any unwanted attention for the next few weeks. She believes we've bought into everything she's said. And as far as she's concerned, she'd only have to back off until we wrap up the murder investigation, and we'd be done with West Winds.

'She's convinced that if we find Perry it will back up her claims about his killing Chester and abducting his nieces. Her priority is getting her daughters back, and I think she's genuinely concerned about their safety. Gabrielle's relying on us being able to find them. She's played the innocent victim card to perfection.'

'Those girls are better off without her,' muttered Broadbent.

'I wouldn't argue with that,' said Ashton.

'I hope Kennedy can talk the super around. It'd be crazy to release Gabrielle when she's facing these latest allegations. If we find proof of what she's been up to the force would be left with egg on its face,' said Jemima. 'But I'm sure Deavers will see sense.'

As they drove past Lucy's house, Jemima glanced sideways and longed to be sitting inside playing a computer game with James until it was time for him to go to bed. It seemed unfair that even now, she had no choice but to work, far later into the day than she wanted to.

They turned into the lengthy approach to West Winds, and Jemima felt her stomach tighten. She'd had these twinges throughout the day but reassured herself that they were just Braxton Hicks contractions, as her due date was some weeks away.

Broadbent stared across at the barns. 'Can't see any obvious sign that the NCA are still there, but there are two Forensics vehicles.'

'It won't be a quick job collecting all the evidence from that crime scene,' said Jemima.

Ashton pulled up in front of West Winds, and the three officers stepped out of the vehicle. Broadbent removed the crime-scene tape to allow Jemima to open the front door of the property.

'The moment of truth,' said Ashton.

CHAPTER 37

Jemima reached for a light switch. It was still possible to see things in the building's interior, but the daylight was fading. 'The kitchen's the first on the left,' she said.

Broadbent was already familiar with the property's lay-out, but Ashton hadn't accompanied them on their previous visit. 'Wow! It's like something out of a magazine. How the other half lives.' He nodded in admiration.

'Keep dreaming, Fin. You chose the wrong career if you want a place like this,' said Broadbent.

'You and me both,' sighed Ashton.

'Do you want to go into the larder first and see if you can find the entrance?' Broadbent's question was directed towards Jemima.

'No. If it's all the same to you, I think I'll leave it to you two. Just give me a shout if you happen to find it. I believe there's a button beneath the fifth shelf down,' said Jemima. Her initial insistence on accompanying them into the base-ment no longer seemed important.

She pulled out one of the bar stools and sat down heav-ily, wishing there had been a more comfortable alternative. Suddenly, everything felt like too much effort, and she decided that she'd get the lads to drop her at Lucy's when they finished the search. Her body was telling her to rest, and the discomfort she was experiencing meant that she wasn't entirely focused on the job. If anything, the other two would be better off without her. All she could think about was putting her feet up. If only she could get a good night's sleep, it would sharpen her mind and allow her to focus on the case and see it through to the end.

'Which of us is going to do the honours?' asked Ashton. It was obvious that he was keen to be the one to find the hidden entrance.

'You go for it,' said Broadbent. In normal circumstances, he would have been eager to be the one to make the discovery. He would have thought of it as a personal coup. But he could see that Jemima was struggling. He had kept a watchful eye on his wife when her pregnancy headed towards full-term. And with first-hand experience to fall back on, he felt a valid reason for concern.

For many years, there had been a special bond between Dan and Jemima. He still felt ashamed about giving her a hard time when she had first joined the squad. On the few occasions he'd spoken to her about his initial shoddy behaviour towards her, she had told him to forget about it, insisting that it was all water under the bridge and that his unedifying behaviour back then was best forgotten about. Jemima wasn't one to hold grudges. Despite the way Broadbent had treated her, she had come through for him in a selfless act of heroism. It had undoubtedly saved his life, but her actions had cost her dearly, as she had sustained severe injuries while fighting off his attacker.

When Broadbent regained consciousness in the hospital, he had discovered what Jemima had done. She had put her life on the line to save him, and he'd been ashamed, a feeling made worse by knowing that he could not say for sure that he would have gone all out to save her if she had been the one in danger.

Jemima and Dan had put all that behind them a long time ago and had gone on to form a strong partnership, safe in the knowledge that they always had each other's back. And that was why Broadbent was more than willing to allow Ashton to explore the larder on his own while he took a few moments to check on Jemima.

'How're you doing?' Broadbent gently touched her shoulder.

'I've felt better.' She managed a weak smile. 'I should have called it a day and told Kennedy that I wasn't up to it.'

'Found it!' Ashton's voice rang out from inside the larder.

'Wait for Dan!' called Jemima. But it was too late. In his eagerness, Ashton pressed the catch, and they both heard the entrance spring open. 'Go with him, Dan. I'll just catch my breath and follow you down there in a moment.'

Broadbent strode towards the larder, eager to set foot inside Gabrielle Johnson's inner sanctum. Suddenly, there was a wetness between Jemima's legs, and she looked down in dismay. Her waters had broken. As a contraction took hold, she doubled over, resting her head against the work surface. It brought no relief.

In the background, Jemima was vaguely aware of a guttural groan followed by a thudding sound. However, the implications were lost on her. All she could think about was her own predicament. There was no denying that the birth was imminent, and this sudden realization filled her with fear as she battled to rise above the pain. As panic took hold, her thoughts raced ahead to what would happen if she didn't make it to the hospital in time. And as another contraction followed, she did her best to breathe through it.

'Dan!' Jemima's voice was high and unnatural. Broadbent failed to respond, and she was unsure whether he had heard her. 'Daaaan!' This time, she screamed his name as loudly as she could. When there was still no reply or the reassuring sound of any approaching footsteps, she looked around in desperation. She spotted her phone further along the work surface. Somehow she found the strength to stretch across to it, determined to call for an ambulance. Her hands shook as she began to type in the code to unlock the device. She had only managed the first two digits when she was stopped in her tracks.

'Put the phone down!'

Jemima blinked to rid her eyes of tears and turned her head in the direction of the voice. Her first clear image was of Broadbent walking towards her with his hands up. Behind him, wearing a sinister look, was Gabrielle Johnson.

Until that moment, it hadn't occurred to Jemima that things could get any worse. After all, she was in labour, and the pain of the contractions was far more intense than anything she had imagined. It took a few seconds for the reality of the situation to hit home.

Gabrielle Johnson stopped a few feet away from Jemima. The woman was holding a knife — a huge knife. Blood dripped from the blade and stained the floor.

She prodded Broadbent in the back with the weapon. 'Cuff yourself to a handle of the fridge–freezer then toss your phone on the floor.' Her pseudo-refined accent had all but disappeared, and her tone was menacing. She pointed the blade in Jemima's direction. 'Get over there with him,' she snarled.

Years of experience brought about a moment of clarity that transcended the pain and fear of labour. Jemima knew that she had to rise above her current situation, no matter how impossible that might seem. They would have one chance and one chance only.

With no sign of Ashton, Jemima had to assume that he was injured. Once Broadbent was cuffed, it would be down to her to disarm Gabrielle. And with the best will in the world, she was in no fit state to do that. She was barely capable of raising herself from the bar stool, let alone kickbox herself out of trouble, which was her favoured form of self-defence.

Broadbent made eye contact with Jemima. The look practically screamed that they needed to bring this situation to a close.

Jemima elongated the little finger of her left hand. It was a non-verbal signal they had used on numerous occasions, meaning that she understood and agreed that they take action immediately.

Broadbent fumbled with his set of handcuffs, sending them clattering to the floor. Jemima knew that her partner had done this on purpose. It was a ploy to draw Gabrielle's attention away from Jemima and buy them both a few seconds.

'Final warning — get those cuffs on, or I'll stick you with this!' shouted Gabrielle. She took a step closer to him and jabbed the knife precariously close to his chest.

The moment had arrived. There was no time for hesitation or for half-measures. Jemima looked around for something — anything — she could use against the woman. For once, luck was on her side, and she grabbed a marble chopping board with both hands from the work surface behind her.

Gritting her teeth against another contraction, she forced herself a few steps forward, swinging the board at head height. The movements were far from graceful but effective nonetheless.

Gabrielle Johnson didn't stand a chance. The woman was just glancing back over her shoulder when the hefty slab hit her square in the face.

Blood splattered everywhere. The knife dropped from Gabrielle's hand, and she went down like a sack of potatoes.

CHAPTER 38

Jemima forced her chin on to her chest as she closed her eyes and groaned. The level of pain she was experiencing was ramping up dramatically as one contraction relentlessly followed another. It was only now that she realized that the discomfort she had felt throughout the day must have been the early stages of labour, and she cursed her own stupidity. There was hardly any time between the contractions now, and the pain was so intense that it radiated throughout her entire body.

'You can do this. Just breathe through it.' Broadbent was doing his best to sound calm and knowledgeable, but his facial expression told another story. Every time Jemima groaned, he winced at the sound she made.

Having been at his wife's side as she gave birth to their only child, Broadbent knew just how scary and traumatic the experience could be. It was one thing supporting your wife while professionals were on hand to oversee events and intervene when necessary. It was quite another thing to know that should anything happen quickly, the burden of decision-making was placed squarely on his shoulders. Until medical help arrived, he had no option but to step up and do whatever was necessary. Dan just hoped that, for everyone's sake, he could do it. A niggling seed of self-doubt told him that he'd be sure to let everyone down in spectacular fashion. His heart rate was already high, and his hands were trembling.

His concern grew with each passing second. He knew he wasn't up to the task as he had a phobia about blood. He had boasted to his co-workers about being there at the birth of his own child, but he'd failed to tell anyone that when he saw the baby's head crown, he'd actually fainted. His squeamishness had been a source of much amusement to the midwife.

Throughout her career, Jemima had sustained significant injuries during physical altercations. Some of these had resulted in broken bones and worse. Many had hurt like hell at the time. However, she had wrongly assumed that these experiences would stand her in good stead for the pain of birth. As yet another contraction crested, she acknowledged that labour pains were an entirely different concept. Physical assaults were short-lived. Whereas these contractions just kept on coming, increasing in intensity and frequency with no let-up.

Lucy had reassured her that it was not unusual for your first labour to last many hours. In a way, that thought had been comforting, but it had lulled Jemima into a false sense of security. She'd spent months convincing herself that no matter how painful it was at the start, she'd have plenty of time to get to the hospital. And once there, they would offer pain relief should she need it.

Jemima was incapable of responding to Broadbent's flippant but well-meaning advice. It was pointless telling her to breathe. Everyone had to breathe. If you didn't, you died. Having attended birthing classes, she knew that he was right, but it was easy to tell someone what to do when you weren't the one who felt as though your insides were being ripped out.

As the pain briefly subsided, Jemima looked at the two other people in the room. Gabrielle Johnson was still unconscious, her nose and mouth a bloody mess. Broadbent bent down and felt for a pulse, his head turned away from the woman's injuries. Jemima knew it was because he was afraid that he would vomit. In other circumstances, it would have amused her, but time was of the essence, and his aversion was definitely slowing him down.

Satisfied that Gabrielle was alive, Broadbent secured her wrist to the nearest handle of the American fridge–freezer. The appliance was wedged between two floor-to-ceiling cupboards and was so large and hefty that it would be impossible for her to break free.

'Did you call for an ambulance?' he asked, his attention now back on Jemima.

'No.' Jemima's voice was unnaturally low. Even a monosyllabic reply sapped her rapidly depleting energy levels.

'What about your sister?'

'Out . . . networking . . . event.' It was too much effort for Jemima to string a sentence together.

'I'll call for an ambulance. You OK to stay put for a few minutes? I have to see how Fin's doing. When you get another contraction, try to breathe through it. I'll be back as quickly as I can.' He retrieved his phone from where he'd dropped it and squeezed Jemima's shoulder in a supportive gesture.

He disappeared before Jemima had a chance to respond. She rested her head on the kitchen work surface, momentarily grateful for the coolness it provided. As the pain subsided, Broadbent's words sank in. He was going to check on Finlay.

Throughout the altercation in the kitchen, there had been no sign of the other sergeant. His absence was unusual and highly concerning. Ashton wouldn't have purposely stayed out of the way. She'd been there when he'd ignored a direct order and run into a burning building to save the people inside. His actions, though reckless, were a testament to the sort of man he was. He would have done everything he could to ensure that Gabrielle was disarmed as quickly as possible. And as this thought occurred to her, Jemima recalled that blood had been dripping from Gabrielle's knife.

Needing reassurance that she hadn't imagined it, Jemima glanced at the floor and spotted the ominous crimson trail. A shiver ran along her spine. There was no way that Finlay would have left them to it for this long. He must be injured, and it had to be serious.

Pressing down on the surface, she struggled to raise herself off the stool. Even though she was weak and in pain, she was determined to do everything she could to help her injured colleague. With both feet on the floor, she took a deep breath and shuffled towards the larder. Every movement required an immense amount of effort and concentration. It didn't help matters that Jemima couldn't stand upright. She was hunched over like an old woman, cupping her hands beneath her abdomen to counteract the unbearable pressure pushing down inside.

Jemima had barely managed six paces when she was hit with another contraction. It took all of her strength to try to breathe through it. Her legs gave way, and she crumpled to the floor. She felt the urge to push. All she could think was that this was so wrong. This was her first time. It shouldn't be happening so quickly.

'Daaaannn!' Jemima shouted as loudly as she could. She felt guilty about dragging him away from Finlay. Still, no matter what state Ashton was in, she needed immediate attention. If it had just been her, she would have gritted her teeth through the pain, but she couldn't cope with this alone. It could endanger the baby. 'Daaaaannnn!'

She was relieved to hear the sound of his footsteps.

'What are you doing down there? You should've stayed put. Here, let me help you up.'

'I can't move. The baby's coming.'

'You've got plenty of time. You just need to hold on. The ambulance is on its way.'

'Don't have time. I need to puuusssh!'

'Oh, shit! This shouldn't be happening. Don't do this to me, Jemima. I've never done this before.' Broadbent was horrified and unable to disguise his fear. 'What do I do? Towels, I need towels and hot water.'

'For God's sake, Dan, there's no time. It's happening. My baby's coming, and nothing's going to stop it. You have to make sure the cord isn't wrapped around its neck.'

'I can't do this. I'm not up to it.'

'You have to do it! You're my only hope, so don't go all flaky on me. There'll be blood, but you'll have to deal with it. Just don't vomit on the baby. Call the emergency services. They'll talk you through it.'

'But—'

'Just do it!'

'OK.' Broadbent turned and ran.

'Dan! Where are you going?'

There was a moment when Jemima thought that her partner had deserted her, but seconds later, he returned.

'Had to make sure the door was open. Don't want any delay when the paramedics get here. And I grabbed some cushions to make you feel more comfortable.'

'Hello! Are you there? Can you hear me?' The voice seemed to come from far away.

'It's the emergency services operator.' Broadbent dropped the cushions and turned his attention to his phone.

Jemima managed a weak smile. At least now, Broadbent would have someone on hand to talk him through the steps he should follow. It was the last clear thought that Jemima had.

Almost fifteen minutes later, Broadbent handed Jemima the baby wrapped in a clean tea towel.

'Say hello to your baby boy,' said Broadbent. Tears of relief rolled down his cheeks.

Jemima gazed at her son's face and marvelled at his tiny fingers. She was about to say something when there was a sound of an approaching vehicle, and Broadbent rushed towards the front door.

The paramedics had finally arrived.

EPILOGUE

Lucy was the first visitor of the day. Jemima had only just placed the baby back in the cot, having fed and changed him. It had been an exhausting night, what with the stringent checks and tests that the medical staff had insisted they needed to carry out on both of them. The little one had woken three times during the night, which Jemima had been informed was perfectly normal. She was excited about entering this new phase of her life but was under no illusion that it would take a while to get to grips with the demands of motherhood.

There had been a part of Jemima that had dreaded seeing her baby for the first time. It was not a thought that most pregnant women had. But given the traumatic circumstances surrounding the conception, she was concerned that when she finally got to meet her baby, it might remind her of the rape. She tried to remain positive, but it was always there in the back of her mind. She had a secret fear that when the baby was born, she would discover that she was unable to love it.

As things turned out, Jemima needn't have worried. The moment her eyes locked on to his tiny face, she experienced a rush of love so overwhelming that she knew nothing would ever compare to it. Of course, she loved James fiercely and unconditionally. She thought of him as her son, despite having missed out on the first few years of the boy's life. This baby wouldn't change how she felt about him — she had more than enough love to go around. But being biologically part of her, she was sure that this baby would help fill the void she had lived with for so many years.

'Congratulations, sis!' Lucy's smile was broad, and she could not hide her excitement at meeting the latest addition to the family. 'Let's take a look at him.' She thrust her arm forward and handed Jemima a balloon emblazoned with the words *Baby Boy*. 'Oh, he's gorgeous, Jem. He's a right little heartbreaker, and he looks just like his mum.'

Jemima smiled, delighted that her sister believed that the baby was as wonderful as she thought he was.

'Oh, I almost forgot, I got you this too.' Lucy distractedly handed Jemima a carrier bag.

'What is it?'

'Take a look. You're going to love it.'

Jemima reached inside and pulled out a little blue vest with the words *I love my mum* on it.

'It's great. Thanks, Luce.' Jemima swallowed hard. She wasn't usually one to cry, but she was overcome with emotion, and tears suddenly rolled down her cheeks.

'Hey, hey, there's no need for that. This is a happy occasion,' cooed Lucy. She sat on the edge of the bed and hugged Jemima tightly.

'I know. I know. I don't know what's got into me. Embarrassing or what?' Jemima wiped her eyes with the edge of the bed sheet. 'I think it's just exhaustion.'

'I'm not surprised. This little man didn't exactly have the perfect birth, arriving the way he did. But then again, his mother's never been conventional. Though, I have to say that I feel cheated to have missed out on his arrival.'

'How's James? Does he know about his brother?' asked Jemima.

'I told him this morning. He missed you at breakfast. He's very excited and can't wait to meet him. The little scamp even tried to wangle a day off school just so he could come with me this morning. I told him there was no way you'd agree to that, but I promised him that if they hadn't discharged you by the time he came home from school, I'd bring him here myself.'

'Did you let Dad know?'

'Of course I did. He's thrilled. He'll be here in about an hour.' Lucy glanced at her watch.

'And Mum?' Jemima already knew the answer but was determined to ask the question.

'Ummm . . . best forget about her.'

'No surprise there.' Their mother had an uncanny knack of taking the shine off even the most exciting moments in Jemima's life. 'She doesn't deserve to see this little one.'

At the sound of approaching footsteps, they both looked towards the door. Moments later, Broadbent, Kennedy and Peters peered around it. Each of them had come bearing a gift for the baby, like a contemporary version of the three wise men.

'I'll give you some space,' Lucy said. 'I've got a hectic few hours today as there are quite a few orders to get out. Dad will be in shortly, and he's already said that he's more than happy to pick you up whenever they discharge you.' She kissed Jemima on the cheek and fondly stroked the baby's head, then quickly gathered her things together.

If Jemima had been more herself, she would have noticed the awkward silence between her sister and the men. She even saw Lucy touch each of their arms as she walked past them but thought no more about it. Later, when she had time to reflect on the scene, she would kick herself for failing to notice that one of the squad was missing.

'How're you doing, kiddo?' Kennedy's voice was softer than usual, and he gave a slight smile as he peered over the top of the cot. 'He's a right bobby dazzler. There's a card and something for him. You don't need to worry — Sally was responsible for choosing them.' He glanced at the others. 'I'll just grab us a few chairs.' He wandered off to find some.

Peters was the next to speak. 'I'm glad everything went well for both of you. Just as well Dan was there. I'm not sure

266

I could've coped.' He cleared his throat. 'I've got you a little something. You can open it later.'

'You're looking better than when I last saw you,' said Broadbent. There were noticeable dark smudges beneath his eyes, and his voice was flat as he raised a weak smile.

'I didn't get a chance to say it yesterday, but thanks for everything you did, Dan. I know it wasn't easy for you. When you think about how things played out, it was embarrassing for both of us, but you were absolutely bloody amazing. I'll never be able to thank you enough. I'm so sorry that I put you through that, but when I needed you, you really came through for me,' Jemima held out her arms.

Dan bent down to embrace Jemima, squeezing her tight as he whispered in her ear. 'I'm just putting this out there to get any embarrassment out of the way. I saw a side of you last night that I hope never to see again. I'm sure I'll need years of therapy to get that image out of my mind.'

They both giggled like a couple of kids, before he continued. 'Seriously though, you're my best friend, Jem. I'd do anything for you. And that little boy will always have a special place in my heart. Just like his mum. Though, I must say, you pushed me to my limits, and I don't ever want to have to do anything like that again. But I'm proud of myself. I never thought I'd be capable of delivering a baby.' As he finished speaking, he pulled away and kissed her gently on the cheek.

Jemima glanced around as a thought occurred to her. 'Where's Finlay?' As she asked the question, she suddenly remembered the bloodied knife that Gabrielle Johnson had been holding. 'He was hurt, wasn't he?' It was the only possible explanation for his absence.

Broadbent and Peters exchanged looks. But before either had a chance to say anything, Kennedy arrived with the chairs. 'Let's all sit down. We've some things to discuss. It doesn't seem right having to talk about these matters in front of this little one, but at least he won't remember or understand any of this,' said the DCI.

'Where's Finlay?' repeated Jemima. She stared at each of them in turn. She sensed that something awful had happened and suddenly felt nauseous.

'The lad didn't make it,' said Kennedy with a simple shake of his head.

'What do you mean? I don't understand.' Jemima was conscious of her voice becoming higher and more emotional with each word. She desperately hoped that she had mis-heard, but deep down, she knew that she hadn't.

'Fin died at the scene, Jem,' said Broadbent. There were tears in his eyes as he spoke. 'I knew he was hurt, but I didn't realize how bad it was. That Johnson bitch stabbed him and walked away without a backward glance. I wanted to go to him, but she forced me into the kitchen. Fin died in there alone.'

'Noooo!' wailed Jemima. She sobbed so hard that it was a few minutes before she was able to speak again.

'I delayed you,' she said. 'I went into labour, and I was scared. If it wasn't for me, you might have been able to save Finlay.'

'You're wrong,' said Broadbent. 'I blamed myself at first, but Prothero did the post-mortem late last night. He con-firmed the cause of death was a single wound to the heart. No one could have saved Fin. It was over for him as soon as the blade went in.'

'We've all got regrets,' said Kennedy. 'I sent the three of you out there without armed backup. I honestly thought Gabrielle was still in custody. So if Finlay's death is on any-one, it's on me. It was my decision and mine alone.

'I should have checked with the custody sergeant. Instead, I went straight around to see Deavers. The man's an arse. He kept me waiting while he was on the phone, and then he insisted that I explain to him in great detail why Gabrielle shouldn't be released. He questioned everything, going over and over the smallest details. By the time I'd established that he'd already ordered her release, it was too late. I tried to warn you, but couldn't get hold of anyone.'

The DCI's words didn't make the news any easier to bear.

'Deavers has blood on his hands,' said Broadbent.

'He'll find some way to worm his way out of it,' muttered Kennedy.

'How's Ingrid?' Jemima knew it was a stupid question. Ingrid was Ashton's partner. The woman would have been devastated.

'Not well,' said Peters. 'I went along with the DCI to break the news. I stayed with her until her sister arrived.'

'I didn't know she had a sister.' It suddenly occurred to Jemima that she had known very little about Ashton's home life. She'd met Ingrid on a couple of occasions but had made no genuine attempt to get to know the woman. They all had busy lives, but that was no excuse. Finlay had been an integral part of their team and possibly the most intelligent person she had ever known. But now he was gone. Like the rest of them, Jemima would not get to see him again, and there was so much about him she would never get to know.

'There's never going to be an ideal time for this,' Kennedy said, 'but I thought you should know about recent developments. Chester Johnson was telling the truth when he alleged that Gabrielle was heading up a major drugs operation. A cursory glance at some of the paperwork recovered from the hidden room shows that she was making millions and was using her haulage company to import consignments. It's no wonder she was horrified that her brother had brought trouble to her door. The people trafficking posed a huge risk to her own illegal activities. Perry Cook had Gabrielle over a barrel making her believe that he'd killed Chester and kidnapped the girls. Those kiddies were her Achilles' heel. The threat that they'd be harmed if she didn't comply was the perfect way of keeping her in line.'

'We all know that people like Gabrielle have the best lawyers money can buy. She'll have a whole network of connections, high-powered people who'll see to it that she walks. We've seen it time and time again,' muttered Jemima. The

269

news of Ashton's demise had hit her hard. Her hormones were dancing the fandango, bouncing her mood all over the place. She was tired to the point of exhaustion. She had no idea how she would get through the next few hours, let alone the rest of her life, especially with the demands a new baby would put on her. This was all too much, too soon.

'She'll go down for Fin's murder,' said Broadbent. 'I saw her stab him. I'm a credible witness. There's no way she'll get away with it.'

'As for the rest of it, Chester has agreed to testify in return for immunity and new identities for him and the kids. While you were at West Winds, I was busy making phone calls to find the necessary contacts to set things in motion,' said Peters.

'We're not going to rest until we get justice for Finlay,' said Kennedy.

Jemima couldn't help but think that these fine sentiments were empty platitudes. There had been occasions when she'd said similar things to the friends and family of victims. Now she appreciated just how facile the words were. No matter what happened from here on in, nothing would bring Finlay Ashton back to them. That gentle giant of a man was gone and would leave a massive hole in the lives of everyone who had known and loved him.

'The drug squad are looking into the possibility of there being a link between Gabrielle's operation and the network of dealers that the Forbes twins are caught up with. It's early days yet, and they'll have their work cut out getting anyone to talk,' said Broadbent.

'Oh, and Charlie Morgan finally deigned to return my call,' Kennedy added. 'They're still uncertain whether it'll be possible to establish the identity of whoever was placed in the barrel of acid. They've got scientists working on it, but the odds of them getting any workable DNA aren't that great. I've informed them of Pavla's death, which should give them the best possible shot of matching anything they're able to extract against her DNA. But I'm not holding my breath on that one.'

'And Perry Cook?' Jemima asked.

'I updated Morgan on our findings, and we handed him over to the NCA. They've reached the conclusion he was a more hapless idiot than co-conspirator and offered him a deal with a new identity if he testifies against McClennen, Henney and Waverley. It'll dent the Waverleys' operation, and it'll rile Leonard Waverley that his youngest will serve time, but who knows . . . As you'd expect, no one's talking much at the moment, but that could change.'

'What about the Czech students?' asked Jemima.

'All good. Remarkably, none of them has any serious physical injuries as a result of their ordeal. As for the psychological effects, well, that's a different matter. They'll have to remain in this country for a few days, as they'll have to be interviewed by Charlie Morgan's team. I wouldn't be surprised if it takes a while, as it's going to be an emotional experience for them having to recount what they went through,' said Kennedy.

'I contacted their embassy to update them on the matter,' said Gareth. 'They'll arrange repatriation, as the women obviously don't have their passports. I think they're making arrangements for family members to come over and support them for the remainder of their stay here.'

'Hey now, I hope you're not tiring my girl out.' Donald Goodman strode into the room carrying a small case.

Kennedy, Broadbent and Peters all stood up as Jemima's father approached her bedside.

'I guess we should make a move,' said Kennedy. 'You take care of yourself and that little one, Jemima. We'll touch base soon.'

'Not too soon, I hope,' said Donald. 'My daughter's officially on maternity leave and my grandson takes priority. Now, I'd appreciate it if you'd all leave Jemima in peace.' Donald deposited the case on the floor and opened his arms wide, shooing them out of the room as though seeing off a flock of geese.

Jemima smiled at the sight of him. 'You didn't need to do that, Dad.'

'Oh yes, I did. Some people don't take the hint. Anyway, how are you doing, love?'

'All the better for seeing you.'

'That's good. Now, let me take a look at my grandson. Oh, he's lovely, Jem.' Donald bent over the cot and gazed lovingly at the newest member of his family. 'Have you thought of a name yet?'

'I have. I was going to call him Luke, but I've changed my mind. Say hello to Finlay Luke Huxley.'

THE END

Thank you for reading this book.

If you enjoyed it please leave feedback on Amazon or Goodreads, and if there is anything we missed or you have a question about, then please get in touch. We appreciate you choosing our book.

Founded in 2014 in Shoreditch, London, we at Joffe Books pride ourselves on our history of innovative publishing. We were thrilled to be shortlisted for Independent Publisher of the Year at the British Book Awards.

www.joffebooks.com

We're very grateful to eagle-eyed readers who take the time to contact us. Please send any errors you find to corrections@joffebooks.com. We'll get them fixed ASAP.

Lightning Source UK Ltd.
Milton Keynes UK
UKHW040725020223
416362UK00004B/395